I0584085

ALL FOR SUMMER

PARMAN REYNOLDS

Black Rose Writing | Texas

©2021 by Parman Reynolds
All rights reserved. No part of this book may be reproduced, stored in a retrieval system or transmitted in any form or by any means without the prior written permission of the publishers, except by a reviewer who may quote brief passages in a review to be printed in a newspaper, magazine or journal.

The author grants the final approval for this literary material.

First printing

This is a work of fiction. Names, characters, businesses, places, events, and incidents are either the products of the author's imagination or used in a fictitious manner. Any resemblance to actual persons, living or dead, or actual events is purely coincidental.

ISBN: 978-1-68433-883-2
PUBLISHED BY BLACK ROSE WRITING
www.blackrosewriting.com

Printed in the United States of America
Suggested Retail Price (SRP) $20.95

All for Summer is printed in Jensen

*As a planet-friendly publisher, Black Rose Writing does its best to eliminate unnecessary waste to reduce paper usage and energy costs, while never compromising the reading experience. As a result, the final word count vs. page count may not meet common expectations.

To Mary
For All of Her Patience

ALL FOR SUMMER

ONE

DOUGLAS COUNTY JAIL
MAY 1983

Turns out killing people is real time consuming.

On the TV shows, they get it all wrapped up in less'n an hour, maybe two on the outside. Being in jail now for 'bout five long months awaiting my trial, seems like here the wheels of justice could use some WD-40. I figured I needed to explain things to the rich attorney man, get him fixed on the lay of the land and the general attitude of the citizens of this particular Texas county, by telling him about what happened to Carl on account of Clarice.

I said, "See, Carl lived down the road a piece from me and Suzie in a trailer he got after his momma died. Had the aluminum siding nearly beat off in that bad hail storm we had 'bout nine years back. Couple of old cars sat out by the driveway, left where they quit runnin'. The county sold off the place a while ago for back taxes and the new owner cleared off the weeds and junk, but I imagine the cars went—"

The rich attorney man stirred a little. "Luther, I don't see how this—"

"Hang on, I'm gettin' to that. Carl had this wife, Clarice was her name. Good lookin' woman, too, built, you know..." I started to hold out my hands in front to show him, but I figured that wasn't the kinda thing I shoulda been doing, so on I went with my story. "Had this mother, Gladys, I recollect her name was. Word around town was her and Clarice didn't get along so good, so next thing you know Clarice married Carl. Didn't have

1

much money, but they had them a nice weddin' reception out at the Elks Lodge, the place where the highway comes in from Beaumont? Some real pretty napkins, too, kind that had the initials printed in gold, two 'Cs' locked together."

I hooked my index fingers so he'd get him an idea of what I meant by the fancy design, but by then the rich attorney man was looking down at his yellow tablet. It was the kind lawyers use with the thin blue lines so your hen scratching's all straight and neat, so he missed out on the finger deal.

"Suzie and I went to the weddin' on account of her knowin' Clarice pretty good back in high school. That Clarice, I tell you, could drink more beer than any man you ever seen. Later on, when things wasn't goin' so well between her and Carl, she went out alone one night, honky-tonkin'. Guess that's what caused the trouble."

"Trouble?" The man's head bobbed up like a float tied to a hook a ten-pound bass had spit out. He hadn't hardly written down a damn thing I'd said. Barely paying attention before now, from what I could tell.

"Carl come home that evenin' early 'cause he got fired from his job or something like that, I don't really remember for sure, and lo and behold there was Clarice humpin' Scott Blackburn. Scott's the son of the Chevy dealer, see, and his family owns a fair stretch of land here in Douglas County, most of it rented out to Mrs. Davis' kids, who've worked it for years. Scott's always had him a girl on his arm, but the single ones weren't enough, I guess, seein' as how he ended up bangin' a married woman. Carl said at the trial they was goin' at it when he walked in on 'em. Scott's on top, see, and took the first one in the back. Went all the way through him and buried up in the wall."

The attorney was getting irritated with my detailed explaining, like maybe the story I was telling didn't really matter.

"Were you involved in any way in the murder of this, uh, Scott…"

"Scott Blackburn. 'Course not." I wondered how could he ask a question like that, maybe thinking I went around killing people for recreation?

"Then why are you—"

I flung up an arm to show him how it happened, like it was told in court. "Clarice jumped up right after Scott bought the farm and started cussin' and screamin' at Carl, callin' him all kinds of names and sayin' if he was ever home and acted like a proper husband this whole thing wouldn't a-happened."

I stopped then and considered some on what I'd told the man. "Least that's what Carl said she said at the trial, Clarice not bein' there to speak on her behalf and all. People in the courtroom talked about how he looked at the floor all the time, not showin' much emotion. He said he must've lost his mind, gone crazy, him pointin' his 0.44 magnum at her and sayin', 'If you don't shut the fuck up I'm gonna shoot you in the face.' He said that right out in the courtroom, too, with a bunch of women hearin' it and all."

The rich attorney man, Mr. Garner was his name, started in again. "Well, I'm sure that—"

"Said she kept on screamin' and cussin' and so he shot her in the face like he promised."

"Oh?" the man said, kinda puzzled-like.

"Oh, what?" I asked, not knowing where maybe he was headed.

"That's it?"

"That was it for Clarice."

"And what in God's name does that story have to do with you?"

"The bullet went in here." I pointed to my left eye, "and came out the back 'bout here. Heard the doctor testified Clarice's head must've been like a rotten cantaloupe hitting the floor, all overripe and squishy, brains and blood spillin' out the big hole in the back and soakin' into that white carpet. See, she liked white and had most of their trailer done in it. Suzie said Clarice always made Carl take off his shoes when he come in the house. I doubt they ever got it up, it bein' white and all, the blood soakin' right through into the pad. Gets real sticky when it dries. Probably had to cut out a square and patch it back, makin' sure the nap run the right way so you couldn't see the seams. 'Course, Scott Blackburn contributed to the mess, what with parts of his liver all over the wall."

Mr. Garner pulled down on the end of the sleeves of his white shirt so the big cufflinks poked outta his coat, looking to me like maybe he was showing off, subtle-like. They was real pretty, the cufflinks, black squares all bordered in gold with some kinda twisty gold "K" in the middle, looking real sharp with that pin-striped suit. I figured he had a couple thousand dollars worth of stuff on, maybe twice that. I don't know for sure, but I guess high-dollar clothes aren't a problem if you're used to making two, three hundred an hour, which is better'n I get in a whole week janitoring, even with that last fifty-cent raise.

"I don't mean to seem rude, Luther, but—"

"Oh, sorry, the point. I'm gettin' to that. The defense's line was that Carl had gone crazy jealous and couldn't help shootin' the both of them, but the jury was havin' none of it and he got the 'lectric chair anyway. 'Course if he'd waited 'til now he'd got the needle instead, and talk in here is that's a better way to go. So, anyway, what I'm sayin' is that kind of defense don't work around here. Assuming that's what you were thinkin' of for me. Pleadin' insanity, that is."

Mr. Garner thought on what I'd said a bit, then come up with, "Mr. Holman, have you ever been charged with a felony before?"

"Call me Luther."

"Okay, Luther, have you—"

"See, Luther's my given name and I never liked it much, but I was named for my granddaddy, who was a Luther, too, but my daddy wasn't, so I couldn't be a three. Just another Luther."

"Your middle name is Edward. Why not go by Ed?"

I shook my head. "I couldn't do that, what with Momma givin' me the first name of her husband's daddy. If Luther was in the middle, no problem, but it bein' at the first and me not usin' it, it woulda showed her I disliked it and I wouldn't hurt her feelin's for the world."

"Mr…Luther, about that question—"

"Nope."

He scribbled a bit more on the yellow pad. "I'm going to see Judge Harder about a continuance and that ridiculous bail amount."

"Good luck, but it won't work," I said.

"Why not?"

"'Flight risk' they called it. Afraid I'd run off if they let me outta here."

Mr. Garner said, "I need to go interview your wife. Thanks for you time, Luther."

I rose and shook his hand 'cause that's what I was taught to do if you got manners. "Thank you for comin' here to see me, Mr. Garner. I sure 'preciate it."

"The letter your mother sent us was very moving. Our team decided this was one case we wanted to look into. Especially considering the unusually high conviction rate here in Douglas County."

"That's real nice of you to wanna help, Mr. Garner. Tell Susie I love her and I miss her. Okay?"

"I certainly will."

"Thank you, Mr. Garner."

The rich attorney man nodded like he was already thinking of something else. Right after he left, Gene come out and took me back to the cell.

◆　◆　◆

I didn't have anything much to do the rest of the day except think or sleep, seeing as Barry, Carl's older brother, was on the bottom bunk snoring off a drunk-and-disorderly. I thought about Susie and how I missed her and when I closed my eyes I could feel her soft cheeks in my hands. Maybe I'll be with her again, but it don't look good, even with Mr. Garner on board, what with me accused of murdering the mayor's kid, and him found with a bullet from my daddy's 0.38 stuck halfway inside the mush used to be his brains.

TWO

THREE YEARS EARLIER

Delbert's Family Diner enjoyed a dedicated clientele, thanks mainly to Delbert's chicken fried steak and enchiladas, as well as the cheap prices. The worn and tacky décor, and the celebrated fights between Delbert and whatever staff member who happened to face his wrath that day, were less of a draw. Today, in the midst of the lunch rush, Delbert and Clarice were arguing over whose mistake the steak served to Table 12 was. Accusations and their counters were hurled with abandon. Clarice, already on edge that day, was having none of Delbert's shit, and the shouting rose in volume as the patrons either tried their best to ignore the confrontation, or alternately, enjoyed the show. As neither party was inclined to give in, an ultimatum was given.

"You can't talk to me like that!" Delbert's small eyes narrowed, him gasping a bit for breath after the sustained argument. Determined to show everyone who was boss, he reached a conclusion. "Get the hell out! You're *fired.*"

Clarice jerked the string on the apron's bow and ripped the stained fabric off in one motion. Throwing it down between two chrome counter stools topped with cracked black vinyl seats, she yelled, "Got straight to *hell,* Delbert!"

"You damn *bitch!*" the cook screamed back. "You can't talk to me like that!"

Clarice ground the apron into the grimy floor with her nurse's shoe heel. "Maybe this'll give them cockroaches something to party on instead of the tables."

The patrons, previously titillated by the exchange, glanced down at the plastic tops with the anxiety of someone waking up from a naked-in-front-of-strangers dream.

Suzie touched her arm. "Clarice, come on. He isn't worth it."

"The *hell* did you say?" Delbert demanded, digging for the dirty cloth on the floor, bunching it up in the middle with his stubby fingers.

"Nothing." She took Clarice's arm. "I'll walk you out the back."

Muriel Kirkland, a veteran of twenty-five years of hard-core waitressing, evaluated the situation in her usual pragmatic way. "Okay, who needs coffee or tea?"

Several glasses and cups took to the air.

◆　◆　◆

Outside, Suzie held Clarice's hand as she began to shake.

"Goddamn bastard." Clarice pulled a cigarette from the pack in her side pocket. The filter, cramped between her thumb and first finger, danced like a mosquito in a determined breeze. "Why'd he have to go and do that? In front of all those people? What an asshole."

"Because he *is* an asshole," Suzie said. "You ought to know that by now."

"Yeah, I should." Clarice took a deep breath, squeezing her eyes shut, trying to dismiss the tears she had managed to hold onto until now. "Guess maybe I don't get a good reference, huh?"

"You'll find something better."

Smearing the wetness with the back of her hand, Clarice said, "Shit. Soon as Carl finds out he'll be pissed..." Her voice faded off as the end of the cigarette quit moving. "You're right. Something better. I never liked cleaning up after cheap jerks anyway."

Clarice sucked in a breath, tainted by the sour stench of the nearby garbage cans, as her thumb absently stroked the back of the younger woman's hand. Clarice exhaled after her tongue shoved the white tube to one side. "You're a good friend, Suzie Holman."

A tired smile flicked across Suzie's face. "Go home, take a hot bath. Tomorrow'll be better."

Clarice considered the glum kindness floating in Suzie's eyes and wondered how someone that had been through what... "Water heater's busted," she said. "That soak'd be mighty cold."

Fresh wrinkles furrowed together at the ends of Suzie's patient eyes. "Good luck anyway, Clarice."

"Thanks a bunch." Clarice, her quick cry now over, hugged the small woman hard, causing Suzie to stand on her tiptoes. After a moment, Clarice released her. "I must look like a damn mess."

Suzie's eyes darted to the back door. "Hey, I...gotta go back in..."

"Sure. See ya."

◆ ◆ ◆

The Trans Am started after four cranks, the dual exhaust pipes rattling against the muddy frame as they spewed thick puffs of dark blue smoke into the still, hot air. Clarice gunned the car, hearing the clicking noise, louder now, the one Carl said was the valves or something that would screw up the engine soon and don't race it, goddamn it. She punched the accelerator to the floor, not giving a shit.

"Honey," Clarice said, "You got yourself some living to do."

◆ ◆ ◆

Halfway down Main Street, Clarice spotted Denise coming out of Bascomb's. After pulling into an open angled parking space, the front tire bumping off the curb, Clarice laid on the horn.

Denise, decked out in a short black skirt and aqua blouse, grinned and waved, the sacks on her arm swinging like a sailor sending a semaphore.

Squeezing through the gap between the Trans Am and an old Malibu, Denise stuck her head through the open window, "What you doing here, girl? Aren't you waiting tables today?"

"Was," Clarice said. "Until I got fired."

"Fired? You're kidding."

"Only regret I got is I didn't cut Delbert's dick off 'fore I left."

Denise giggled. "This story I gotta hear."

"By the way, why aren't *you* working?" Clarice said.

"Hel-lo? Emancipation Day? Freed the slaves?"

Clarice stared at her. "That's an official holiday? In Texas? You're fucking kidding me."

"First year. Shit, girl, the stuff you don't know could fill a book."

Clarice nodded. "You got that right."

"Now, with our own special holiday, us Black folks can have lives just as shitty as you white people." Denise raised her arms and waved her packages again. "Wanna see what I bought?"

"Sure. Get your skinny ass in here."

After shutting the door, Denise said, "Let's go over to my house. Have ourselves a drink, celebrate your lack of gainful employment."

Clarice shot the car out of the parking space and managed to apply two short rubber strips on the asphalt before the transmission lurched into second gear.

THREE

"Luther, I don't have good news."

"That so, Mr. Garner?"

"Judge Harder refused the continuance. And he insisted the half-million dollar bond amount remain."

"Wouldn't expect any different."

"But that's ridiculous. And we need more time— "

"Mama and Suzie tried to raise some money, but the bondsman said he'd need ten percent in cash. Heck, that's more'n my whole house is worth. So I don't see as I got much choice in the matter 'cept to sit tight. Folks here in the slammer call the judge Hard-On Harder. He says the problem with the law today is justice needs to be swift and sure and he's going to see to the swift part and it's the jury's responsibility to see to the sure. He's probably real upset Bob Franklin's not defendin' me anymore."

Mr. Garner gave his head a short shake. "The judge says we've got three weeks before the trial and not a day more."

"Good," I says. "Glad to get it over and done with."

"Luther, I wouldn't be so anxious. The state has given me a list of their witnesses and a look at their evidence, like they're required to, but there are a number of matters that need to be investigated. The private detective we've hired won't be here until tomorrow. We need more time to prepare for the trial. A lot more."

"Your man won't find out much. Little towns like this one don't cotton to big-city people nosin' around. Maybe Momma shouldn't have written you, but she probably figured what the hell, Franklin wasn't doin' nothin' for me."

Mr. Garner nodded. "The Rural Legal Defense Fund was formed to address cases like yours. Cases in which we suspect the defendant doesn't get a fair trial or may be represented by incompetent counsel."

"You hit the nail on the head there, Mr. Garner. Incompetent's too good a word for Franklin. See, he's the one who defended Carl, the one I told you about, on that murder charge? Talk was a little more smarts on the legal side and Carl could've been a lifer peelin' potatoes over in Huntsville. Then there was John Barker. He was up for doin' Mrs. Sharpston a few years back and Franklin didn't use the evidence he had to help get John off—"

"Luther, I don't want to talk about other cases right now. Only yours."

"Okay, sure," I said, seeing how I can come across as what you might call a rambling talker if you're not used to me. "You see Suzie yesterday? She comes by here every day on her lunch break. Gets thirty minutes off is all, and has to wait 'til after two when all the farmers is out of the diner. Been workin' double shifts since I was arrested 'cause we need the money and after the night meal it's too late for visiting. But she'll be here, right after two."

"What I want to talk about is your daughter," Mr. Garner said.

I clammed up fast as hell.

"Mr. Holman?"

"Summer's in heaven, if there's any justice in God's universe, which the Good Book says there's plenty of, but the livin' of it makes you wonder." I turned my head, pretending I had a sudden interest in the top of the scrawny willow tree outside the thick wire glass window. Mostly I didn't want to look at Mr. Garner. Mostly I didn't want to cry in front of a stranger.

"Luther," he said, persistent-like a couple of times, and I saw he wasn't going to let up on talking this through.

"Yes." I faced him now, blinking like maybe a load of dirt outside had sudden-like blown into my eye and me being left having to scratch it outta the corners. He didn't believe it one bit, but didn't say nothing about the tears and that's a mark for him, despite all the money he spends on his clothes.

"Luther, we've got to discuss your daughter some time. That's the key to the prosecution's case, your motive for killing Mark Reinhardt."

"I didn't kill Mark Reinhardt."

"I believe you, but the state has a lot of circumstantial evidence."

"Such as?"

"The plaster cast of the mud in the alley behind Reinhardt's house matches your truck's tire pattern. The ballistics of the bullet that killed Reinhardt match your pistol. It had your fingerprints on—"

"'Course it did. It's my pistol."

"And your alibi is—"

"Suzie told them I was with her all night, the night Reinhardt got himself shot."

"I'm sorry, Luther, but that's not enough. The jury may feel that as wife will—"

"It's enough for me and it ought to be enough for the damn jury," I said, interrupting Mr. Garner, even though that was not very polite, but I was looking him in the eye, hard, so he'd know for sure I meant it.

Mr. Garner's face wandered down like he expected something miraculous to appear on the papers he'd been scratching on, but nothing did and when he turned his head back up at me, the silver hair on the side of his head glistened like light on a frozen pond after a cold snow. Not that it snows much down here, but I seen pictures. I figured him for sixty, sixty-five and why the hell was a rich man doing this kind of work? He licked his lips a couple times to let me know he heard what I said but wasn't making much of it.

"Luther, can I be frank?"

"Sure."

"Unless we can develop an alternative to the state's case, we're in serous trouble. I don't want you convicted of a murder you didn't commit and I know your family doesn't want that, either. Give me the information I need. If you don't, I'll have to find it out elsewhere."

Staring into his watery blue eyes, I was trying to decide how to reply. He was good, no doubt, and that would help at the trial. I needed to quit being stubborn, as usual, seeing as how I wanted more'n anything to be with my Suzie again, but talking about Summer and how we lost her was too much for me right about then.

"Anything else you might want to know?" I asked before my mind could run away from me. I know that cold, dark road real well. Been down it lots of times. Sometimes I get so mad I could… I stopped and took me a breath.

Mr. Garner said, "Did you go out anywhere the night Reinhardt was shot? To get gas, maybe?"

"I's at home with Suzie all night, watchin' TV. I can even tell you all the shows was on."

"Did anybody see you there? Call on the phone? Maybe drove by your house and saw your pickup parked in front? Maybe a neighbor noticed you were at home near the time of the murder?"

"Nobody's come forward so far, so I guess not."

Mr. Garner moved his jaw around some like he was a cow chewing his cud but he didn't have nothing in his mouth but spit. Then he says, "What can you tell me about Mark Reinhardt?"

"He's the mayor's kid. Lived here all his life."

"What was his reputation? Did he have any enemies? Bad debts? Problems with women?"

"Tell your investigator man to go look up Billy Yates, over on Third Street, second house from the corner of Mon-roe. Run-down place out back, little shack really, is where Billy lives, if'n he's in town. Long as he's not drunk at the Night Crawler."

"What does Mr. Yates know?"

"Be sure and have cash on hand or he won't say nothin'."

Mr. Garner nodded. "All right. But I need you to tell me about Summer. In your own words."

I stood up and walked over to the window and pretended to inspect that scrawny tree outside, but it didn't do no good at easing my mind and he straight-away asked me again. For all I could tell he was yelling down a tube a thousand miles away.

"Then I'll have to ask Suzie. And it might be harder for her to tell me."

I quick-stepped back to him, mad as hell for him thinking I wasn't enough of a man to spare my wife's feelings. The blood flushed up in my face like I was a hot dog on a spit.

"Don't you ever—*ever*—accuse me of hurtin' my wife."

He studied me for a long minute and didn't look away or seem afraid, but considering he's most likely seen a lot of bad-asses in his time, I probably wasn't much compared to people real practiced-up on that kind of behavior.

"Please tell me what happened," he says and stretches his hands across the table, looking like he wanted to take ahold of both of mine.

Damn, he was good.

"Maybe tomorrow, but I can't…today."

FOUR

Clarice sucked down the smoke, feeling the hot gas slamming through her lungs, enjoying every second of it. People who thought cigarettes tasted terrible were crazy. "What I said is we should do something bad."

"Like what?" Denise asked, suspicious now, a bit over-concerned now after her third Crown-and-Coke.

"Fuck if I know. Maybe rob a bank."

"You shitting me?"

"No. Hell, no."

Denise closed her eyes to think. "What about Carl? We might not have time to pull off grand theft 'fore he gets home and wants dinner."

"He's working the double tonight. Won't see him 'til tomorrow some time."

Leaning back into the sofa cushion, Denise was enjoying thinking about the idea, the complete stupidity of it. "How'd it look, the sheriff's secretary holding up a bank, huh?"

"Listen, it's gotta be easy. Stupid shits do it all the time and don't get caught, and we ain't stupid, are we?"

"No. Well, maybe about this...and they *do* get caught. Some of them, anyways."

"We'll put on plastic masks, Halloween type, wear men's clothes, disguise our voices. Or maybe we stay quiet and hand them a note made outta pasted-on letters, then show 'em our guns. Money-or-your-life kinda shit. We're in and out in forty, fifty seconds. I hear they train those people to give you the money quick. Listen, you got any weed?"

"What makes you think that?"

Clarice ground her cigarette against the navy blue insides of the glazed ashtray, watching the white and gray flakes dance off the end, highlighted against the strong color. "I didn't ask you where you *got* it. I asked did you *have* any?"

Denise, right about now having trouble concentrating on the question, stood up and stumbled as one foot came down on part of the other one. "Look, you know I'm not into that. But I *do* happen to… Hey, anyone ever say—"

"Just tell me where it is, dammit."

Clarice watched Denise swaying like she was caught in a breeze that had suddenly come up in the living room. The woman never could hold her liquor. "No way I'd ever say… Hey, you're too fucked up to even go *get* it."

"Like you'd know where it was," Denise said, sliding by Clarice on the end of the green corduroy sofa, touching the other woman's arm to reassure her, missing her with the last pat of the two. "Back in a minute."

The minute turned into five. Denise tottered for a moment in the small kitchen, steadying a hand on the Formica countertop before launching herself back into the living room. She carried a sandwich bag half full of green moss.

"Here you go," she said, stopping as she handed it off to Clarice.

Opening the bag, Clarice took in the aroma. "Good stuff. And fresh. How'd you come by it?"

"B.J. and Cooter took down some fellahs trying to move into town last week. Dopers up from San Antonio, he said, wanting to start up a local trade. I accidental-like saw him and Cooter in the back room, cutting it. Said it was top quality, maybe I would like to have some, the evidence people didn't need all of it, so they let me have…"

Denise collapsed onto the sofa, the cushion's air wheezing out in an asthmatic moan. "Shit," she said, rubbing her temples with a middle finger and thumb, "I shouldn't a-told you that." She reached out for the sweaty drink sitting on the coaster, the long pink fingernails flashy against her tan skin. "I gotta eat soon, else I'm gonna throw up. What time is it?"

"Six. We been here all fucking afternoon. You got any rolling papers?" Clarice said, looking through the clear plastic at the bag's contents.

"Now, about that bank," Denise, trying hard to figure out the best angle, straightening out the index finger from the rest of her hand cramped around the whiskey glass, "How would that work?"

"We'd need shotguns."

"How the hell you hide shotguns?" Denise said.

"Under our coats. Seen it on TV a bunch of times."

"It's a hundred fucking degrees outside. We go in wearing coats, everybody'll know right off something's wrong. Jesus, Clarice, I'm half drunk and I know *that* wouldn't work."

Her friend reconsidered. "Okay, maybe pistols. Nine millimeters, like the gangbangers use. Got any extras lying around the office?"

Denise exhaled, "You one crazy bitch, you know it?"

Clarice nodded. "I'm still thirsty. How 'bout we go to the Night Crawler, have us some more drinks?"

"Maybe later. It's not open yet. And that bank idea? Shit, Clarice, they're already closed. We'll have to do it tomorrow, on my lunch hour. Now, who's gonna drive?"

"Tonight when we go eat or tomorrow when we hold up the bank?"

Denise pressed the palm of her hand against her forehead, mashing it down hard enough to leave a temporary spot that faded as soon as she lifted her hand. "Tonight's all I'm interested in."

"Me, of course. You left your car downtown, 'member?" Clarice stood up, one finger clamping the marijuana bag against her drink. "I'm asking you again, bitch, do you got any rolling papers?"

"Yes," Denise said, one question behind.

"Where?"

Denise shook her head. "I mean no."

"What kind of person's got weed and nothing to roll it in?"

"Hey, it's not like I smoke on a regular basis."

Clarice, putting the bag in her purse, said, "We'll stop by the convenience store, buy you a chili dog or some cheese nachos, settle your stomach. But we're going by my house first, get me outta this damn waitress outfit." She reached down for the woman on the sofa, knowing without extra encouragement Denise would stay right there all night. "Let's go, girlfriend."

"I gotta change. Got all sweaty out shopping, it being so hot—"

"Christ, hurry it up, Denise. Time's a-wasting."

FIVE

Right after two in the afternoon Suzie dropped, on time as always. She sat there with her hand held up to mine, like the cheap Plexiglas panel with the speaker in the middle wasn't between us, and we was actually touching, feeling the warmth of each other, and I can't figure out why they let you sit out with your lawyer all morning long here and shake hands with him and then they won't let you even touch your own wife.

Suzie's short, maybe three inches over five feet on a good day and small boned and looked like a slow nudge would knock her off her feet. I could see a food stain on her white uniform, down near her waist where she was carrying maybe fifteen dishes at the same time. I always wondered why waitresses and painters wear white. Maybe they like to show off their mistakes.

"Luther, I miss you."

"Me, too, baby. I can't wait to hold you again."

'Fore I spoke again, she added, "Oh, Luther, what's gonna happen to us?"

Then I seen the tears had sprung out all over and her face was screwed up and the end of her nose was turning red like a hornet stung it. It near broke my heart to see her feel so bad and I couldn't do nothing about it.

"Baby, don't cry. It'll all work out. You wait and see."

She nodded and sniffled, then bucked up and wiped the tears off and gave me a little smile, kind a wife gives a husband when there's things between 'em no one else can share, and they both know what's meant without speaking a word. Her brown roots was starting to show under the cheap blonde dye job. I told her a hundred times not to do that herself and go to the beauty shop and get it done proper but she says it's too expensive and won't go. I decided maybe it wasn't the best time to mention her hair color, seeing as I was going to trial for murder in a few weeks.

"I'll try," she said.

"How's your feet?" I asked, since she's got problems standing up all day and now it's two shifts and her feet have got to hurt a lot by the evening, what with me not there to rub 'em for her like I always do.

"They're all right."

"Quit that second shift. I mean it," I said, raising my voice a little, but she paid no attention, that being the way she was when she made up her mind and there wasn't no use me trying to change it.

"We need the money."

"Borrow it. Go see Fred at the bank. He'll loan us some."

She shook her head. "Not when we can't pay it back."

"We'll find a way."

"I won't do it."

And that was that. Maybe we could've borrowed the money from the bank, but I doubt it. The two of us working for low wages, we hadn't accumulated much in the way of collateral, as the banker likes to call it.

Then she says, "A letter came from the school system yesterday. Said you've been terminated."

I nodded. "Guess they don't want a murderer wipin' up pee in the stalls."

Gene the deputy came by and said time was up and I had to go back.

"'Bye, baby. See you tomorrow," I said, and got up and walked away without looking back 'cause if I hadn't Gene would've had to drug me back.

◆　◆　◆

Like I said before, I share a cell with Barry, the brother of Carl that shot Clarice in the face, and it's not a big mystery jail's his second home seeing as how crime runs in the Telford family like brown eyes does in others. Barry used to be called Buzz 'cause of his short hair but once he got his real career of thieving going good, he let his hair grow long and greasy so Buzz wouldn't work anymore and now he's just plain Barry. I've got the top bunk 'cause Barry says he don't like heights, and, besides, one day I'll understand about wanting the lower one once the sheriff gives me The Explanation.

◆　◆　◆

Sheriff B.J. Sanders come by after dinner, leaning into the cell door and acting real friendly-like. Everyone used to call him "Blow Job" when he was younger, after his initials and all, but since he become sheriff twenty years back he took to busting open the heads of those of the criminal persuasion that persisted with the "Blow Job" remark, so they stopped saying it, but they still think it plenty.

B.J. looked like Smokey The Bear, except that the cowboy hat didn't work and most of the fur was missing. He pressed in against the door, his belly pouching through the steel bars in two or three spaces, B.J. always having trouble pushing away from the dinner table soon enough.

"Luther, come on down here," he says.

I got down and walked over.

"You started smoking, boy?"

I saw B.J. looking at the pack of cigarettes in my pocket and I said, "Yes, sir, I have. Helps to pass the time."

"Hear you got yourself a new lawyer."

"Yes, sir, I did."

"Bob Franklin not good enough for the likes of you?"

"Bob's fine," I says.

"Then why you got somebody else?"

"Legal Defense Fund sent the man over and I thought it was the polite thing to do, taking him up on representing me. Mr. Garner seems like a good lawyer, near as I can tell."

B.J. reached out and grabbed my neck with his big fat hand and started squeezing. "Trash like you don't need to bring in outsiders. Tomorrow you tell the man you want Bob back, hear?"

I was having some trouble answering right about then.

"Tomorrow. Else me and Cooter come for a real visit." He let go and watched me fall back against the concrete block wall. "Ask Barry. He'll tell you what happens you don't listen." He laughed and left.

After rubbing my throat for a while I asked Barry was that The Explanation he was talking 'bout before and Barry said hell no and believe me you'd know it when it showed up.

Six

Denise slumped onto the side of the bed, feeling the booze, her head swimming the backstroke. Then the arm behind her collapsed and she fell backwards onto the spread.

Sitting alone in the living room, Clarice finished her drink and listened for Denise. Not hearing any movement, she said, "Shit," and got to her feet. Rounding the corner into the bedroom, Clarice spied Denise sprawled out on the grass-green expanse, her short skirt riding up with her panties peeking out between her legs.

"Hey, get up. I mean it, goddammit," Clarice said.

"No…I'm staying here," Denise moaned.

"Hell you say." Clarice walked to the dresser, opening and slamming drawers in succession. "What color outfit you want to wear?"

Massaging her forehead, eyes closed, Denise remained mute.

"Red looks good on you." Clarice fished through the underwear, finding a thong and throwing it over on Denise's face, then headed for the closet.

"I mean it," Denise said, listless, not even moving to remove the underwear.

"Shut up, you drunk bitch."

The hangers scratched across the galvanized pipe. Clarice inspected the possibilities, finding a stretch outfit, cardinal red, looking like it would maybe fit a ten-year-old on a diet.

"Here. Put this on."

Eyes open now, Denise's words fell from her mouth like vomit. "Told you, I'm not fucking *going*."

• • •

Fifteen minutes later, they emerged from Denise's house, Clarice still in her white-with-powder-blue-trim waitress uniform, tugging on Denise, all in red, stumbling along in spiky strap heels.

Denise's shoulder nudged the inside of the car door, her head resting against the window. "I'm throwing up in your fucking car in maybe five seconds, tops. Serve you right. Telling you, I feel like shit."

"You'll be fine," Clarice said, backing out with a lurch that almost snapped Denise's head off.

• • •

Denise, sipping a bicarb, looking like maybe she'd live a while longer, lounged on the arm of the frayed chair she'd pulled in from the living room. Clarice was down to her granny panties, bent over looking for a new bra.

"Where's that other one?" Clarice said. "Goddammit."

"What you gonna put on? We gotta look cool."

Clarice raised up, her heavy breasts settling on her chest. "Shit, I remember."

She returned from the bathroom, the bra already hooked in the front, sliding it around and sacking up her boobs. Finished, she turned sideways, sucking in her stomach.

"One thing about you, girl," Denise said. "Always had a nice rack."

"Yeah," Clarice said, "but they're saggy now." She turned a little more, putting an index finger on the front center of one cup. "Down about an inch in the last three years. By the time I'm sixty, they'll be slapping my knees."

Denise laughed. "Least you got big ones. Me, I must've inherited from my daddy."

"But you got that little ass to go with it. Men like a skinny broad. Makes them look big and important."

"You think?"

"Sure."

After Clarice pulled off her panties, Denise said, "Hey, don't Carl ask you to shave some of that?"

"Fuck Carl."

"But I mean, don't men like that?"

"I never asked. He'll have to take me natural."

Denise said, "Yeah, but least you got a man. I'm still looking, you know."

"That why you wear those damn thongs?" Clarice asked, pulling on a pair of underwear matching the ones she'd taken off.

"No panty lines, girl. Besides, makes me feel sexy, string up the crack of my ass, nobody but me knowing. Like a naughty secret."

"Secret, hell. I couldn't stand that." Clarice stepped to her closet, paging through her clothes, unsatisfied. "I need a new wardrobe."

Denise rested an arm on the top of the chair and pressed the cold glass across her forehead with her free hand. Finished with the temporary treatment, she waved the bicarb around as she talked. "You get you a thong, maybe a garter belt and stockings, flash ole Carl when he comes home. Man, he'll go crazy."

"All he wants to do is drink beer and watch NASCAR," Clarice said, sighing.

"Hey, you two having trouble?" Denise said, concerned now.

"Oh, it's…" Clarice stopped, holding onto an empty hanger. "You ever stop and think about your life, wondering how you got where you are? Look back, seeing all the mistakes? Settling too soon, knowing all along it wasn't what you wanted?"

Denise, uneasy now, dropped the glass to the top of her bare leg. "Sure. I mean, everyone does some time."

"I been at it a lot lately." Clarice continued back through the hangers.

Denise tottered up on her five inch heels. "Tell you what. Put on that brown sharecropper rig there and we'll go shopping for you a real dress, kind that shows off that figure, even if your tits *are* halfway to the floor. Then we'll get us something to eat, maybe go out to the city park, watch the sunset. You tell me all your troubles and I'll pretend to feel sorry for your dumb ass. How's that sound?"

"That'd be real nice, girlfriend," Clarice said, a shimmer of tears working their way across her lower lids.

Seven

"Our investigator tracked down Mr. Yates yesterday. He found the man at home, drunk from what I understand."

"Then you found Billy," I said.

"He promised to meet my man tonight at nine. After he's sobered up, and as long as we brought a 'consulting fee.' At a place called the Night Crawler. You know it?"

"Juke joint out on the south end of town off the highway. Lots of loud music and nobody much willin' to say what happens in the back room."

Mr. Garner nodded. "I'll let you know what we find out. Now how about you tell me that story I asked about yesterday?"

"No," I said and wouldn't budge 'cause I couldn't face telling that story today and besides my throat hurt a little from the visit by the law last night.

"Mr. Holman, I'm a persistent man. I'll keep asking."

"Fine. I'll keep saying 'no' 'til I'm ready."

I got a look, The Square Eye Momma always called it, but who knows what that really means since most people nod their head when you say "The Square Eye" like they understand it but they don't and act like they know to keep from looking ignorant. But if ever I seen The Square Eye, this was it.

"I'll do everything I can to defend you, Luther, but I need your cooperation."

"Yes, sir," I said and stood up and shook his hand 'fore he left.

◆ ◆ ◆

Suzie showed up the next day at the regular time. I didn't tell her about the throat incident 'cause I didn't want to worry her.

"How's Mop and Broom?" I asked. You see, we got ourselves these two cats, about the same age, one we paid two dollars for and the other was free. I named them myself, in honor of my profession and all.

"Mop still looks for you every night," she said, "Like a dog. Strangest thing I ever saw. Broom spends all her time in my lap."

"Okay," I said, not knowing what else to ask about.

"I've got something here to show you," she said, and what do you know but she unzips her waitress dress down to her bellybutton and she didn't have on no bra and showed me her little bare round titties real quick-like before she zipped back up.

I laughed out loud and then Gene the deputy caught on to what she was doing and said if she ever done that again she couldn't never come back in for a visit.

After Suzie left, Gene took me back to my cell and said in a low voice he wished he had a woman loved him as much as Suzie did me, that being a mighty fine thing for a man to come home to.

◆ ◆ ◆

That night all I could think about my little wife and holding her tight and what she done for me this afternoon and I ended up spending part of the night petting the one-eyed snake. I asked Barry polite-like if he minded the bunk squeaking a little and he laughed and said he done it, too, to pass the time, and it was the most pleasant night I'd had in jail. Assuming there is such a thing.

◆ ◆ ◆

Turned out later Billy Yates wasn't of much help, considering Mr. Garner said Billy was discovered a couple days later, out in the tall weeds behind the Night Crawler, his head busted in by persons unknown. Billy was the kind most decent folk aren't gonna miss much and I don't expect the sheriff to waste much of his valuable resources looking for the ones who done it.

EIGHT

"You ever think about killing yourself?"

The tip of Denise's knife stalled in the middle of the dinner roll, its warm insides sucking the soft butter down like a whirlpool in the bathtub. "Say what?"

Poking her fork at the remains of her sirloin steak, Clarice said, "Simple question."

"No, I mean…" The knife started again, maneuvering the remainder of the butter into the now-closing halves of the roll. Denise set the bread down, staring at it before meeting Clarice's eyes. "You *really* thinking about it?"

"Used to. Not so much any more."

"*Used* to?"

Nodding, Clarice said, "When I was younger. Fourteen or so. Lots of girls do that, right?"

"Maybe."

"Meaning you didn't?"

"I'm not saying never. But it didn't exactly occupy all my time." Denise refocused on the roll and moved it into her mouth to wait for a break in the emotional logjam.

"You got butter on your chin."

Denise dropped the bread to her plate and fished for a napkin. "Why would you…did you think about something like that?"

"Never mind," Clarice said, wanting a cigarette, bad. But she was stuck in the non-smoking section of the Country Sizzler. Clarice scanned the restaurant, checking out the arrangements with an expert eye. Salad wagon in the center, good choice, but the soup tureens should be on the other side, away from the greens, where people needed more room to stand and ladle out the soup it wouldn't drip on the floor. And the payout counter, too near the kitchen door that needed a bigger glass to prevent collisions…

"No, I want to hear." Denise cleaned the stray drip off and leaned forward. "You and me been best friends for what, maybe fifteen years?"

"Yeah," Clarice said, still looking away, hoping for a change in the subject.

"So don't you go dissing me now, *bitch*. I had me plenty of opportunities to throw you back in high school, uh-huh, I mean."

"What the hell you saying?"

"The Black girls I ran with? They were always on me, telling me to dump the honky."

Clarice's eyes glowed. "I'd known that, I'd kicked all their damn asses."

"Why you think I stayed quiet?"

Clarice laughed, deep down, a raspy smoker's scratch catching the last of the sound coming up from her throat. "Maybe a good choice."

"Why'd you keep it from me?"

"What?"

"Thinking of killing yourself. Pisses me off now I hear it. I'm your closest friend, right?"

"Right," she said, finally answering Denise, the word whispering out from lips barely apart.

Clarice thought back about seeing Denise for the first time, in junior high, her looking real young and scared of herself. Denise was shy and wide-eyed back then, like maybe half the time she wasn't sure how she got to school in the first place. They'd met in the cafeteria, Clarice sitting by herself that day because she was pissed off about something. Despite the Black kids keeping pretty much to themselves those days, Denise had ginned up the courage to come over and ask, hey, would it be okay maybe I had lunch with you, those other girls don't like me so much. Clarice had been ready to bark out a negative reply, but there Denise was with her old woman glasses and long braids tied up, looking like she was expecting another rejection. Clarice instead said, sure, what the hell, have a seat, it's a free country. Soon, they'd become friends, then, later on, best friends. They both were innocent back then, back before the world had stepped all over them.

A brown hand extended across the red plaid plastic tablecloth, finding Clarice's fingers, folding them into hers. "Love you, girl."

Clarice blinked to scare away the tears starting up. Shit, she thought, three fucking times in one day.

Watching her friend, Denise said, "Remember, when we was younger, we said everything happens to you happens to me, too?"

Swallowing, Clarice nodded. "Yeah. I remember."

"So tell me why you thought about killing yourself."

"I forgot the reason," Clarice said.

"Bullshit."

Clarice folded her napkin and took the time to lay it beside her plate, thinking how she hated customers at the diner who dumped their napkins in the middle of their plates, letting the juices soak up into the paper, and her having to separate out the mess most days, except when they had a busboy, which wasn't often. Some of them even stubbed out their cigarettes in the plates, disregarding the ashtray on the table. Well, she didn't need to worry about that shit anymore.

"Let's go. I'll get the check." Clarice reached for the downturned slip.

Denise's hand landed on the ticket first. "Last I heard you're out of a job, girl. I'll be taking care of this."

"The hell you say," Clarice said. "I'm not a charity case."

"You get a job, you're buying next. And I'm not talking no half-price early-bird tough shit like this, neither. I'm thinking filet. Maybe lobster, too."

"Done," Clarice said. "But I'll get the tip."

Denise watched as her friend dropped close to thirty percent on the table. "How about let's go buy you a real dress, then go see that sunset?"

NINE

Momma come to see me middle of the week before the trial started, which was awful nice of her considering the gout was working hard on her. First I seen her she was rounding the corner, shoving her walker ahead and making a face ever time she took a step. The bottom part of her left leg was swole up half again the size it was supposed to be but she come anyway, to see her son, and I thought that was pretty special for her to go to so much trouble.

"Hey, Momma, you didn't have to come," I said.

"Oh, go on." She heaved down in the chair in front of the glass, grabbing at the counter top to steady herself, then stretched her bad leg out to the side. "Had to come see my baby boy." She gave me the same big wide smile I always get from my momma.

"You come by yourself?"

"Carlene carried me over. She's out in the lobby knittin' a sweater for her grandkid. 'Course he won't never wear it and she knows it and I can't figure out why in the world she keeps at it."

"Tell her I said thank you."

"I will."

We looked at each other through the dirty glass, covered over with fingerprints that a dab of Windex would've cleared right up.

"Son, how you doin' in here? It's been a long while."

"It's jail, Momma. Not much better or worse than you'd think."

"They been feedin' you right?"

"I get three squares a day if I want 'em, but they come early. Breakfast starts at six and supper's over by five. Lights out at eight. You get used to it 'cause you have to."

"Looks to me like you lost fifteen pounds, maybe more," she said. "Not like you had a lot to give up in the first place."

"Maybe, Momma. I don't know."

"We all miss you over at the house for Sunday dinner after church. Just Suzie and me and half the time she can't hardly eat nothin', she's so sad worryin' after you." Momma waited, then said, "There's somethin' I could do about all this. If'n you'd let me."

When I didn't reply, she added, "I suppose we've all got to be patient for what's comin', though the Lord knows it's hard. When's the trial start?"

"Next Monday, nine-thirty, Mr. Garner says. Didn't Suzie tell you?"

"I recollect now maybe she did, but I need to be reminded of things these days, from time to time. Not like my mind's goin', though. Least not yet. I plan on bein' there, in the front row, right behind you."

I shook my head. "Momma, you stay home and take care yourself. That leg of yours looks like it's about to bust wide open."

"You crazy?" she asked and didn't wait for an answer 'cause that's the kind of question a mother asks her kid and never expects a reply. "I'll be there, right next to Suzie. Both of us'll be pullin' for you. Besides, I might need to stand up in court and tell that knothead Harder a thing or two."

"I can't see you standin' up about much of anything much right now."

She frowned to hush me up. "I'll get this leg doctored on 'fore then, never you mind. What about that new lawyer? He's any better'n that Bob Franklin no-account?"

"I 'spect so. He's asked a lot of the right questions. He's got him an investigator snoopin' around town and says next week he'll see to it a reporter from one of those big-city newspapers shows up for the trial 'cause it might help later if we get us some publicity."

"Suzie say anything about him to you?"

"No," I said. "Why?"

"I don't know. Nothin'."

"What's that mean?"

Momma shifted in the seat, looking like she was thinking 'bout how she wanted to give her reply. "She said that attorney looked at her kinda funny, like maybe he knew her from before."

"Didn't mention it to me."

Momma said something low I couldn't quite make out, then added, "I gotta go. They give me fifteen minutes and it took near all that to get me in here."

"Thanks for comin', Momma."

"Sure, Luther. I had to see you. You're still my little boy."

Momma smiled and then struggled up and a deputy come over to help her but she wasn't having none of it, pushing him away with that walker like it was a spear. But that's how my momma is, she's got plenty of spunk and it's a shame her mind can't make her body work the way it used to. She's only sixty-five, but the years've been hard on her and I sure wish she'd get some rest.

◆   ◆   ◆

That night Sheriff Sanders showed up with Cooter, his nephew deputy. I figure they call him Cooter 'cause Shithead was already taken.

Next thing I know I was down in the interrogation room with my hands handcuffed to two thick rails under the seat of a wooden chair bolted to the floor, and I could see I wasn't the first one to experience their version of persuasion 'cause there was places along both sides where the cuffs had slid back and forth and worked off all the varnish.

Cooter took one of the cigarettes outta my pocket without asking could he have one please and lit it up. Then they both started asking a lot of questions 'bout why didn't I get rid of the new lawyer like they told me to and what does the lawyer know and what the hell did I think I was doing. I answered best I could but they must've not been satisfied with my comments since Cooter pretty soon puts on the brass knucks and begins leaving marks where they don't show. I remember thinking I wished he would've put his cigarette out first 'cause when he slung into me hot ash near as not went right down my shirt collar.

◆　◆　◆

When they drug me back to the cell a while later, B.J. hollers at Barry and says maybe I need the bottom bunk tonight 'cause I'm feeling poorly seeing as how I tripped on the stairs that don't exist and can't seem to stand up so good.

I laid down best I could and tried to concentrate on how one breath was going to follow the next and Barry said from up top that he'd stay there for a couple days more 'til I got to feeling better and now I know what The Explanation is and I don't have to ask about it no more.

After I got easy I told Barry there was something I needed to get ahold of and maybe could he help me out with it. He said casual-like it wouldn't be no problem excepting maybe if I needed a female companion snuck in, and who knows maybe that might be arranged, too, for the right price. From what I could tell, that's how you act when you're a steady customer of this place and know how it works as well as anybody.

After I gave him my list, he asked what the hell did I need a razor blade and some glue and rubber bands for unless I wanted to cut my wrist and then glue up the joints after I happened to change my mind. I said no thanks, I wasn't ready to die just yet and if I left this earth it sure wouldn't be from the likes of no razor blade.

TEN

Clarice ran her hand across the emerald green dress Denise had talked her into buying, touching the fabric, feeling its texture. It was beautiful, low-cut and shorter than she would've bought on her own. It was the best looking dress she'd ever owned, and the most expensive. Under it was a new set of sexy black underwear.

"Carl sees the bill, he's gonna shit," Clarice said.

"Fuck Carl. Isn't that what you said before?" Denise said, giggling from the influence of the joint, having only smoked half of one.

Clarice rolled another joint as the roach was dying out. "Yeah, somebody's got to. Long as it isn't me."

"What you talking about?" Denise asked, paying attention now, the mellow feeling fading.

"We haven't done it in six weeks."

"How come?"

Clarice flicked the glowing stub out of the open window of the Trans Am, watching it hit the gravel and the sputtering ember fade to black. They were parked at the edge of the city park's lake, facing west, watching the sun falling into the earth. It had cooled off some, more like ninety by now, still hot and sticky except for the slight tickle of a breeze coming off the water. The clouds were tinged pink high up in the sky, fading down to golden brown near the earth, so beautiful yet forever untouchable. In a few minutes, the sunset would trigger an invasion of mosquitoes, ready for blood, and they'd have to leave.

"My fault," Clarice said, staring through the windshield, a vacant look on her face.

"Why, girl? What's happened?" Denise turned sideways in the car, bunching her eyebrows together.

"Something that happened years ago. Can't get it out of my mind."

Denise laid her hand on Clarice's. A newborn marijuana cigarette, ready to go, sat forgotten in the console ashtray. "Got anything to do with what you wouldn't talk about before?"

Clarice rested her left elbow on the top of the door, her open palm holding the side of her tilted head. "'Member when we were fourteen and Gladys had that boyfriend for about a year? Lived with us in the house?"

"Yeah, I remember. What was his name?"

"Anthony."

"That's right," Denise said, nodding. "Middle sized man, sort of chubby guy, brown hair. Not that much to see."

"Except for the eyes," Clarice said. "He had hawk eyes."

"So? What about him?"

"Anthony molested me."

"*What!*" Denise said, her friend's news so unexpected, she had a hard time connecting the words to what they meant.

Clarice turned to Denise, the slow tears now cutting ruts in the freebie makeup the department store woman put on after she bought the dress. Clarice's mind flashed a view of the two them, sitting there as a passer-by in the aisle would have seen them, Clarice and Denise laughing and cutting up at the cosmetics counter like when they were still back in high school. That pleasant vision evaporated, replaced by the long-repressed older one.

Taking in a shaky breath, Clarice said, "Twelve times. I can still remember each one of them, clear and separate, like they happened today. I even numbered each one, in my head, as they happened. So I could keep track."

"Why the *hell* didn't you tell your mother? If she'd known, she would've—"

39

"That's the shit of it. Gladys knew. And she didn't care." Clarice's lower lip began to tremble. "Not enough…enough to save her daughter."

Taking the crying woman in her arms, Denise said, "You could've told me, dammit. You could've *told* me."

"I know," Clarice said, sobs racking her chest, "I know that now."

The sun hurtled down over the tops of the trees, the multi-shades of the clouds fading together into a dull brown in a prelude to the future blackness. Soon the frogs would start up with their rough songs, accompanied by the crickets making their own special night music.

Clarice sat up and took a deep breath, her strength gone, laying her head back against the faded headrest, Denise not saying a word, knowing her friend, her need to collect herself before talking some more.

"I developed early, you know. Had a set of tits before most of the girls." She waited before she spoke again, listening for the night sounds, just starting but getting stronger, more intense. Both of the women were fixated on the confession, knowing how special and long remembered it was going to be and not wanting to spoil it. "He'd been there about four months and he kept looking at me, strange-like. I had any sense I'd known what was coming."

"Shit, Clarice. You were *fourteen*."

"The first time he came in my bedroom, real late, and he said, I'll never forget it, 'There's something I've been meaning to give you,' and he unzips his pants and pulls out his dick. It was already hard. He'd been waiting for an opportunity to get at me."

"God," Denise said, seeing it.

Clarice rushed ahead. "It hurt bad, mother asking me what was wrong the next day, looking at me walking funny, and at him, too. She knew right then, from the start."

"And she never said nothing?"

"Not one fucking word. Not ever. Too concerned about losing her new boyfriend, needing a meal ticket and having me to sell to get it." Clarice jabbed the joint in her mouth, lighting it up, then held the smoke deep in her lungs.

"How'd it ever stop?" Denise asked.

Clarice coughed out the smoke. "Last time, number twelve, he comes in, already naked, holding his cock like always, saying 'I've got what you want right here,' rubbing it with his hand, up and down. That night, I was prepared. I had a butcher knife under my pillow waiting for him. Pulled it out while I was feelin' my teeth knocking together in my head. I said, 'You touch me and I'll stick this in you all the way up to the handle.'"

"Goddamn, Clarice, what happened?"

"He called me a filthy fucking whore. Can you imagine that? Yelling at me, saying I led him on."

"What'd Gladys do? She had to hear y'all yelling at each other."

"Pretended to be asleep."

"Through all that?"

Clarice smiled, sad as much as hurt, remembering it. "She was a peach, wasn't she? After Anthony moved out the next day she asked why couldn't I get along with her boyfriend and had to screw up their relationship." Clarice took another pull on the joint, the story almost gone now. "Right after that I took up with Carl. He seemed okay, good enough. But now, when I see him on me, naked, it's not Carl but Anthony."

Denise waited to talk, trying to think of the right thing to say. "You need some counseling, girl, tell somebody about this. Time goes on, it's only gonna get worse you don't."

Clarice looked at Denise, a smile frozen on her face, the evening mosquitoes chewing on her arm and her not even knowing it. "I *have* told someone. *You.* You're the only one will ever know."

"Come on," Denise said, opening her door and fanning away the bugs. "Get out. I'll drive. You're in no condition, hear me?"

ELEVEN

Next day Mr. Garner was early as usual and asked what was the matter since I was limping some as I come in and I said I had a little fall last night but there wasn't nothing to it. Cooter stood around near the wall and smiled at what I said, then then he walked through the door to get himself some coffee and five donuts and left us alone.

Mr. Garner said he had to hear the story about Summer since it was almost trial time and he and the investigator had heard it talked up around town and wanted to know the real McCoy. It knew it was way past time to tell him so I started in quick-like so I could get it over with and never have to tell it again. Least, not to him.

"Summer was born on May the ninth, the perfect evening to bring a perfect little girl into this world. Today she'd be twelve years, three months, six days old. I think about her sweet little face, the last time I saw her alive and that dimple on her left cheek that deepened way down ever time she smiled."

I must not've thought about it conscious-like, but there my finger was, poking my cheek in the same place. "I sometimes go to thinkin' on what she'd look like and what she'd be sayin' and doin' with her future all ahead of her. But now she's singin' with the angels or maybe sleepin' in the cold ground, waitin' for the Lord to call her home. I don't know which. All I know is she's gone."

"I'm so sorry, Luther," Mr. Garner said.

I think, looking at his face, maybe he was sorry, and that give me a little strength to go on, but my old heart was falling out of my chest, the way it does every time I think of her and about what happened.

I got up and looked out at that stupid scrawny willow tree again and at the stupid brown sparrows sitting on the branches in the heat, them swaying with the breeze and riding it out. Maybe one of them was her, come back as a bird and staring through that window at me and giving me some courage to tell my tale, and God knows I needed it. The lawyer stayed where he was, not needling me anymore, but looked in my direction, a kind concern pasted on his face and it was maybe all made up, but that helped me with the telling, still.

"Suzie said our little girl was so perfect, wasn't any use us havin' any more kids since there wouldn't never be none better and I had to agree. She was everything a parent wanted. Kinda funny the way she used to run to the door when I come home, so happy to see her daddy..."

I stopped again and considered what to say next to a man had never met your baby, but what was the point trying to tell a stranger how special your little girl was. He never seen her or spoke to her or watched her play in the backyard.

"When is the last time you saw her?" Mr. Garner said, innocent-like.

"In her casket, since you asked."

"Sorry. I meant when she was alive."

"Middle of August, almost four years ago. It was hot and sweaty like now, and she was goin' to ride her bike over to Mary Johnson's house, four blocks away, since they was both in Girl Scouts and they had them a project to work on so they could get a merit badge. That's what cost me my daughter, Mr. Garner. A merit badge."

"Luther, I'm sure—"

"We told her to be careful and watch the intersections and the cars pullin' out of driveways and she said she would. She was gonna be gone about an hour and a half tops but it was two days later 'fore they found her, out in the woods north of town."

Mr. Garner cleared his throat and didn't say nothing.

"Next time I saw her, it was in the funeral home before they cleaned her up. Sheriff Sanders said the doc told him she was molested and then strangled and they took samples from inside her body to check out who might've done it, do a blood test. Me and Suzie have read about that new test they have, they call it DNA, but it's not ready yet, and I hear it costs a lot, so that wasn't somethin' we could look to back then." I paused, thinking it through. "They never found out nothin' for sure. Couple other girls about the same age had disappeared 'fore that, maybe the same man, I don't know, but those other times there wasn't much to go on, no bodies was ever found, not like with Summer. But when you lose what little evidence you got I guess it don't matter much if you had it to start with, does it? All we got back was her blue dress in a garbage bag, it all stained with mud and leaves. Can you believe that? A garbage bag."

The attorney was looking down at his hands now like maybe he'd grown a couple new thumbs since he last checked but I saw he hadn't.

"They never, ah… They lost the evidence? Didn't do a blood test?" he said.

"Contaminated, they said."

"The sheriff bungled it, then?"

"Sheriff Sanders said it was the lab's fault and besides he laid the murder off to a traveler and said it don't matter the evidence got messed up 'cause we'd never find the man that done it anyways, him gone away for good and never to return." I shrugged. "Maybe the lab got careless. Or maybe someone told them to."

"What does this have to do with Mark Reinhardt?"

"Word around town was maybe he had something to do with it."

"With losing the evidence?"

"With killing my daughter."

"Did he?"

"He never stood trial for it."

"Did you kill Mark Reinhardt, Luther? Because of what happened to your daughter? Because you believed he murdered Summer?"

"You think if it was Reinhardt that done it and I knew it for sure I would've waited this long to kill him?"

"You didn't answer my question."

"I told you before I didn't murder the man."

"Luther, you have no alibi for that night, except for your wife's testimony. The state alleges that your motive was vigilante revenge, pure and simple, without any real proof that Reinhardt was even guilty."

"What do you think, Mr. Garner?"

"I think we've going to have a helluva time proving your innocence, Luther. Right now, they're offering second degree manslaughter with fifteen years. Seems odd they're eager to put this behind them so soon. But if you're convicted on capital murder, you might very well be sentenced to death. There's also temporary insanity, if you'll consider it, despite how it turned out for Carl Telford. I think, based on the circumstances of your daughter's death, that would be a viable defense strategy."

"I don't want you to bargain for my life. I want you to help me get the truth out, and not end up with me killed for somethin' I didn't do."

Mr. Garner shook his head and rubbed it with his hand, massaging the temples as he went, the skin piling up in waves in front of his fingertips like it does when a man gets older and the skin starts to sag 'cause then you got more'n you need but there's no place for it to go but to hang on your face.

"The investigator hasn't turned up much so far. And Billy Yates didn't live long enough to talk to us."

"Billy's dead and there's no going back on that, but you might try Jack Roberts. He and Mark Reinhardt run together on occasion."

"Who? Jack Roberts?"

"That's right."

"Where does he live?"

"He runs the Night Crawler."

"What does he know that might help us?"

"He and Reinhardt was drinking buddies for a spell. I think even Jack finally had enough of Reinhardt."

The attorney folded up his stuff and stood to leave and I tore off a little piece of paper and wrote a few words on it and slid it across to him. He looked up and started to reply and I gave my head a quick motion to shush him. That's when I turned around and saw Cooter drinking the last of his coffee, looking through the glass at me. Mr. Garner shook his head and I took the paper back and wrote a couple more lines down and he stared at them and tore the paper up and left.

• ◆ ◆

Later on that night I was talking to Barry about my lawyer and he asks what I said to Mr. Garner and then he interrupts me.

"You stupid or what?"

I asked why he said that and he says you ever look up at the ceiling and I said no and he says the speakers up there can be reversed and made into microphones if you switch the system right and Cooter could hear everything we said, if he wanted to, 'cause he's been known to listen in before.

The thought of that made me think I swallowed a trash can full of old cafeteria fish. I spent the rest of the night trying to remember for sure the words I said in there and thank God I didn't make that last request out loud.

TWELVE

"So why not some African-sounding name, like maybe Shaneequa?" Clarice asked.

Denise and Clarice sat on adjacent barstools at the Night Crawler, despite Denise's earlier suggestion that maybe they should call it a night, Clarice saying, shit, I'm not ready to go home yet and I need me a second tequila sunrise, all while taking her time chain-smoking the long cigs with the tan filters.

"You know how things were back then, most Black folks not wanting to attract any attention, not come up with different names for their kids," Denise said, looking down at the bar top through the liquid gold of her original Crown-and-Coke. She was safe nursing this one along, watching the ice cubes shrink down, knowing she couldn't handle mixing her liquors. "Besides, she had this cousin of hers she liked a lot, name of Denise, up in De-triot."

"Get you ladies something else?" the bartender said, wiping down the glossy surface with a wet white rag.

"Not for me," Denise said, waiting, knowing she could have maybe one more if necessary, her determined now not to get shit-faced twice in the same day. The cheap steak was settled in her stomach, soaking up some of the booze, giving her a temporary reprieve.

"Give me a minute," Clarice said, and watched the man move away.

"Your turn," Denise said.

"Not sure. Didn't ever talk to Gladys about it my name. 'Course, I didn't talk to her about much of anything, now as I recall. Knowing her, though, she gave it to me as punishment for future sins."

"Well, at least we're two 'ices'. Together like always."

"Right. Yeah."

"Clarice, you know, what we talked about in the car?"

Clarice stared straight ahead, her three foot thick emotional wall concreted in place, knowing what her friend meant but not acknowledging it, saying instead, "We talked about lots of things in the car."

"Your situation, what happened when—"

Clarice cut her off. "Forget it. I have."

"I mean, girl, you need to get help to handle that."

"It's handled. Has been for years."

Denise twisted the glass 'round and 'round, working on a way to start the conversation back up, knowing how Clarice bottled things up inside and you needed a crowbar to budge them.

"See that man, the one in the corner?" Denise bent her head, after a long pause in their conversation, to show the direction, Clarice looking around now in her direct way, not self-conscious at all.

"Yeah? So what?"

"Keeps looking over here. Must be liking what he sees, a good-looking woman in a sexy green dress."

Clarice's critical eye sized the cowboy up. Short, cheap snap-button western shirt, a stupid downturned hat ringed with a dark sweat band, pants frayed from letting the floor do the hemming, legs straight out under the table like he just got off a horse and couldn't bend them yet. The man was raising his Lone Star, eyeing them. "Looks like a piece of crap to me."

"Don't be doing that," Denise said. "Keep an open mind, see?"

"Long as we're comparing men, how about that Black dude in the side booth back there, having eyes for you ever since we came in?"

"I didn't see no—" Denise stopped, her head stuck halfway around. "Goddamn, Clarice, he's handsome. I mean, shit, better than handsome.

Gorgeous. And he's…smiling at me." Denise gave the man a timid wave, then turned back, self-conscious about what she'd done.

"Uh-huh."

The cowboy broke out of the booth and approached the two women, waving the longneck around in one hand, trying to be casual-like.

"Hey, how y'all doin'?" Cowboy said. "How'd y'all like to party?"

"No, thanks," Clarice said, turning her back to the man, staring at herself in the mirror on the wall, most of it covered up with wood shelves holding liquor bottles sporting their colored labels.

"You and me could have us a good time," Cowboy said, standing there, looking down Clarice's dress, seeing the rounded insides of her big breasts for the first time. "Nice pair, I *mean*. Say, I got this place not far from here and—"

"Fuck off," Clarice said, not even looking back.

The man, getting upset now, not wanting to give up, said, "Hey, you get rid of the nigger and I'll show you what a real man—" He stopped talking, his face locked in pain.

Clarice looked past him at the Black dude standing behind Cowboy like he'd always been there, Cowboy's fingers now bent part of the way back by the dude's huge hand.

"Pardon me, ladies," the man said with a voice from deep down inside his chest somewhere, full of authority and ease, "This man's annoying you, I'd be happy to ask him to leave."

Cowboy's knees hit the floor, one hand grabbing for the extended arm, his mouth screwed up in a silent scream as the big man increased the angle of the bend.

"That'd be real nice of you, Mr…" Clarice said.

"The name's Green, Bobby Green. Pleased to meet you."

"Clarice," she said, stretching out her palm, watching the man work, the redneck almost out from the pain and his other hand flailing against Bobby Green's big arm. Bobby reached across Cowboy, seeming like he wasn't even paying attention to his victim, Clarice feeling his strength but a soft touch, too, as his huge hand enclosed all of hers.

"Miss Clarice," he said, "The pleasure's all mine." He released Cowboy and stepped over the writhing form, around Clarice's back toward Denise.

Denise, levitating off her stool, said nothing, her mouth open and eyes wide.

"And who might this vision of loveliness be?" he said, taking her extended fingers, a thumb almost covering all of them, kissing the back of her hand.

Denise wasn't able to speak.

Clarice looked down at the floor between the woman's inward-turned shoes, half expecting to see a puddle of pee between the high heels. "This here's Denise, Bobby. She's having some difficulty saying her name right now." She glanced in the other direction, watching Cowboy drift off toward the front door, damaged fingers locked under the opposite armpit, spitting out fuck, fuck, but not loud enough for Bobby Green to hear.

"Mister...Green," Denise got out, a hurricane required to tear her eyes away from the man.

"Please, call me Bobby, Miss Denise. You ladies mind if I sit down?"

"Not at all," Clarice said. "You can, too, Denise."

Denise settled back, staring at Bobby as he took the stool adjacent.

Clarice said, "What can I get you to drink, Bobby? For saving two damsels in distress?"

"I'd like a Heineken, Miss Clarice," he said, "But I insist on buying a round for the pleasure of your company."

Clarice lifted her glass. "Barkeep, another sunrise and a Heineken for Mr. Green—"

"Me, too," Denise breathed out, eyes locked on the man's face, "A Heineken, just like Mr. Bobby Green."

"Shit a brick," Clarice said, laughing as she poked a new cigarette filter into her mouth.

Thirteen

Before Mr. Garner could get going the next day, I slipped him a note about the speakers and his face got real red and his mouth formed up tight as a hatband.

"Are you sure?" he asked.

"Word is that's what happens."

"But that's—"

"Yes, sir, it is." I says, and give him a glance upward to tell him to be quiet about it and he did.

'Bout that time Mr. Garner's arm accidental-like hits his open briefcase and knocks it sideways. The case slid to the side of the table, then it tilted and fell, the contents scattering out all over, including the notes and folders and the law book in there.

We had quite a time picking it all up but I was glad to help out since there in the wreck of his papers was the thing I asked him for in my note from the last time. I slipped it into my orange jumpsuit while I was picking up the other stuff.

Lying on the floor was a little tape recorder in a silver case which I hope hadn't busted. Mr. Garner picked it up and placed it on the table.

"Luther, I've brought this in to record some of your remarks. The deputy sheriff there—" He looked past me through the window at Cooter, busy checking us out, "says that the tape recorder can only be used if I bring it in and take it out each day. He's allowed to examine the tape each time I enter or leave with it."

"Okay," I said.

"I need to record a couple of things like the fact that you didn't kill Reinhardt and where you were when in happened. Things like that."

I nodded and it didn't take no time at all to finish up and then Mr. Garner put the recorder back in his briefcase and he stood up and I did, too, and asked him a question been worrying me for a while.

"Mr. Garner, why you doin' this kinda work? Can't be the money. Kind of clothes you got on don't get bought with no public defender money."

Mr. Garner give me a strange look. "People like you, Luther," he said. "People like you."

FOURTEEN

"What brings you to our little burg, Bobby?" Clarice said.

Mr. Green said, "Thinking of starting up a business. Contracting, maybe."

"Oh?"

"Yes, ma'am. Adding on patios, small remodels, pouring driveways, what have you."

"Think you can make a living at it here?" Clarice asked.

"Bobby'll do fine," Denise said, a dreamy smile on her face for the last half-hour, offering breathless answers back to most of the man's questions.

Clarice said, "I'm only saying, Bobby, this town's not very big."

"I've been successful before in small markets," Bobby said, finishing off the second Heineken. "I'm from Detroit originally."

"Really?" Denise said, "I got this cousin up there, name of Denise Masters. Same first one as mine. Maybe you might happen to know her?"

"Sorry to say, no, but I'm sure if that Denise is anything like you, I've missed out on quite a lot."

Another giggle from Denise.

A Ray Charles blues tune flowed over from the juke box, a few couples coming onto the floor now, slow dancing, but not many of them since it was a Wednesday night.

"Ray's a favorite of mine, Miss Denise," Bobby said, taking her hand in his, "Would you favor me with a dance?"

"Yes, I believe I would, Mr. Green," Denise said, coquettish, but already up off the stool.

Clarice watched them moving together in the dark bar, Bobby holding her close, their fingers intertwined. It wasn't long before Denise's arms were around his neck, holding on tight, the pink fingernails standing out against the man's dark skin, her head now on Bobby's chest, eyes closed, them swaying together as one, never wanting it to end.

Turning back, Clarice took a drag and thought of Carl, wondering if they'd ever felt that way toward each other, even at the beginning, and knew the answer without having to think about it.

◆　◆　◆

With Bobby gone to the john for a minute, Denise said to Clarice, "I think if he asked me to, well, whatever, maybe, I'd—"

"What you waiting on, girlfriend?" Clarice said.

"I can't leave you here. Not by yourself."

"I'll be fine. Make this my last one."

"You sure? But, I mean, he probably won't—"

"You're falling for him. Hard," Clarice said.

"Yeah, like never before," Denise said, her mouth partway open, excitement gushing out of her.

"Word of advice, sweetie? Be careful, go slow. I know he seems nice, but..."

"*Nice?* You *kidding?* He's the best thing ever—" Denise began.

"*All* I'm saying, you don't *know* the man. Not really. Hear me?"

"Sure," Denise said, deflated.

Bobby was back by then and before he sat down Clarice said, "Bobby, would you mind doing me a favor?"

"Of course, Miss Clarice."

"Could I perhaps get you to take Denise home? I've got to run, soon as I finish this drink, and that'd save me a lot of time. Me and Denise came in my car."

Denise slow-smiled at Clarice, the unspoken truth that the girls lived maybe five, ten minutes apart. This last remark now added to the many secrets they'd shared since junior high, except that last one, the one she heard Clarice tell for the first time tonight.

"Clarice, Bobby doesn't need to—"

"I'd be honored to take Denise home," he said in that deep voice of his, Denise having talked him into dropping the 'Miss' part.

"Thanks, 'preciate it," Clarice said, looking down at her watch, "My, look at the time. I need to be home in fifteen minutes."

"Would you like to leave now?" Bobby asked Denise.

"Sure, right now," she said, almost forgetting her purse in the excitement, hugging Clarice goodbye and whispering a wet "thank you" in her ear.

Bobby laid two twenties on the counter, more than enough, and helped Denise off the stool like she was a china doll.

Clarice watched them walk out, Bobby's thick arm across the back of the red stretch dress, his hand tight against Denise's waist, her leaning into him. One of those special moments, she realized, bound to be spoiled some way, sooner than later, but the sight of them together stirred hope in her anyway.

She turned back to the mirrored wall as her chin gave a nod up. "Barkeep? What's a girl need to do around here to get herself a whiskey sour?"

FIFTEEN

Monday come around and I was plenty glad for the trial to start up, despite what Barry told me. Why it can't begin at eight, same time as normal people go to work, I don't know, but maybe the lawyers and the judge gotta get their morning coffee down and straighten up the papers on their desks and sit around and shoot the shit a while, no need to get on with it like maybe a man's life's at stake in the next room.

Mr. Garner saw to it that I got a nice haircut and a new dark blue suit and white shirt and striped tie to wear, and shiny new shoes that hurt a little when I walked. I wished I had on my work boots instead but I figured those wouldn't look so good with the new suit.

'Bout nine-thirty I come into the courtroom by the side door with a bailiff holding my arm and me in handcuffs looking like a career criminal and that's what most of the audience thought when they seen me. After everybody had a good look, he took the cuffs off and I sat down at the defense table.

Mr. Garner was already there, standing behind it in another nice high-dollar suit and talking to Suzie and Momma and smiling a lot like he had this thing licked and of course that was all a load of bullshit, but if it made them feel good, so much the better.

I leaned over the railing and touched Suzie's hand and kissed her cheek and the bailiff run up and said stop, no contact would be tolerated between the accused and the spectators even if one of them was my wife, but I still got to touch her and that was the first time in six months. The memory of the smell of her stayed with me all morning.

Mr. Garner watched us, paying real particular attention to the look on my wife's face, but didn't say nothing about what he'd witnessed and had a sad kind of smile on his old face.

Suzie had on one of her Sunday dresses but she was pale and thin and tired-out looking and her brown roots were showing more than ever. I knew how hard this all was on her and I asked was she working today and she said Delbert gave her the mornings off for maybe the entire week if she absolutely needed to and said not to worry about being fired 'long as she worked the night shift instead and I said that was real nice of Delbert.

Momma sat there beside Suzie with her leg propped up on a stool she said they like to not let her bring it in, and a pillow tucked under her butt to ease the soreness from those hard oak benches.

The courtroom here is, I guess, typical of most, but I don't know seeing as how I've never seen another. It's on the second floor of the courthouse, so you got to take the stairs or the elevator to get up there. I suppose it's handy that the sheriff's office and jail are next door, so they can march a man across the yard so the spectators can get a good look at him. My ride up in the elevator was private-like, since the bailiffs wouldn't let no one in there but me and them, but that left the spectators plenty of time to gawk at me 'fore the doors closed.

I'd never been inside the courtroom other than the time they charged me with Reinhardt's murder. It's not that big of an affair, small I guess, 'cause the county's population isn't much compared to the big cities. After Harder's bench high up in front, and the witness stand and jury box, and allowing for space for the defense and prosecution tables, there's not a lot of room left, them having only five rows of benches to take care of the audience. It's plenty of room in most situations but this time scores of people wanted in. I figure they must not have had have much else to do.

After waiting some more, Judge Harder shows up and the bailiff makes everybody stand up like Harder's special, him instead being a grouchy old turd in a black robe, but we stood up anyways and then got to sit right back down. I figure if he'd been born a hundred years earlier he'd had on a white sheet instead and be riding around at night tormenting the Black folks. Harder is the district judge who travels around the nearby counties, holding court where he needs to. I 'spect they had to wipe the dust off the benches here since this room is seldom used.

Lawyer talk is that seating the jury is one of the most important things to do right. *Voir dire*, they call it, which Mr. Garner says comes from French, and why they can't say it in English instead, it being America and all, I don't know. I watched the lot of the potential jurors fidgeting in the benches off to my right, waiting their time to say they was too busy to serve or their mother was sick or they had little kids to tend to or they got vacation already planned or whatever, them being set on getting back home quick-like and needing to stop their valuable time from being wasted on a trial of a janitor everybody in town already knew was guilty of what the newspaper called a heinous crime. I had to look "heinous" up after it was told to me, so I'd know what people were telling on me.

The judge and both lawyers went through a slew of the outstanding citizens of the county, arguing over this and that and asking various questions like whether had they made up their mind about me yet and could they consider me innocent and could they assess the death penalty if I was found guilty and they all said yes or no in the right places but it could've all been a lie since most of them figured I must be guilty for sure, since the duly-elected government officials said I done it.

Picking the jury took most of the day and 'long about four in the afternoon they had twelve uncomfortable people locked down in those ass-busting oak chairs that squeak when they swivel and need some grease on the bearings to clear that up.

Some of Mr. Garner's griping around near the end of the whole process came over Scott Blackburn's daddy, Terry, being selected, seeing as how his son'd been killed recent, so he might have himself a biased attitude against another gunman. Mr. Garner was out of strikes by then, so they let Blackburn on the jury, him swearing he'd be fair, so I couldn't see what a big deal it was.

I was all-fired ready to start up with the real part of the trial but by then it was declared too late in the day to continue. We was recessed 'til Tuesday and we all had to stand up again and watch Harder walk out and I couldn't help thinking if we'd started at a decent time we could have got something else accomplished today for sure.

The jury had to promise not to read about the trial in the paper and keep an open mind and not discuss the case with anyone, not even their family, otherwise they'd be in big trouble, and as a punishment they'd get what Harder called sequestered. I assume that's kinda like putting the jury in jail along with me. They all said sure, no problem, they'd do as they were told, but when two of the hard-shell Baptists, near the end of the line as they filed out, laughed a little and said they expected this wouldn't take long, maybe a day or so, which I took as a bad sign.

Mr. Garner gave me a quick pep talk before the bailiff come to take me back. Suzie said she'd be taking Momma home and afterward she'd hop over to the restaurant and I said please go home instead and get some rest and she didn't listen to me one bit.

◆ ◆ ◆

I almost couldn't stand waiting another night in the jail for the trial to start up again. I tried to carry on a conversation with Barry but he said shut the goddamn hell up and get some sleep for God's sake and be glad it wasn't tomorrow seeing as right now I wasn't a convicted felon, only an accused, but in a few days it would be different since by then I'd be headed for prison to die like he saw Carl do and I'd pray to the Good Lord it was still last week and no trial going on yet.

Guess that's what experience does for you.

SIXTEEN

"Oh...Oh...Unnh...Oh, *Goddd!*" Denise's eyes stayed locked shut, one hand strangling a rung of the headboard, the other with a death grip on the back of Bobby Green's head, which was stuck like a tick between her spread legs. Her fingers curled into the short hair on his head as she shivered through the most intense orgasm she had ever experienced.

Denise and Bobby had arrived at her house a half hour before, this the most likely place for further conversation since Bobby was resigned to spending his nights in a motel room until he found a rental. Chivalrous as before, he offered to leave after walking Denise to the door.

Of course, she was having none of that.

Denise went in first, telling him he could see she liked green, lots of stuff in her house that color, must be a sign. Within seconds she was all over him.

Finished now, Denise breathed like she'd been mountain climbing on K2. Bobby moved up, lying against her now, supporting almost all of his weight with elbows and knees, but knowing she felt the length of him against her.

"My God, Bobby, I..." Denise said, her breaths coming quick together.

"Was it good for you, baby?" he said.

"Shit, *yes!*" She kissed him, her tongue searching for the back of his mouth, tasting herself along with his scent.

"That's the appetizer, baby. You ready for the main course?"

"I...uh..."

"Something wrong?" he asked, concerned now.

"No, it's just…you're so big…"

"Baby, don't worry 'bout that. If it looks like it'll be a problem, you tell me and I'll stop."

"You mean it?"

"I wouldn't do anything to hurt you. Promise."

She reached down and grasped his erection, stroking it as she kissed him. Bobby rolled onto his back as she took his cock in her mouth, moving up and down on his shaft as he caressed her head. Finished, she straddled the man and said, "Let me," as she guided him inside of her.

◆   ◆   ◆

Denise was wrong about one thing. She had assumed that her first orgasm was the peak experience she would ever feel. Now the two of them lay together, Denise's head supported by her arm, while she fingered the short curly hairs on Bobby's chest and they talked about the sex their lovemaking.

"Bobby, I don't want you to think…"

"What?" he said.

"You know. I'm that kind of woman."

"What kind?"

"Kind that jumps into bed with a man first time they meet him. Honest, I don't do this sorta thing—"

"I'd never think that. Not about you."

"You sure? You really mean that?"

"Yeah."

Denise thought about Jerome, her boyfriend of a couple years ago. Always after her, soon as they first went out, saying, "When you gonna gimme some pussy, huh?" After enough pleading, she gave in and concluded that a couple of minutes spent making love was way overrated. After that, he begged for it all the time, making her even more reluctant to comply. Finally, it took some persuasion from B.J. and Cooter to make Jerome sniff around elsewhere.

"Bobby, you're new in town and I don't know anything about you. Tell me you're not married or stuff like that."

"No wife, that's for sure. I move around some, hard to keep a steady relationship, know what I'm saying?"

"No girlfriend, either?"

"Not 'fore now."

She smiled, wanting to believe him, amazed at her discovery. Stretching out, she squeezed closer and laid her head on his wide chest. "How can a man like you not have him a woman?"

"Oh, I had lady friends before."

"Yeah, you sure know how to please one."

"That so?" he said.

"'Fore you? I had me just one man, name of Jerome?" she said. "He told me no Black man wants to go down on a woman. Only white boys do that."

Bobby shook his head. "Clear that boy doesn't know what he's talking 'bout. All I got to say is this Jerome must some kind of knucklehead, giving up a woman like you."

"Sugar, you're one sweet talker," Denise said.

"I mean it."

"I sure hope so."

He turned on his side to face her. "You don't believe me?"

"I want to."

He slid his hand down her side and between her legs. "Maybe I need to make another attempt at convincing you."

"That'd be great, but…"

"What's the matter? You tired?"

"No, I…I'm a little sore is all."

"You mean I hurt you, baby? Listen, I told you to tell me—"

"I know," she said. "But I didn't want you to stop. I need a little time is all. Then I'll be ready again."

"Tell you what," he said. He turned again, onto his back, pulling her over on top of him. "Lay that pretty little head of yours down and let me touch you, enjoy us being together."

She lay with her face against his chest, content, knowing nothing could be better than what she was now experiencing. Bobby stroked her back with one hand and her rear with the other, gentle and slow, like he was afraid she would break if he pressed too hard.

"Oh, Bobby. You know..." Denise's voice fell off, her trying to concentrate on where she was in her cycle, figure her chances of getting pregnant, her not expecting something like this to happen. Now, with her eyes closed and the touch of Bobby's big warm hands, she was having an impossible time counting up the days.

SEVENTEEN

District Attorney Cunningham was sorting out stuff from his briefcase and making stacks on his table when they led me in and he acted like he barely knew I was there next door even though he'd been in the room with me the whole day before. From what I could tell, he figured I was some kinda pesky cockroach he'd get around to squashing sooner than later.

Momma and Suzie sat behind me like yesterday and the rest of the seats was taken up by the witnesses and members of the curious public got nothing better to do than gawk at a janitor on trial for murder. There was a man I didn't recognize, who later Mr. Garner told me was the big-city reporter he'd asked to show up and write a little piece for the state's general readership. He spent a lot of time yawning.

Sheriff Sanders had a seat along the wall and caught my eye a couple times and frowned and gave an eye-slider glance and nod toward my attorney like I was supposed to know what that meant, which I did, but I didn't pay him no never-mind.

Harder wandered in and we all get to stand up and sit down. Mr. Garner stood up after that and asked Harder if it pleased the court could we have the witnesses stay out in the hall until their turn came so as not to hear what each other said, but Harder said no and let's get on with it.

Cunningham got to give his opening statement to the jurors and according to him the evidence would prove that the accused was the lowest, meanest, rottenest sum-bitch murdering bastard that ever lived, having with malice aforethought snuffed out the life of a leading citizen for no reason at all. The jury paid close attention to all of that, some of them nodding at his more forceful points.

Next it was Mr. Garner's turn and he got up and said what the district attorney claimed was all a big lie and there wasn't any witnesses placing me at the murder scene, just a bit of circumstantial evidence that was all suspect anyways, and the jury needed to keep an open mind about what the state would say concerning the defendant, 'cause he'd show it was all full of mistakes and conjecture and when he thought about it, he couldn't believe we were even having a trial in the first place. Then it was time to get things going.

"The state calls Shirley Johnson."

EIGHTEEN

The Night Crawler falls back several blocks from the dirt road that passes in the vicinity of the place. A robust weed patch shielded the view of the gravel parking lot, helping block the customers' cars, all parked at random angles. No neon sign or bright marquee broadcast the bar's existence. The sole identification was its street address, mandated two years ago for 911 purposes, now painted beside the front door in crude black numbers invisible at night.

The Crawler remained the single place in town where a person could legally indulge in an adult beverage, the beneficiary of Texas' goofy local option laws that allowed each precinct to decide if liquor could be sold there. For some unusual reason, this seemed to be the solitary spot within thirty miles that had managed to vote booze in. Ownership of the bar was murky at best. Jack Roberts ran the joint and offered an occasional reference to his well-heeled silent partners when asked if he wasn't for sure making a killing off the place.

Inside, the bar décor was primitive, but being so made it easier to clean up from the regular messes that littered the grimy wood floors. The permanent lighting was sparse and always dimmed, making it compete with the neon beer signs for its share of the minimal illumination. This condition made it difficult to see people from across the main floor, which was the whole point. The booths along the side wall were tattered and patrons often ran their hands along the plastic cushions before sitting down, checking for sticky residue left by past occupants.

If you really needed to pee, the bathrooms in the back sported the same relative level of attention as the main building; that is, they always smelled of urine and featured overflowing trash cans filled with the discarded paper towels that didn't instead land on the floor. Most users of the facilities, at least those conscientious enough to wash their hands, knew that management was casual at best about filling up the towel dispensers. It was best to plan on slinging the water off on the way back to the main floor. Such depressing conditions were accepted because of the Crawler's unique role in getting the local citizenry drunk or high.

That same feature guaranteed that the bar was the town's consistent moneymaker. Where else could you get most anything, legal or illegal, that a person might wish to partake of? On occasion, a patron managed to get himself beat up, cut up, or killed here, but the grand jury tended to no-bill the culprits as long as a witness to self-defense could be dredged up, which was often possible if sufficient payment had been made to the correct parties. Most times the Crawler kept a low profile, the lower the better.

Finishing the last of her whiskey sour, Clarice grew tired of staring at the rough plank walls framing the bartender's mirror, and weary of watching the unrecognizable and fleeting shadows crossing the cluttered mirror. She and Carl had been here a few months back, but not lately. In fact, she hadn't been anywhere with Carl for a while. The juke box was silent now, its noise no longer overshadowing the tic-tic reciprocating sounds of the rickety swamp coolers that struggled to cool the place.

She pushed Bobby's money across the bar. "This be enough?"

"Fine," the bartender said, wiping out one of the interminable shot glasses with his rag.

As she rose to leave, a man from the booth in the corner approached her. She had missed him before, having only noticed Cowboy and Bobby Green because she spent most of the night staring into the bar mirror.

"Pardon me, ma'am," he said. "I saw you sitting alone over there and wanted to see if you would like to share my booth for a minute."

Better line than Cowboy, she thought. "Sorry, I was leaving."

"Fine," he said. "Maybe next time. I was just looking for a little company. That's all."

"Yeah, sure."

"Honest, I was. I finally got up enough nerve to ask you, and here you are heading for the door. Bad timing, I guess."

Clarice held up her left hand, her thumb rotating the thin gold band. "See that?"

"Uh-huh."

"Means I don't sleep around, understand? I came here for a drink with my friend. That's it."

"Well," he said. "I'm gonna have me one more and I'm headed home, too."

Clarice, looking the man over, hesitated. "Do I know you?"

He thrust out his hand. "Scott Blackburn. My daddy started the Chevy dealership here. I own it now."

"That's it," she said, nodding. "Me and Carl came in a few years ago and tried to buy a car. I 'member seeing you sitting in the corner office. You're older now."

"Aren't we all?" Blackburn said with a shake of his head, then, "Any luck? With the car, I mean?"

"Nope. Payment was too high."

"I'm real sorry about that. Next time, ask for me personally. Sometimes those salesmen...well, you know how it goes. Who might I look for if you come back?"

"Clarice. Clarice Telford."

"Yeah," he said, nodding his head. "Thought you looked familiar. I remember you now. You were a couple of years behind me in high school, you and Carl getting married right after graduation as I recall."

"That's right," she said. "You've got a good memory, Mr. Blackburn. We didn't run in the same social circles, you and me."

"So how's old Carl doing?" Scott asked.

"He's working a double at the plant tonight. Better get home before he shows up and wonders where I am."

"I understand," he said. "Pleased to see you again, Clarice. Tell Carl I said hi."

"Sure. I will."

Part way to the door, Clarice realized that it would be another eight hours before Carl would be home, that she didn't have to get up early tomorrow since she no longer had a job, and there wasn't anything to do at home except watch distorted late-night TV brought in by the hail-mangled antenna atop the house. She reversed course and headed back to Scott's booth.

"Tell you what," she said. "I might take you up on one drink."

Scott stood up and motioned her into the booth. "Have a seat, Clarice. What can I get you?"

"How 'bout a vodka collins?"

"Coming right up." He motioned to the bartender. "Mack, a vodka collins for Mrs. Telford. And I'll have another scotch-and-water."

"Sure thing, Mr. Blackburn."

NINETEEN

Shirley come up the aisle in a new print dress I 'spect was bought at Bascomb's Department Store, since that's where most of the women in town shop when they want to make an impression. Her hair was all dolled-up and lacquered together. She was carrying a white handbag and had on white shoes, which was acceptable because it was summer time, but I remember Momma saying that no decent woman wore white after a certain time, so I'll need to check on that and see when the cutoff is.

Shirley was a busy-body and everybody knew it, but today she was the star of the stage and seemed real eager to tell her story. She sat up straight in the witness chair like a rod was stuck down the back of her new dress straight through into her butt. Maybe if her husband hadn't run off and left her ten years ago she'd be interested in things other than testifying in a murder trial.

Cunningham started in. "Mrs. Johnson, were you at your home on December sixteenth of last year?"

"You know I was."

The prosecuting attorney frowned. "Mrs. Johnson, please answer yes or no."

"Yes, of course," she said, then corrected herself with, "Yes."

Things weren't starting out real smooth for ole Shirley.

"Can you tell the court what happened at approximately 10:00 PM that night?" Cunningham asked, having stood up and proceeded to shuffle his papers around like he might've forgotten something.

"I heard a noise outside the house."

"What kind of noise, Mrs. Johnson?"

"Loud. Sounded like a couple of gunshots coming from across the street."

There was a little gossiping in the spectator area about how the good stuff was starting up right away, and Harder tapped his toy hammer a couple times and said for them to be quiet.

"Was this a sound you heard often, Mrs. Johnson?" Cunningham asked.

"Heavens, no. I'd never heard such a thing."

"What did you do next?"

"Well, I went and looked out my kitchen window. It's across from Mark's, uh, Mr. Reinhardt's, house."

"And did you see anything unusual?"

"No, sir. But I called the police, of course."

"Tell me, Mrs. Johnson, do you have a general idea of what happens around your house?"

"Of course, I do," she said, and a few of the audience snickered since Shirley thinks everybody else's business is hers, too.

"Do you recall seeing a pickup truck parked in the alley beside Mark Reinhardt's house that night?"

"Yes, sir, I do."

"And what would give you cause to notice this vehicle?"

"Well," she said, trying not to sound so nosey, "Like I said, I've got this kitchen window that looks out on the street, across from Mark's house, and anytime I'm washing dishes or getting a drink of water I can see right over there. I remember getting some water from the sink, before I heard the shots, and seeing a vehicle parked in the alley."

Shirley went on to say she'd seen a dark blue what looked to her like an old Ford truck parked in Reinhardt's alley once before, too, late at night, but the truck didn't seem to belong to Reinhardt or none of his friends, near as she could tell, as they always parked in his driveway, or all along the street, and on occasion in her own driveway, and in those cases she often as not had to run them off, polite like. Then the D.A. introduced as evidence a big color photo of my truck, which of course is dark blue and over fifteen years old, but still runs good. And Shirley up and said, yes, that's the one.

"Thank you. No further questions. Your witness."

The D.A. sat down and Shirley seemed a little disappointed, seeing as she got all decked out in a new dress and her moment of glory's only lasting a couple of minutes so far.

Mr. Garner rose and eased over to the witness stand. Shirley looked kinda nervous like he was a snake about to bite her head off, but Mr. Garner smiled a big smile and told her that her dress was real pretty and she blushed at that and said thank you. Maybe she wasn't used to people going on about her looks, unless it's Herb Goodwin, who from what Momma says sees Shirley on the side when Herb's wife is out of town tending to the sick parents. He parks his car in her garage so no one will know he's there, but they still do anyway.

"Mrs. Johnson, you have testified that you believe that the truck in this photo," he said as he picked up the big glossy picture, "is the same one you saw parked in Mr. Reinhardt's alley that night, before you heard what sounded like gunshots. Is that correct?"

"Yes."

"Okay. Now, how many times did you see the truck in that location?"

"Well," she said, patting that hair of hers that wasn't going to move no matter if a brick fell on it, "it's not like I keep a record or anything."

"How about a guess?" Mr. Garner asked.

"Once before. But it's not like I keep track. It could've been there more than that."

"So the night Mr. Reinhardt was killed is the second time you saw a vehicle in the alley?"

"Yes."

"Did you call the police or tell Mark Reinhardt about this vehicle being in the alley previous to his murder?"

"No," she said, ducking her head. "Looks like I should have."

"Mrs. Johnson, did you ever get the license plate number of this vehicle?"

"No." Shirley got flustered. "I'm sorry to say I—"

"Now Mrs. Johnson, I'm not here to reprimand you. If the vehicle was parked in the alley, crossways to you, then you wouldn't have been able to see the plate. And I want you to know that I think it's quite decent of you to come forward with information that might help us find out who killed Mr. Reinhardt."

Shirley had taken a handkerchief out of her white bag and was busy dabbing at her eyes, so when what Mr. Garner said sunk in, she looked real surprised.

"You are?" she said.

"Can you tell me if your city street light is near the middle of the block or at the corner instead?"

"At the…" Shirley stopped and thought for once before she started talking. Her finger wandered in the air, trying to find the pole location. "At the corner. Where the streets come together."

"And does it work? Does it come on at night?"

"Yes, I suppose so."

"Is it bright, bright enough to see all around your house?" Mr. Garner asked, all innocent-like.

"No, of course not," Shirley said. "Lots of people around town get the electric company to come add one in their alley so they could see what's going on out back."

"Do you or Mr. Reinhardt have such a light?"

"No, we don't. I can't afford—"

"Then can we establish that the truck, which you said was parked in the alley once before, and also on the night Mr. Reinhardt was killed, wasn't that easy to see? Sideways to your viewing angle?"

The witness thought on that a little, and said, "Yes."

"How wide is the space between the side of Mr. Reinhardt's backyard fence and the house next door?"

"Heavens, I have no idea."

Mr. Garner headed back to our table and pulled out a piece of paper. "If it please the Court, defense would like to enter this survey as Exhibit B."

Cunningham had him a look-see at the sketch and said okay, that seemed about right. Mr. Garner handed the paper to Shirley. Mr. Garner said that they're less formal here, in the small counties, about the handling of the exhibits and procedure, but I guess it don't matter much how you handle 'em long as you get 'em in.

"Mrs. Johnson, the information here on the survey indicates that there's only five feet of alley width visible from your side of the street. And your house is well over a hundred feet away from the alley across the street. Does that sound correct?"

She nodded, uncertain of what to say. "Okay."

"So based on this, you could see only part of the side of the vehicle in the alley. Isn't that correct?"

"Well, I…I suppose so."

"Based on that information, isn't it possible that you might not be able to identify the type of truck for certain, having seen just a little bit of the pickup?"

Cunningham objected, saying Mrs. Johnson testified before that she felt sure she had correctly identified the truck in the alley, and the judge agreed.

Mr. Garner went on like nothing had happened. "Did you ever see who might be driving the truck? Or if there was more than one person in it? Ever see anyone get out of it?"

"No."

"Could you tell what year model this truck was?"

"I don't know pickups that well."

"Is it possible then that the truck might have been black, or maybe dark green, instead of blue? After all, you testified that it was quite dark in the alley."

"Oh, I don't know. I suppose so."

Mr. Garner returned to our table and fetched some papers and handed them to Harder.

"If it please the Court, I would like to enter into the record a list of the late model black, blue, and green Ford pickup trucks registered in this county. As Exhibit C, Your Honor."

Up jumps Cunningham and objects, but Harder had to let it in. I guess Mr. Garner's investigator had been doing something useful these last few weeks after all.

Mr. Garner hands the sheet to Shirley and asks her could she read out how many of the subject vehicles there were and she says it says here there are thirty-six and Mr. Garner says thank you very much.

"Mrs. Johnson, you said you heard gunshots on the night of the sixteenth, about 10:00 at night? Is that correct?"

"Yes, sir."

"Had you ever heard strange sounds coming from Mr. Reinhardt's house before?"

"No. Well, not counting the parties."

"Parties?"

"Mark—Mr. Reinhardt—used to entertain from time to time," she said and dropped her head like she'd let out a big secret but of course everyone in town knew the story about those parties and talk was you could get anything there you might have a hankering for if you had the courage to attend.

"Mrs. Johnson, didn't you say during your deposition that it might have been one or two shots you heard fired? That you weren't sure of the number?"

"Well, yes, but then I figured it was only one, seeing as that's all they found evidence of."

"Tell me, Mrs. Johnson, have you ever shot a gun?"

"No."

"Ever been around one while it was being fired?"

"Not that I can remember."

"I see," Mr. Garner said, and looked like he was up a stump, though most everyone in the courtroom except Shirley knew where he was headed next, especially Cunningham, who was looking real pissed off right about then.

"So, if you aren't accustomed to the sound of a gun being fired, and haven't ever heard one fired, how did you know the sound you heard was a gunshot?"

"The sheriff said so."

"Ever wonder if the sheriff was wrong?" Mr. Garner said.

Over my shoulder, I heard Momma say to Suzie how dumb could that woman be and it no wonder she was ignorant enough to believe Herb might divorce his wife and marry her. Momma had a habit of saying what she thought and didn't worry much that others might hear. Long about that time, the rest of the audience took up blabbing, too, making the judge impatient with all the noise so he hammered his gavel and pointed it at a few of the louder ones and let 'em have it and they shushed up.

"Mrs. Johnson, after you heard the sound that the *sheriff* later said was a gunshot..." I liked the way he got that one in, "...you said you looked out your window?"

"Yes, that's what I said."

"Your kitchen window, if I remember right? The one across from Mark Reinhardt's house?"

"Yes."

"And what did you see?" Mr. Garner asked, innocent-like.

"Nothing."

"Pardon me?"

"Nothing. Like I said before."

"So the vehicle you believed you saw parked in the alley earlier, behind Mr. Reinhardt's house, was no longer there?"

"Yes," Shirley said, still confused by the questions.

"About how long was it after you heard the sound that you got up and looked out the window? Approximately?"

"Well," she said, thinking it through, "I was sitting at the dining table paying some bills, and that's the room next to the kitchen. So I'd guess maybe, oh…" Shirley was counting in her head, and every time she counted a second her head would bob up and down. "Maybe six, seven seconds."

"Six or seven seconds?" Mr. Garner asked.

"Yes, sir."

Like before, most everybody but Shirley could see the next one coming.

"May I ask, then, how a person could shoot Mark Reinhardt, run out of the house, through the backyard, to his pickup in the alley, start it, and drive away, all in a very few seconds? Maybe the vehicle you thought you saw wasn't even connected to the murder. Isn't that possible?"

"Objection!" Cunningham yelled. "Calls for a conclusion by the witness. It's not like Mrs. Johnson had a stopwatch and was timing the situation."

"No further questions," Mr. Garner said.

Shirley stepped down, deflated like a balloon when all the air squeaked out of it, slow-like so that you didn't realize what'd happened until it was almost flat.

I told Mr. Garner when he sat back down that he done good straightening her out, but he said never mind, we was only getting started.

TWENTY

"You're a funny man, Scott Blackburn," Clarice declared, still laughing over his latest story.

"Look, I'm telling you what happened. It's all true."

"What'd they say about it being wrecked?"

"Said they changed their minds and didn't like the color."

"You're fucking kidding!"

"Swear to God."

Clarice shook her head. "Some people got lots of nerve."

The evening was ending on a pleasant note, Clarice getting to like the man sitting across from her, finding him funny, intelligent, friendly. Scott wasn't what you'd call handsome, but had an easy way about him. For his part, Scott acted like he simply enjoyed her company, including the view down the front of Clarice's dress, those big breasts jiggling as she laughed, lying there on edge of the table, just out of his reach.

Clarice glanced at her watch, noticing the time, realizing that the one drink had turned into at least four more. Despite her renowned tolerance for alcohol, she was feeling woozy.

"Look," she said, "I've got to go."

"No, stay and have another."

"Can't. If I do, they'll have to roll me out. How much I owe you?"

"Forget it. I'm in here enough the bartender gives me a special rate."

"That so?"

He nodded. "I'm ashamed to admit it. Don't tell anyone."

"Secret's safe," she said. She edged across the plastic seat cushion, steadying herself on the curved wood between the booths, working on her upward rise. When her legs locked, she staggered.

"Hey there, lady," Scott said. "I believe you need a hand."

"No...I... Wow, I must've had more'n I thought."

He stood beside her, touching her arm as if the slight pressure would be enough to stop a falling woman. Clarice blinked several times, then started forward, weaving a bit.

"Easy there," he said. "Looks like you shouldn't be driving."

"'Course I am," she said, back over her shoulder, as she pushed out the front door.

She fished through the clutter in the bottom of her purse, still pawing for the large key ring that had always before been a simple capture for her groping fingers. A moment later, Scott was at her elbow.

"You drive home like this and kill somebody, that'd mean I've lost a chance to sell you a car."

She smiled, closing her eyes. "I promise to dodge all your future customers."

"My car's over there," he said, pointing to a new Cadillac with dealer plates.

"I thought you sold Chevys?" Clarice said.

"Doesn't mean I have to drive them. Come on," he said, taking a firm grip on her arm, guiding her. Clarice found it easier not to resist.

◆　◆　◆

Scott opened the car door. Clarice turned sideways and fell in. With careful effort, she swung her legs inside, the hem of her new emerald green dress exposing most of the sides of her legs. She considered tugging on it to cover up more skin, but decided it wasn't worth the effort. Scott shut the door and hustled around the back of the car.

Once inside, he started the engine. "Where abouts you live?"

• • •

"Listen, thanks for the lift," Clarice said.

They were sitting in the front yard of Carl's mobile home, Clarice embarrassed by the mound of clutter that Carl always promised to clean up but never did. It didn't help that two old cars sat out in the tall grass, having refused, back when this place belonged to Carl's mother's, to ever run again. It wasn't that Carl didn't notice the mess. He told her he figured there wasn't any reason to take the time to make it more presentable.

Clarice knew she needed to get out of Scott's expensive car, quit smelling the luxurious leather, seeing a dashboard where all of the gauges worked and having to listen close to tell the engine was running.

"Happy to help," he said, not making a move to get out. "You doing okay now?"

"Fine. I'll be asleep in no time."

"Oh," he said, disappointed.

Clarice noticed his sad puppy-dog face. "Member, I said I was married."

"I remember. I was hoping *you* might not."

"Not likely. Too much luxury in here for me, though. Hell, if I stayed, I might get used to it."

They shared a laugh.

"Thanks again," Clarice said, reaching for the door handle.

"Here, I'll walk you to the door," he said, hopping out and sailing around the back of the car.

"Thank you, sir." She took the offered hand, rising out of the seat cushion, steadier now than in the bar, her reaching for the hem of the dress, trying to make sure her underwear didn't show as she stepped out. The clouds in her heads were starting to dissipate. As usual, she sobered up in a hurry.

At the door, Clarice turned back to Scott. "Maybe I'll see you again."

"I hope so. Say, I don't guess there's any chance…"

"Sorry," she said, giving him a short wave as she unlocked the door and pushed it open.

"I understand. Good night." He reached for the knob as she crossed the threshold, turned on the living room light, then closed the door, giving him a last smile for his troubles as the slit between the door and the jamb disappeared.

Scott waited, listening as footsteps crossed the living room, hearing another door open. He released the knob, pushing the door a few inches inward to prevent it from latching. Avoiding the permanent trash piled close to the side of the trailer, he circled around back, checking the windows. The small one at the back was lit. He could see a shadow through the frosted glass and heard Clarice shuffling something on the counter, then water running.

Satisfied, he retraced his steps, opened the front door, then closed it behind him, in the process almost tripping over Clarice's discarded high heels. The bathroom door was closed, light showing under it. Good. He switched off the living room light and crept forward, guessing the master bedroom would be off of the bath. Finding the edge of the bed in the dimness, he stopped and began unbuttoning his shirt.

The poor single guy routine worked most of the time, allowing him to enter women's lives and bodies with a minimum of effort. Tonight, even the stories, the chivalrous behavior, the booze, and the sad look hadn't worked. He decided long before that Clarice Telford and her big tits weren't just walking away from him after she drank up half of the booze in the Night Crawler. That kind of outlay demanded payback, a substantial return on investment.

He listened near the bathroom door, hearing her taking a pee, wondering what she looked like with her panties down. He shrugged. He'd know soon enough. Returning to the bed, he unzipped his pants and squeezed his growing erection.

TWENTY-ONE

"The State calls Sheriff B.J. Sanders."

A few seconds later, B.J. was sitting in the witness chair next to the judge, after duly swearing to God he wouldn't never tell a lie.

Cunningham rose from the prosecution table and fiddled with some papers, which seemed to me amounted to nothing but wasting time, then started talking. "Sheriff Sanders, can you tell us what happened on the night of December sixteenth of last year at Mark Reinhardt's house?"

"Yes, sir, I can," Sanders said.

"Please proceed."

B.J. had him a good spit swallow to prepare for the ordeal and then began to talk. "The department dispatcher called me on the patrol car radio at 10:07 PM and said they'd gotten a report of a disturbance at Mr. Reinhardt's house."

"What kind of disturbance?" asked Cunningham, who by now had managed to make it all the way to the front of the courtroom and was leaning against the rail in front of Sanders like he was tuckered out from the effort.

"Shirley Johnson had called and said she heard something that sounded like a gunshot."

"And did you investigate?"

"Certainly."

It seemed pretty silly to me to be going over things this way, but Mr. Garner told me before that the prosecution would have to make the case in detail, step by step, filling in the holes and trying to not leave anything out so that I couldn't get an appeal going if I was convicted.

"Tell the court what happened after that, Sheriff."

"Me and Deputy Sanders arrived at Mr. Reinhardt's house about 10:12 and stopped out front. The house was quiet."

"Were there any vehicles parked in front of the house, Sheriff?"

"No, sir."

"In the alley?"

"No, sir. Not at that time."

"Did you see anything suspicious?"

"No, sir."

"Please proceed."

"We approached the house and rang the doorbell and got no response. We knocked and no one came to the door."

"Did you try calling the house?"

"The dispatcher did, 'fore we got there."

Cunningham had perked up a little after his rest break and started over toward the jury, sliding his hand down their rail like he was appraising it for a garage sale.

"Then what happened?" he asked.

B.J.'s butt must've been starting to wear on him while in the hard seat, since he shifted around like his pants was wet and he couldn't get them up enough to air-dry.

"We went 'round the back of the house and looked through the windows, into his office. That's when we saw him."

"Him?"

"Mark Reinhardt. He was slumped over his desk."

There was a murmur that went through the spectators, who was following the story pretty close, and here we was, already in the middle of the murder. Most of the jurors sat up straighter to listen, except for Mrs.

Murphy in the back row, who looked like she was drifting away despite all the excitement.

"Slumped over his desk?"

"Yes, sir," B.J. said.

"Did you investigate?"

"Damn right we did," B.J. said, and then looked at the judge, embarrassed like he'd been caught letting a squealer fart in church during the part when someone's giving themselves to the Lord. The judge nodded toward the sheriff and said please watch your language from now on and B.J. said yes, sir. It must be wonderful to be so proper and correct and not need to use bad language while you're tying to send a man to Death Row.

"The back door was locked, so we had to break the glass to enter the house. We checked on Mr. Reinhardt, then phoned for the ambulance, but it was too late. He was already dead."

A moan rose up outta the audience and sure enough it was from Richard Reinhardt, the deceased's father and more or less permanent mayor of this town. Harder acted like he didn't hear it and on he went.

"What did you do next, Sheriff?"

"We searched the scene for clues."

I had me this vision of B.J., holding a big magnifying glass, all stooped over like a detective, examining things. That idea sorta made me want to laugh but I swallowed that down, seeing as how that kinda public reaction wouldn't go toward helping my cause, what with me laughing at the spellbinding story the sheriff was a-telling.

"And did you find anything?" Cunningham said, pausing like he didn't have no idea of the answer.

"Not inside the house. But we found fresh tire tracks in the alley."

"Tire tracks?" Cunningham asked, real surprised at the revelation.

"Yes, sir. It had rained the night before, so the ground was still soft."

"I see. Did you take photographs and make impressions of these tracks?"

"Of course I..." B.J.'s voice trailed off, seeing as the first thought outta his head was maybe how stupid do you think we are, so he added, "Yes, we did."

Cunningham headed back to his desk and drew out a stack of papers. "I'd like to enter the photographs of the tire tracks, and the photograph of the plaster casts of the same tire tracks, as Exhibits D and E, if it pleases the court."

Harder looked over at Mr. Garner, who said no objections, so that was over and done with. I was kinda surprised Mr. Garner didn't make any kind of fuss about all that incriminating evidence, as they call it, being made official.

"Were these photographs and the associated casts examined by an expert?" Cunningham asked.

"Yes, sir, they were."

"Thank you, sheriff. Your Honor, I reserve the right to recall the witness at a later time."

Harder nodded and said very well and asked Mr. Garner to cross.

"Mr. Sanders," Mr. Garner said, not calling him sheriff on purpose so as not to give him any stature with the jury, least that's the way he explained it to me beforehand, "can you tell me why you investigated the death of Mr. Reinhardt instead of letting the city police handle it?"

"We got ourselves an agreement," B.J. said. "Town's small enough that they stick to writing tickets and we handle the serious stuff."

B.J. was right about that. The town's just got two cops and both of them are Barneys that'd be hard-pressed to find one bullet between 'em.

"Did you personally take the photographs and plaster casts?"

B.J. gave Mr. Garner a stare and says, "No, Deputy Sanders did that."

"Deputy Sanders? He has the same last name as you do. Any relation?"

"He's my nephew."

"I see. The same person as Cooter Sanders?"

"I only got one deputy named Sanders," B.J. said, looking around the courtroom and laughing a bit to himself and so did a few others at such a silly question.

My attorney said thank you and, like Cunningham did before, said he wanted to wait 'til later to talk to the sheriff again. B.J. left the stand and gave me The Snake Eye again as he waddled past, which I took to mean the worst for me was coming right up.

TWENTY-TWO

Cooter entered the Night Crawler by the usual way—his personal key in the locked rear door. The short hallway, which passes by the restrooms, ended in Jack Roberts' office. The deputy pulled out his revolver and grabbed the door knob, shoving inside the cluttered room all at once, startling Jack who was seated behind the desk counting out cash.

Jack jumped, then frowned at the sight of the drawn gun. "Goddamn, Cooter, you scared the shit out of me. How many times I gotta tell you knock 'fore you come in?"

"Checking your heart out, Jack." Cooter said as he holstered his weapon. He loved scaring people, using his law enforcement position to project power onto anyone he chose.

"What are you doing here?" Jack said.

"Came by for the weekly pickup, that's what." Cooter worked his ass into the chair across from Jack.

"Bullshit. That's not due 'til Friday."

"I's in the neighborhood. Thought I'd stop by, get a jump on things. Besides," Cooter said, "nothing much going on here from what I can see in the parking lot."

"It's quiet, that's for damn sure. We're having a bad month."

"That so?"

"Fuck yes it's so. Listen, you tell B.J. that I can't keep this up."

Cooter's thumb shuffled the edge of one of the outdated magazines thrown on the end table beside his chair. "Jack, I don't want to hear your shit. I only want our money."

Roberts grunted and turned to his credenza, extracting a worn book filled with yellow accountant's sheets. He opened it near the middle, ran his finger down the page, and stopped at a line. "Says here we only cleared ten grand so far and the month's almost over with."

"And?"

"I'm telling you—"

"Which one of your piece-of-shit bosses told you to talk that way to me?

Roberts' face sagged in disgust. "I spend my whole fucking life down here, and all I get what's little left over after all y'all bastards are bought and paid for."

Cooter grinned. "I'm crying inside, Jack. Really I am. Listen, I'm going to get me a free beer while you count out the split. Be back in a minute."

"Go to hell."

Cooter laughed, then exited Roberts' crowded office and sauntered into the main part of the building, but first he put on his dark green aviators with the gold rims. He knew they made him look dangerous, in control, people uncertain of what a man was thinking behind the shades, even if it made it double-tough to make anything out inside the dark bar.

Mack saw Cooter coming and had a Budweiser ready by the time the deputy sat down. Cooter accepted the bottle without comment. He leaned his back into the bar, surveying the sinners. His middle finger pulled the aviators down on his nose, far enough to see over the top of them, and spotted Scott Blackburn near the back, seated across from some woman in a green dress.

"What's your boss doing?" Cooter asked the bartender.

"What else? Hustling pussy."

"Yeah, what flavor?"

"That there's Clarice Telford."

"No shit? Carl's wife?"

"Same."

"Didn't recognize her from the back. Fuck she doing here without Carl?" Cooter asked.

"Hell if I know. Came in earlier with that colored secretary of yours, Diane?"

"Denise."

"Whatever. She left earlier with some big buck, name of Bobby Green. Clarice decided to stay and drink some more."

"Never heard of no Bobby Green before," Cooter said, upending the bottle and draining most of its contents, his throat working up and down like a piston.

Mack wiped out a tumbler and stared across at Scott and Clarice. "Me neither. Said he was some kind of contractor, thinking of starting up a business."

"Humm. Reckon he's in need of any protection from the criminal elements?"

"Not that I can tell," Mack said, setting down one whiskey glass and picking up its twin. "Seemed able to handle himself." Mack related the story of Bobby and Cowboy. "I had my hand under the counter, ready to pull out the sawed-off, 'bout the time he let Randy go. The man didn't even look down when he stepped over poor ole Randy."

"Bobby Green," Cooter said, committing the name to memory. "I may need to have me a talk with the man, explain the way things work around here. Who's that over there, by the side entrance?"

Mack narrowed his eyes, struggling to see across the dance floor. "Haven't seen those two here before. Behind the wall, that's Billy across from 'em."

"Believe I'll go see Billy, ask how he's doing." Cooter belched and left the unfinished beer on the bar for Mack to pick up.

Out of the corner of his eye, Cooter caught Clarice, bright in her green dress, staggering out of the booth, Scott helping her get steady, then watched the man follow her outside. "Pus-sy to-night," he muttered to himself. "I should be so lucky."

Approaching the booth, Cooter could see the couple, sitting together, turn their heads his way. The tall guy was Luther Holman, the dip-shit janitor at the high school, and next to him was his cute blonde wife, Suzie.

"Evening," he said, pushing his cowboy hat up to reveal a forehead with the lower section dark brown and the upper part a dead white, like a fish's belly.

"Hi," said Suzie as she rubbed his hands together in her lap. Luther only nodded.

Craning his neck around, Billy Yates almost hit Cooter's belly, startled at finding the deputy so near. "Yeah, uh, hello," Billy said.

"Now I wonder what brings this particular group of people together?" Cooter said.

"Nothing much," Billy said. "We's just talking."

"'Bout what?"

Billy's fake smile froze on his face, his eyes rolling over to Luther and Suzie.

Luther piped up, saying, "We was asking Billy did he know anything about…"

Cooter fixed on Billy's eyes, seeing them widening.

"…any good fishing 'round here these days. Me and Suzie was thinkin' about going this weekend."

"Yeah," Billy said, nodding, too relieved to hide it. "I was telling 'em—"

"Come on over here a minute, Billy. You and me need to have us a talk," Cooter said.

Billy slouched out of booth, saying, "I'll be right back. Don't run off."

◆ ◆ ◆

Billy and Cooter sat at the bar, talking so low that Mack had a hard time overhearing.

"Call me suspicious, Billy," Cooter said, "but you're always up to no damn good."

"Bullshit," Billy said, his voice weak, Cooter noticing a little sweat working its way out of the man's forehead. "They came over, asked me that about the fishing, seeing as I—"

"Billy? Shut the fuck up."

"Yes, sir."

"Now I'm going to tell you once more. No whispering around about that dead damn kid of theirs and how it happened, regardless of what you think you know."

"Hey, I didn't—"

Cooter reached out, squeezing the small tricep on Billy's scrawny arm, pinching through to the bone, watching Billy's face contort as he suffered. "What you didn't do was listen to me when I told you to shut the fuck up."

"Okay, okay," Billy said, his eyes squeezed shut in pain.

"Next time I ask you to do something, you do it. Understand?"

Billy nodded, unable to speak.

Cooter released the man. "Time to say goodnight, Billy."

Billy hurried out the back door, his shirttail flapping over the back of his grimy jeans, holding onto his arm like it was broken. Cooter looked over at the Holmans, staring long enough that they got the message, leaving now after Luther dropped a bill on the table, Suzie in front with Luther pushing her along, heading out the side door.

"Mack, how 'bout you go back and see if Jack's got my package ready?"

"Okay."

Cooter belched. "But gimme another beer first."

TWENTY-THREE

The medical examiner, Dr. Matthews, said he worked out of Beaumont but also takes care of the little towns nearby that ended up with dead people needing to be cut up and studied on. While the man was on the stand letting out how he had spent years training in medical school and taking courses in forensics and sifting through lots of cold innards, I wondered what kind of doctor might be attracted to seeing dead patients. Leastways they don't never complain about you being late for their appointment.

"Tell the court what your examination concluded, Dr. Matthews," Cunningham said.

"Mark Reinhardt suffered a gunshot wound to the forehead, causing massive brain trauma and immediate death."

"Did you recover the bullet?"

"Yes. It lodged inside the victim's skull."

A few of the jurors shook their heads about how terrible that must have been, but the way I look at it, it was better to get the dying story over with quick if you've got to do it. Cunningham sat down, looking pretty pleased.

After wasting some time looking at his notes, Mr. Garner started in on Matthews.

"Dr. Matthews, how far away from Mark Reinhardt would you say the shooter was?"

Matthews didn't hesitate and come back with about four feet, give or take, based on the lack of powder residue on the wound and how far the particular bullet penetrated into the brain and such.

"So, based on the angle of the bullet, and if the victim was found seated in his desk chair, then the person that shot him was likely standing across the desk from him, correct?"

It was clear Matthews was a veteran of courtroom fistfights, so he said, kinda cagey-like, probably, yes, he was.

"Would that not indicate that the victim knew his killer?"

"Possibly. Or perhaps he was threatened by an intruder and made to sit in his chair. Impossible to say for sure."

"Do you find many cases when the victim is shot in the exact center of the forehead?"

"No, not many."

"Would you say, then, that such an action takes a steady hand and good aim?"

"Probably."

"Not a nervous person? Not likely to be someone who'd ever committed murder before? Not likely one whose hand shook from emotion?"

Dr. Matthews took a few seconds to answer. "It's unlikely that an emotionally upset person would have the control over the pistol that would allow such precise aim. Unless they were lucky, which, of course, is certainly possible."

"Did your examination indicate that Mr. Reinhardt had any other problems?"

The doctor rubbed his chin. "Such as?"

"Physical problems? Say, heart disease, cancer, stroke, high cholesterol?"

"No. He was in good health."

"Any evidence of drug abuse?"

The crowd stirred around on that question and Cunningham objected, saying, "Must the court listen to a litany of questions regarding intimate details of Mr. Reinhardt's physiology and personal health? I believe Dr.

Matthews has answered the question as to what caused Mr. Reinhardt's death, which is all that this case is concerned with."

Harder scowled down at my attorney. "Mr. Garner, the Court agrees that this line of questioning seems tedious at best."

"Would Your Honor direct the witness to answer my last question?"

"Very well, Dr. Matthews?"

"No. No evidence of drug abuse."

You'd think all this talking to witnesses took maybe ten minutes or so, but by now it was already noon and we recessed for lunch for two hours. Momma and Suzie told me everything looked like it was going real swell, but I think they was only trying to cheer me up. I went back to a side room to have me a cold sandwich and a talk with Mr. Garner.

◆　◆　◆

"How come you didn't ask any questions about the tire tracks?" I asked Mr. Garner.

"That will come later."

"You got old Shirley pretty good."

"She's a nice lady. Only trying to do her citizen's duty."

"So you think it was a truck like mine that was parked in the alley?"

"I didn't say that," Mr. Garner said, and slants his eyes over to me.

"You think maybe it was mine?" I asked.

"I didn't say that, either."

"What *are* you saying?"

"Luther, you're innocent until proven guilty, or at least that's the way it's supposed to work. All we're trying to do is establish reasonable doubt that you were the one who murdered Mark Reinhardt. We don't have to prove that you are innocent, only not guilty."

"But that means if I get off everybody in town will still think I did it, just there wasn't quite enough evidence to convict."

"I can't help what the public thinks. My job is to get you released."

He was right of course but that wasn't what I wanted to hear. I wanted to be found "innocent," not "not guilty."

"Sounds like things are goin' good," I said, to change the subject. "You proved the driver of that pickup couldn't have shot Reinhardt and got away 'fore Shirley saw them, and then that medical examiner, the thing about the shooter being nervous—"

"Luther, don't get complacent. We've only been able to show some inconsistencies in the prosecution's case so far. That's all. Now they realize you have someone on your side that's actually trying to defend you. Cunningham will step things up and be more cautious from now on."

"But, I—"

"Don't get your hopes up so high. Not so soon. Despite how it seems now, this isn't going to be an easy case to win."

"Why would you say that?"

"I've tried a lot of cases in my career, Luther. You'd be surprised at how things turn out."

"You sayin' I won't get a fair trial?"

"I'm saying that no one knows ahead of time how a jury will decide a case. About the time you think there's no way your client can be convicted, they do. Or maybe something comes out of left field and wipes out your entire case. Anything can happen."

"Okay, then what's next?"

"The prosecution will present the rest of their side and then it'll be our turn."

"We have anything to present that'll get me off?"

"I hope so, Luther. I hope so."

I reminded myself that ever time I thought things was going to turn out okay in my life, that's when they didn't, and why should now be any different from the rest of it. About then the bailiff said come on back in 'cause it was starting up again.

TWENTY-FOUR

"Clarice!"

Denise's head and torso jerked upwards off of Bobby's chest, her eyes wild.

"What the matter, baby?" Bobby said, startled awake.

"I had this…this dream, maybe, I don't know what." She scrambled off Bobby and lunged for the phone. Denise sat on the edge of the bed, the receiver crammed against her ear as the ringing tone repeated, again and again. "Shit. She's not home yet. How could that be?"

"Maybe she stayed a while longer," Bobby said, reaching out to stroke Denise's bare back.

"No, she was going home…" Denise hung up, realizing that Clarice had faked the time limit on her drinking to let Denise go home with Bobby. She could see her still there, wasted and alone, thinking about that Anthony guy and needing her friend. Denise slid across the wrinkled sheets, saying, "Bobby, you got to take me back there."

"Okay," he said. "Let me get my clothes on."

Denise, already slipping on the stretch dress, said, "Sugar, you see what happened to my thong?"

◆ ◆ ◆

Bobby's pickup pulled into the Night Crawler lot in a flurry of dust and haste, Denise looking out the windshield, anxious, for Clarice's car.

"Thank God," she said, seeing the dusty black Trans Am where they'd left it. "At least I know she's still here." Denise leaned back against the seat, relieved.

"Want me to walk you inside, see if I can be of some assistance?" Bobby said.

"Thanks, baby, but no, I can handle it. Be better just me, considering Clarice's condition tonight."

"Oh?"

"It's a girl thing," Denise said, not looking at Bobby but at the Trans Am, remembering their day together and the hard news they had shared.

"Tell you what," Bobby said. "How 'bout I stop by tomorrow, your place of work, take you out for some lunch?"

Denise nodded, turning to him now, her mind still on Clarice, but needing to reply to his kind offer. "That'd be real nice."

"Where 'bouts you work?"

"Downtown, near City Hall. I'm the sheriff's secretary."

"Aw, *shit!*" Bobby said.

Denise, seeing his reaction, said, "What's the matter..." Then the truth hit her, in a rush too obvious to ignore. "Oh, God, I should've known. From out of town, no job, you in the Night Crawler..." She squeezed her eyes shut, realization about the kind of man she was falling for flooding through her.

"What you mean?" he said.

Pounding her thighs with her fists and sobbing, she moaned, "You're a damn drug dealer."

"Hey, I'm no drug dealer."

"Then why'd you say that to me, about where I work, if you go nothing to hide, huh? Why?" Her face upraised, hoping for a plausible answer, any answer, wavered in front of him.

"Can't say. Not now."

"Bobby, look, I know we just met, but I think maybe I'm..." She saw the anguish on his face, an emotion mirroring her own feelings. "I, maybe...maybe I'm falling for you or something. I don't know..."

Bobby, his left forearm wound around the upper part of the steering wheel, stared past her.

"I mean, I thought we..." She stopped, embarrassed at letting her feelings show so soon, feeling stupid, used, alone. She turned away from him, tears streaking her face in a waterfall, remembering what Clarice told her tonight about things moving too fast. "I owe you an apology, Mr. Green. I had no right to assume...." She closed her eyes, sobs racking her chest as she pulled at the door handle. "I...I...need to get Clarice home. Thanks...for the lift." She hesitated, hoping for even a single word of encouragement or tenderness. Anything.

A glance at Bobby showed his tortured face, but no words came out of his lips.

Grabbing the handle and pushing the door open with her shoulder, Denise scrambled out of the pickup and ran toward the Night Crawler, stumbling along as her thin heels punched through the rocks, scarring the sides of the red shoes, her heart left behind in a million broken pieces on the floor of Bobby Green's truck.

TWENTY-FIVE

"Mr. Stengel, could you describe the bullet removed from Mark Reinhardt?" Cunningham said.

Stengel nodded. He was a skinny guy in a cheap suit kinda like mine, bald except for a faded brown fringe. When Cunningham asked him questions, he thought on the answer a while 'fore he spoke, unlike most of 'em that said the first thing that hit their head. Stengel was a smart one, and not much for going on after his first answer.

"The bullet was a 0.38 caliber, pistol round, standard load."

"Was the bullet destroyed by the impact with Mr. Reinhardt's skull?"

"There was some deformation, but it was intact enough for examination and identification."

Cunningham fetched a picture of a bullet lying there against black velvet or something, with a little scale under it to show how long it was and some ID stuff in the corner. It occurred to me it doesn't take much in the way of metal to end a man's life. Least ways, not when it's traveling awful fast.

"Is this a photograph of the bullet removed from Mr. Reinhardt?"

"Yes, sir, it is."

"And what could you tell that from your analysis?"

"The rifling grooves inside of barrels leave marks on the sides of bullets fired through them. It's a matter of matching up the unique grooves and scratches on the bullet with another test bullet fired from the same weapon."

"You make it sound so easy."

"It takes years of practice to be definitive," Stengel said, and gave the district attorney a little smile to reward him for all the flattery.

"The state would like to enter this photograph as Exhibit F."

Harder said okay after Mr. Garner didn't object.

"And this bullet, the one that was fired into the forehead of Mark Reinhardt, causing his immediate and unfortunate death, which weapon did it come from?"

"From the 0.38 caliber handgun on your bench, sir."

Cunningham wandered back to the table, held up Daddy's pistol, which had a white tag dangling off the trigger guard, and said, "This one?"

"Yes, sir."

"Let the record show that this was the pistol seized from the home of the defendant, Luther Holman. Your Honor, the state would like to submit this weapon as Exhibit G."

Before you know it, the worst they had against me was sitting there, all in a neat row.

"No further questions. Your witness."

I was surprised to hear it but Mr. Garner didn't have a question one, so away goes Stengel.

"The state calls Charles Winters."

Winters was a big part of the prosecution's case, Mr. Garner told me. He would be the man that put my truck in Mark Reinhardt's alley. Winters was the professor type, middle height and stooped a little, looking like he was always thinking about something other than what a body was asking him about.

Cunningham let on that Winters was a real smart man and spent a while working through his lengthy resume', as they call it, meaning that the average guy was supposed to take his word for anything he might choose to comment on.

"Dr. Winters, did you examine the photographs and plaster casts taken from the alley?"

"Yes, I did," Winters said, adjusting his glasses and nodding like it reminded him that he really *had* examined something way back when.

"And what did your analysis conclude, Doctor?" Cunningham must've been feeling tired again and leaned over so he could hear the man good.

"The tire pattern was created by a very common tire utilized on pickup trucks. It is a 215/75R15, to be exact."

"How many of these tires were sold in the United States, Doctor?"

"Millions. Of course, to be certain of the particular purchase, I'd have to know when the replacement tires were purchased. But it was a very common size, even now."

"Millions!" Cunningham let out, acting like he was so amazed at the figure that he had to hold his hands out to the side to get ahold of all them tires. "How in the world could you possibly identify a particular tire from such a huge supply?"

Winters smiled because he was expecting a question like that, the answer to it making him look real smart. "Every tire, when driven, develops discriminating marks, such as gouges, cuts, chips, wear patterns, or other peculiarities that occur from daily use and abuse. These marks identify it and make it unique."

"Is that right?"

"Yes, sir."

"Despite the odds, the *enormous* odds, of locating that particular tire and identifying it above all of the others of its type, Dr. Winters, were you successful in determining which vehicle this particular tire came from?"

"Oh, yes," Winters said. "The vehicle drove away forward, covering up the front tire marks, but we had tracks from both rear tires."

"*Both* sides you say?" Cunningham asked.

"That's right."

Cunningham managed to stand up again. "And which tires, out of the millions of possibilities, matched the prints taken from the alley behind Mark Reinhardt' house?"

"The rear tires on a 1966 Ford F100 pickup, registered to Luther Holman, matched perfectly."

TWENTY-SIX

Clarice curled her toes against the old linoleum, feeling its scratchy surface. Maybe she should carpet the bathroom, like she had the rest of the trailer. It took two years of saving up, but she'd managed the down payment for the carpet, and they had only six more payments to go. No, maybe not carpet in here, not with Carl throwing water everywhere since he forgets to pull the shower curtain all the way shut half the time, and still peed on the floor on occasion. She needed tile, but that would cost more than cheap carpet, even if Carl laid it himself. 'Course, the room also needed painting, the original crappy stuff starting to peel now from the sustained humidity, but paint was cheap compared to the cost of a new floor.

It was a fortuitous chance, a lucky meeting, for her to see Denise out shopping today, unexpected that they ended up at the Night Crawler, weird that Denise would latch on to a man like Bobby Green, a surprise when she saw Scott Blackburn and had such a nice conversation with the man. Not what she would've predicted and ending like that for this day, starting out bad with her being fired by stupid-ass Delbert.

She had pretended not to know Scott at first. Fact was, she remembered him real well, from back in high school, him talking to the girls in the hallways, his back against the lockers while they circled him, holding their books against their inflated chests. He'd spoken to her once or twice, out of courtesy, maybe, but she was way out of his class. Scott was an average man, unremarkable in most ways, not really handsome but interesting looking. He had always been popular and funny, all the kids laughing at his jokes and crazy ways. It didn't hurt, too, that his daddy was rich. But why wasn't a man that desirable already married with a couple of kids by now? Well, matter of fact, she couldn't have children, either.

Clarice used to worry about getting pregnant, carousing around with Carl in the backseat of the black Pontiac she now drove. Maybe they were lucky, maybe not. After a few years of marriage, they'd quit using birth control. By now, even Carl had figured out she was going to have a hard time making a baby, showing his true feelings by saying, "Shit, you mean all them rubbers was wasted?"

Wishing she had brought her cigarettes into the bathroom, Clarice's fingers rubbed together in an unconscious swirl around the imaginary oral stimulation. She pressed the heel of her hand into her brow ridge, still feeling a bit drunk. It hurt, and felt good, too, like pushing on a sore tooth. Like making love to Carl.

Carl. What was she going to do with him and their life together? Maybe now that she had told Denise about her past, she could put it behind her, like old clothes left in a shabby motel room. She knew, though, it would take more than one conversation to work her way out of all of that hidden pain.

Anthony's face replicated itself from her memory, her seeing him again that last time, at Gladys' graveside, after she had choked to death on her own vomit while passed out cold on the floor from drinking all day. Anthony stood back from the crowd, staring at Clarice the whole time, a hawk soaring, way up high, watching a rat's ineffective scurrying about on the ground, the victim having no option about what the end would be. Waiting, waiting.

Carl elbowed her, asking wasn't that the damn guy lived with you and Gladys a while back, Clarice nodding, yeah, seems like, her acting like it could be someone else, she wasn't for sure, knowing instead the instant she saw those hawk eyes. After the few mourners, scattered family and Denise, all broke up, Anthony walked over while Carl was talking to a buddy, saying to Clarice it's a shame about Gladys, but it'd been a long time and he'd sure missed her. She was thinking of the million things she wanted to say to him, to curse him for her lost innocence, wanting to scream in his face, kick him hard in the nuts. But nothing happened. She stared into those hawk eyes as he touched the side of her neck with his open palm, skimming it across her skin, saying he'd always remember their times together. Scenes of the encounters shuttered through her blurred vision like a slide projector on automatic as she melted into solid stone.

Then he was gone.

Carl came back over, saying let's go have us all a damn drink, Gladys sure as hell would approve. Clarice remembered watching the gravediggers standing a long way back, respectful but impatient to get on with filling in the hole so they could go home. She looked down, down, past the edge of the suspended casket, down into the black hole where it would soon rest, thinking the thoughts a daughter has for a mother she loved and hated at the same time, any chance for them to reconcile now gone forever. She felt faint, thinking she would topple into the hole, falling for minutes or more, and hit the bottom hard. The gravediggers wouldn't see, covering her up with the dropping casket, shovelfuls of dirt hitting the lid like a fist...

Carl squeezed her arm and said, come on, shit, let's go, this fucking place gives me the creeps.

Clarice wiped and wriggled her panties up as she stood. She had resolved to take off her new underwear and get ready for bed, but she couldn't give them up just yet. They made her feel special, different from usual, and different was good. She'd go lie on the bed for a few minutes, think things through, decide what to do about Carl, then she'd find herself an old t-shirt to sleep in.

She studied herself in the small mirror over the vanity. Not bad looking, but fraying. Some new lines in the face, around the mouth and the corners of the eyes. In another five years, she'd look a decade older.

Opening the bathroom door, she puzzled about the dark bedroom and the living room beyond. She remembered turning on the switch in the living room. Maybe she was drunker than she realized. Her nose told her that rain was coming soon, but she smelled a faint something else, something out of place, but familiar.

Two steps outside of the bathroom door, one arm encircled her neck as the other reached across her. The hand squeezed her breast, then fumbled inside her bra for the nipple.

"Hey, Clarice. You didn't think you could get rid of me that easy, did you? I got something here for you. Been meaning to give it to you all night. Trust me, you'll wish it had been your idea before we're through."

Lightning broke the sky, its flash-bulb effect illuminating the two of them in silhouette in the dresser mirror, showing the naked man behind her, his erect penis prodding her back.

That's when she started screaming.

Anthony had come back.

Twenty-Seven

"Dr. Winters, the court has heard your credentials listed earlier. Are you satisfied that they are accurate?"

Winters had sunk into a reverie between lawyer interrogations and acted surprised at the question.

"They're accurate," he said, adjusting his glasses.

Mr. Garner started rubbing the wood handrail like Cunningham had. I guess lawyers have a thing for polished wood. Maybe since they're so particular about them, they ought to take a wet brush along with 'em and spruce up the flakey spots missing the original varnish.

"Dr. Winters, have you ever been mistaken? That is, about the examinations of tire marks?"

"No, not that I am aware of."

"Then we can be certain that these tracks that you examined are from the defendant's truck, correct?"

"They match his current vehicle tires perfectly."

My guy acted like he had to think hard about his next question, which made Cunningham a little nervous 'cause he'd been around Mr. Garner long enough now to know the man wasn't thinking about what he was going to say at all, only waiting to make his point.

Mr. Garner walked over to the evidence table and selected the photo of the tire tracks.

"And these are the tracks that the impressions were made from?"

"I believe so," Winters said, squinting and getting a little suspicious, too, now.

"You believe so?"

"Well, I didn't take the photographs. I was called in after that."

"I see. And you didn't take these impressions yourself, either?"

Cunningham was up and objecting that B.J. had already set things straight about Cooter taking the impressions. Mr. Garner pretended he had forgotten and apologized.

Mr. Garner forked over the photograph to Winters. "Can you tell me, Dr. Winters, what are the deformations here, in the tread pattern?"

"These here?" Winters asked, holding up the paper and pointing out some shadows that I couldn't see meant much of nothing.

"Yes?"

"They're from gravel. Gravel in the alley made the small lumps in the pattern."

Mr. Garner said, "Gravel, you say?"

"Yes," Winters said. "There's a fair amount of it in the impressions."

"Some," Mr. Garner said, and retrieved the photo Winters was looking over. He returned with the one of the alley.

"Is this the alley the impression was taken from?" Mr. Garner held up the same old muddy alley photo.

"Yes, it…" Winters stopped before the thought got all the way outta his head.

"Dr. Winters?"

"No, it can't be."

Cunningham got real red-faced seeing his prize peacock getting his feathers plucked out from behind, unexpected-like.

"No? Why not?"

"This alley has no gravel base. It's all mud."

Harder got after the little hammer again and hushed up the spectator bunch, who was busy conferring over the turn of events.

"I have here a photograph of Mr. Holman's front yard, Dr. Winters." Mr. Garner said, fanning Cunningham with it as he walked by. "I'd like to enter this as Exhibit H."

"Mr. Cunningham?" asked Harder.

After taking a peek at the photo, Cunningham said, "No objection, Your Honor." But he was mighty pissed.

"Dr. Winters, in your expert opinion, would you say the tire impressions, alleged to have been taken in the alley behind the deceased Mark Reinhardt's house, were instead likely taken in front of Luther Holman's house?"

Winters squinted away and said, "Well, based on this photograph, the incidence of gravel appears to be about the same as the ones in the impressions I examined."

Mr. Garner turned around, waving the photo at the jury. "Then we can conclude, sir, that the set of tire tracks that you examined, offered by the state as *proof positive* that Luther Holman's truck was parked in the alley behind Mark Reinhardt's house immediately after the murder, weren't taken in that alley after all?"

"I—"

"Objection!" Cunningham said. "Dr. Winters was not present when the impressions and photographs were taken, did not closely examine the alley in question, and therefore cannot offer an opinion, without further field examination, as to where these tracks might, or might not, have come from, including the alley in question."

"Sustained. The jury will disregard the witness' speculations," Harder said, then to Mr. Garner, "Get on with it."

Mr. Garner nodded. "Did you receive any other impressions to examine, Dr. Winters?"

By that time Winters knew that he had screwed the pooch for the prosecution.

"Dr. Winters?"

"No, no other impressions."

"Then, your testimony is based on photos and impressions that are likely not even from the alley behind Mr. Reinhardt's house, correct?"

Mr. Garner was using the approach he called "driving the point home," which I guess is a polite way of saying those without much imagination need to be reminded, over and over, of how things had already turned out.

Cunningham was on his way back up to object again about speculation on the part of the witness again, and the judge was getting pissed about my attorney disregarding his instructions, so Mr. Garner apologized and give up on that line of attack. Turning around to B.J. and Cooter on his way back to our spot, Mr. Garner stopped and give 'em both The Square Eye long enough that there couldn't be no doubt what he thought was going on.

Once back at the table, he said, "No further questions, Your Honor."

Cunningham rose and said, "State recalls Sheriff Sanders."

TWENTY-EIGHT

A huge arm grabbed Denise by her waist. She turned to see Bobby's face.

"Let me go, *damn you!*" she yelled, both hands pulling hard at his arm, but her struggles made no difference at all.

Thunder rumbled through the sky following the lightning flash, nature appearing disinterested in the two people below. Fat drops beginning to pelt them.

"Can't let you leave like this," he said.

"Please, please, let me…" she said, crying hard, collapsing back against him.

"I need to explain. If you'll let me."

"No, I need…" She stopped talking and grabbed breaths in short gulps.

Bobby scooped Denise off of the ground, cradled her to him, and headed back to the pickup. Despite herself, Denise clung to him, an arm around his neck, tears mixing with the raindrops. Once they reached the truck, the rain came faster, insistent, demanding proper recognition and respect for its power.

Opening the passenger door, Bobby slid inside, still holding Denise. As he shut them away from the outside, a wave of rain washed over the pickup.

Denise sat still, quieter now, not knowing what to say.

"I must apologize, Miss Denise," he said, holding her securely. "I never wanted…"

"How many times I got to tell you leave off the 'Miss' part?" she said.

He looked down at her face, seeing the ravages of the tears, and wiped off her cheeks with a thumb as big as a tablespoon. "My momma see the way I treated you just now, she'd take a switch to me."

Denise nodded, thinking about the scene, saying, "She must be awful big, get by with that."

"No, she's real small, like you. But she had our respect. All that mattered."

Unwinding herself from the big man some, Denise remained in his lap, sitting up, her head bumping against the roof of the truck. "Bobby, what I said before…"

"'Bout your feelings for me?"

"Yes."

"What I meant to say is, well, I hope we have us a future together. I sure do. But it doesn't look like it right now." Denise turned away, hands moving into her lap, and watched the water cascade down the side window, obscuring the view of the Night Crawler. "Guess I'm stupid, Bobby, but I don't understand you."

"Sometimes, I don't, either."

She waited, giving him time, while he rubbed her back.

"You see, I got this job to do," he said.

"What job?"

"I can't say. Don't want you to know."

"Your business, I guess."

"No, it's not like that," he said, stopping his hand, feeling awkward beside her.

"Listen," she said. "I was talking crazy before. I see that now. I'm sorry 'bout how it came out, me talking off the top my head."

"What you said 'bout you falling for me. Maybe even being in love with me?"

"Yeah," she said, breathing in deep, almost in control again, feeling exposed and ashamed of how she'd let her feelings show so soon. "That part."

He pulled her to him, resting her small form against his as the thunder explosions continued, the rain slashing across the ground like it was spit out of a reciprocating machine.

"I'm gonna tell you something," he said, "Something I shouldn't, but I want you to know."

"Why?" she asked, her head buried against him, his warmth enveloping her, her feeling safe for the first time in her life.

"Because, Denise Jones, I'm falling for you, too."

◆   ◆   ◆

After he finished the story, she understood, maybe too well.

"Now," he said, "let's go in and get Miss Clarice and take her home."

"No," she said, "I need to do it myself."

"You sure?" he asked.

She nodded. "Hard to explain."

"Okay," he said. "I'll drive you over."

Denise looked out of the window, seeing the brief, hard rain almost stopped now, and said, "Don't be silly, Bobby, it's only a few feet." She reached for the door handle.

"You will not," he said. "Not while you're my woman."

He placed her on the console, no effort, opened the passenger door, and trotted around the front of the pickup to the driver's side.

My woman, she heard again, the words ringing inside her head like a big church bell.

Bobby started the truck and rolled across the lot, the front of the pickup now almost touching the front door of the bar. "This be close enough?" he said.

"Yes, baby. It'll be fine." She kissed him, long and hard, then broke away, flustered by the surge of her feelings, knowing she couldn't stay here forever but still wanting to.

"How 'bout I walk you in?" he said.

"No, that's okay. Bye." She unwound herself and opened the door, her coy smile replying to his big grin. "You promised me lunch tomorrow, big boy."

"Be there 'fore noon."

TWENTY-NINE

Cunningham wasn't about to let the tire deal go south on him, so he got to work right off.

"Sheriff, we've heard the last witness state that the tire tracks might've been taken in front of Luther Holman's house, and not in the alley behind Mr. Reinhardt's house. Do you have an explanation for this?"

B.J. shifted his fat butt a mite 'fore he got comfortable and was able to get out an answer. "Well, Mr. Cunningham, all I've got to say is that impressions were made at both locations. Under my direct supervision."

"Both locations, you say?"

"Yes sir, absolutely."

"Then how do you account for—"

"I don't reckon I know what happened. Maybe they were accidentally discarded. Or someone stole a set of 'em—"

Mr. Garner was up and complaining about the sheriff talking about evidence that couldn't be produced, and Harder had to shut them all down. Still, the jury had heard his lie and you can't tell me they forgot about it like they was told to.

Cunningham went on like nothing happened. I guess to be a good lawyer you have to act like nothing surprises you or changes your mind, even if Jesus Christ himself was standing there saying you were full of it.

"Sheriff, what made you think that Luther Holman might have perpetrated this awful crime?"

"Lots of things," B.J. said.

"Such as?"

"Half the county knows the Holmans thought Mr. Reinhardt had something to do with their daughter's death."

"Oh? *Half* the county?"

"Yes, sir. They'd been asking around—"

"Your Honor," Mr. Garner started in, "the defense objects to these general statements by the witness. There is no proof at all that substantial numbers of the population knew anything about my client's beliefs, or that in fact those were his beliefs—"

Cunningham turned to the judge. "If the defense would prefer, we can produce any number of witnesses verifying Sheriff Sander's assertion, Your Honor."

Harder sighed and said it seemed to him expedient to avoid calling most all of the locals to the stand, but that the witness needed to refrain from making sweeping statements. B.J. looked like he wasn't sure if he had won or lost and why the hell was this all taking so long.

"Sheriff, are there any other reasons that you believed Luther Holman would want Mr. Reinhardt dead?"

Cunningham seemed pleased with that question and I soon knew why.

"Certainly. Luther Holman came to my office four months ago and said he had evidence that Mark Reinhardt murdered his daughter and if I didn't do something about it, he sure would."

THIRTY

"Telford! *Telford!*"

The shout from the safety man didn't distract Carl from tightening the large nut. One of the plant workers had spotted vapor hissing from the flanged joint in a eighteen-inch steam pipe feeding from the boiler house. Carl was assigned to inspect the joint and determine what had to be done. Satisfied that the problem could be cured with an adjustable wrench and a cheater bar, Carl pushed down as hard as he could, sweat shining on all visible body parts, his muscles stretching the sleeves of the faded blue work shirt.

The safety foreman, Maxwell was his last name and everyone used only that, waited a few seconds longer, certain of what was about to happen. The bolt screamed its death protest as the excessive force twisted off the shaft.

"*Fuck!*" Carl said as the end of the cheater bar slammed into the worn concrete surface. More steam than before surged forth from the crippled joint.

"Told you," Maxwell said.

Carl couldn't actually hear the remark, considering that the plastic hearing protectors attached by wire hinges to his hard hat covered his ears, but he could read the lips and see the condescending look.

Slinging down his tools, Carl stepped away to watch the steam plume grow in size, its whistle detectable even with the protectors still in place. Maxwell motioned Carl away.

"How the hell was I to know the bolt was going to twist off?" Carl said once they had moved around the corner of the maintenance shed.

"What were you doing with that damn cheater? You know the work rules don't allow it. A cheater can slip off at any—"

"Yeah, yeah. I *know* what the fucking rules say. Only a man can't get things done around here by following all these goddamn *rules*."

"Those *rules* are here to protect us," Maxwell began.

Carl folded his arms, not listening and not pretending to, either.

"You hear what I'm saying?" Maxwell said.

"Every stupid word of it," Carl said.

"Telford, I don't like you *or* your attitude," the safety foreman said.

The pitch in Maxwell's voice was rising, along with its volume, and Telford knew that it would crack soon, as it always did when Maxwell got really upset.

Three of the plant workers, on their way to the breakroom, stopped to witness the confrontation. Carl picked up the men in his side vision and was determined as always not to be seen as the one backing down.

Maxwell fumed with frustration. "You break your arm doing a stupid thing like that, I bet you'd expect the company to pay for it. And give you time off to boot."

"That's what they got insurance for, ain't it?"

"Remember that sign you pass ever time you drive your dumbass inside the plant?" Maxwell said, thumbing behind himself in the wrong direction. "Days since the last lost time accident? Huh? That's important to the plant brass." The last few words came croaking out. "Damn, you pay attention to *anything*?"

Carl checked his watch.

"I'm *talking* to you, Telford!"

"I got a break coming up. Eat shit and die." Carl shoved past Maxwell to join the other men.

"Telford! Get your *ass* back here!"

Ignoring Maxwell, Carl joined the men on the trek to the breakroom.

◆　◆　◆

In the middle of the story about the three nuns and the traveling salesman, Carl was interrupted by an insistent tap on his shoulder. Carl paid no attention at first, getting to the good part now about what the third nun had to say to the naked salesman caught with his dick in his hand.

"Hey, leave me the hell alone," Carl said, shrugging away the tap by not turning around, expressing obvious irritation at having to interrupt his tale. "Can't you see I'm busy instructing these boys?"

Carl's buddy group whooped their approval, one slapping the tabletop. Never without a colorful story, be it inside jail or out, Carl provided free entertainment and a chance for the other men to reflect on how much calmer, and safer, their lives were than Carl's.

The push now became a shove.

Carl, up and turning into the man, had a fist hauled back to smack the interloper square in the face.

The man staggered back, grabbed by an invisible hook, and threw up his palms in self defense. "Look, I came to give you a message."

"So give it," Carl said, still holding out for the chance that his clenched row of fingers could find a landing spot on the man's mouth.

"Supervisor wants to see you. Now."

Relaxing his arm, Carl said, "Tell him I'm busy."

"He said get your ass up to his office. Right now. Honest, that's exactly what he told me to tell you."

THIRTY-ONE

"Goddammit, Luther," Mr. Garner said, part way through his fourth turn around the conference table. You could tell he was mighty upset, considering Mr. Garner almost never cussed.

"Look, Mr. Garner—"

"How in the hell could you forget to tell me that you threatened Reinhardt in front of the sheriff? Tell me it isn't true!"

Ducking my head, I said, "It's true enough."

I guess maybe the floor got too hot and was burning through the bottom of Mr. Garner's first-class shoes, 'cause about then he jerked the chair out across from me and heaved down in it.

"The judge," he began, "had a lot to say about this situation."

Right after B.J. made his off-hand remark about me and what I said about Reinhardt, Mr. Garner jumped up and started shouting and Cunningham did, too, and it was a legal free-for-all for a while. Harder called them together and they parlayed around the bench for a while, then Mr. Garner asked for a few minutes with his client and Harder said he'd do one better and recess court for the day. Mr. Garner managed to get us some quiet time in a small office off the main courtroom, 'long as the bailiff stood outside the door, which as better'n being back at the jail where Cooter listens in. There weren't any windows, so I guess there wasn't no fear I'd crawl out and hightail it away.

I looked over at the wall where the baseboard meets the floor. Lots of dust bunnies crowded the corners. Seems the courthouse custodial staff could use some jacking up. "I know I should've said something before, Mr. Garner, but I didn't think it would come up."

"Didn't think? That's a fair statement." The attorney rubbed his forehead and stared through the clouded glass in the door, watching the shadow of the guard's back. Then he got down to business. "Okay, so you went to the sheriff's office and threatened Reinhardt?"

"Sort of."

"What do you mean, sort of?"

"Okay, I threatened the man."

"Why?"

"Word was that he had something to do with Summer's death."

"Word? What word?"

"You know, people talk."

"What people?"

"After the evidence they got from Summer's body was...contaminated...and the state lab couldn't do nothin' else, I checked around."

"Where?"

"I might have gone out to the Night Crawler once."

"Might have?"

"Okay, I did go. Suzie and me had us a talk with Billy Yates."

"You involved your wife?"

"Yes," I said, thinking how, when my idea was exposed like that, our plan sounded pretty dumb.

"And?"

"And after five hundred dollars in his pocket, he said he had some information about Mark Reinhardt doin' my daughter. That's the way he said it, 'Doing your daughter.' I damn near punched Billy right there."

"Where'd you get the money?" Mr. Garner said.

"We'd saved up for a year for a washer and dryer, but his info seemed like it was more important, leastways that's the way we saw it at the time."

Mr. Garner started to calm down some when he saw what I was leading up to. He got out his pad and started writing.

"What else did Billy Yates say?"

"Nothin'. The rest of it would cost a thousand. Money we didn't have. 'Bout that time, Cooter shows up and runs his ass off. Next time I caught up with Billy, he said he didn't have nothin' more to say. So I went to the sheriff and told him I had me a person said Mark Reinhardt was involved in my daughter's murder and he said prove it and I said I didn't have the money to. He said get the hell out of his office and I said if he wouldn't take care of Reinhardt I would."

The pen wiggled across the yellow pad as Mr. Garner worked through his notes. Once he reached a stopping point, he looked up and said, "And?"

"That's it."

"You didn't take this into your own hands? Didn't threaten Reinhardt personally? Ever?"

"No."

"Then I've got to ask you why not."

My finger followed one of those cuts in the table somebody made while carving their initials in the top. I spelled out "DHJ" three times before I spoke up.

"I couldn't prove he was guilty."

"And still you didn't confront him?"

"No."

The old wood chair squeaked as Mr. Garner reared back in it 'cause the dry glue lets the joints slide a mite. I've fixed noisy ones like it over at the school, what with the clamps that got the red handles and that big bottle of carpenter's wood glue up on the top shelf beside the paint can with Mrs. Wilson's classroom color.

"I'm not sure I believe that, Luther."

"Well, it's the damn truth."

"You mean to tell me that you thought Mark Reinhardt killed your daughter because of what this Billy Yates told you, and you did nothing else."

"That's right."

"Billy Yates is dead. Is there anyone else that saw you talking to him the night he gave you this information?"

"Cooter did. And the bartender."

Mr. Garner tapped his pencil a while 'fore he got around to speaking again.

"I've reviewed the sheriff's deposition. There's no mention of your threat. The district attorney now claims this is because your previous attorney, Mr. Franklin, didn't specifically ask the sheriff if you'd ever threatened Mark Reinhardt, or if he had any other reason for suspecting you other than 'talk around town.' You seem to have a lot of that around here."

"Yes, sir. We do that."

"This is bad, Luther. We had them on the run earlier for manipulating the tire track evidence. Enough that most juries would have doubt as to the sheriff's motives and the chain of evidence. Now we've got to start over."

"Sorry."

"The worst part is that this is the last thing the jurors heard. It gives them the rest of the day to think about it."

I nodded my understanding. "You sure know a lot about juries, Mr. Garner."

He shook his head. "No. Like I told you before. You can never tell what they're going to do."

"Then if they might do what they're not supposed to, maybe we got us a shot," I said.

"Don't count on it." He waited to speak, looking like he was making up his mind. "Luther, I think we're going to have to put Suzie on the stand."

"Why?"

"To testify of your whereabouts on the night of the murder. And the situation surrounding your daughter's death. I know it'll look like she's taking up for you, but we need to do it. If nothing else, perhaps the jury will have sympathy for her, which could translate to giving you the benefit of the doubt."

"But you told me before they would go rough on her. I don't want that. She can't take testifyin' about Summer. She can't *handle* it."

"Luther, I believe that's what it will take to save your life."

"No!"

"It's not your choice. I'm calling her."

THIRTY-TWO

Carl figured Steve for a successful loser. Stuck halfway up the chain of ladder climbers, Steve's rung broke about ten years ago. He remained suspended in mid-air, hanging onto his job, knowing how far the fall to the bottom was.

Carl slung open the flimsy door with the upper glass stenciled in black proclaiming "Shift Supervisor, Steve Simpson." Carl watched the door bang off of the front of the filing cabinet, the corner of it almost punching a hole through the door frame. He flopped down in the metal chair in front of Steve's desk, dropping his hardhat upside down so that it hit the floor with a hollow bang. The lunchbox took up a position next to the hardhat.

Steve looked up from his computer keyboard. "Glad you could make it, Telford."

"Yeah, well, I knew you was lonely up here."

Steve swiveled around to face Carl, elbows heading for the desktop edge.

"Fuck's the matter now?" Carl said.

"That mouth of yours is part of the problem."

"It's the only one I got. Look, I got work to do," Carl said, halfway out of his chair.

"Sit down. We're not finished."

Carl realized that maybe he had screwed up good this time, knowing Steve refused to get angry unless he'd tried all of the wimpy ways out first. Crossing one leg over the other, his ankle resting on his stationary knee,

Carl pretended to smooth out the crease in his greasy pants. "Okay, what'd I do?"

"More like what you haven't done," Steve said.

"Shit, if it's that fucker Maxwell, I can explain. That steam line was leaking and—"

"Already heard all about it," Steve said, pretending to study the crowd of forms and reports in front of him.

"Well, I mean, fuck, what's the big deal about a goddamn bolt? I'll replace it here in a minute."

"No, you won't," Steve said, still staring downward.

"Got something else for me to do?" Carl asked.

"You remember," Steve said, raising his eyes to Carl's, "when I gave you this job? The shit I got from the suits over it?"

"Sure, yeah," Carl said, a dab of worry water dripping onto the top of his flaming self-confidence.

"You'd just got out of jail. That time."

"If you're saying should I be grateful about this man-killing vision of happiness you call a job, then okay, you want me to suck your dick or what?"

Steve's face flushed. "Goddammit, how about some respect instead of that mouth of yours?"

Carl saluted, still sitting down. "Yes, sir, boss."

Steve continued to hold Carl's eyes. This was a new Steve that hadn't surfaced before. "That's the kind of shit I'm talking about. Always the smartass."

"I gotta apologize to Maxwell, the *prick?* Kiss his butt? That's what this is about?"

"Maxwell's concerned about safety. That's a big priority around here. You'd know if you ever stayed awake in the meetings."

"I prefer movies with lots of tits and ass," Carl said, looking around the dusty office at Steve's in-house diplomas for this and that knowledge school, all printed on cheap paper and framed in dime store black-trimmed frames, most now hanging at odd angles to the ceiling line.

"Tell you what, Carl," Steve said, holding his index finger and thumb up, the pads less than half an inch apart. "I'm this close to firing your ass, so if I was you, I'd shut the hell up."

Carl finally got the message.

"Go home, get some sleep. Working a double shift sometimes makes a man tired, his temper hard to control. I'll put it down to that, save your ass again."

Carl sat mute.

"You got a problem with what I've said?" Steve asked.

"I thought I was supposed to be quiet."

"Get the hell out of my office."

"Shit, Steve, I need the OT. Me and Clarice got some late payments to catch up on."

"You're not getting any overtime acting like this. Be glad I didn't fire you right off."

Carl skulked out of the upstairs office, offended by the unfairness of it all, planning vague revenge on Maxwell, the fucking snitch bastard. Must be some way he could hurt Maxwell good, make it look accidental. Like they did to snitches in jail.

That thought comforted Carl as he drove home, speeding all of the way, despite the heavy rain that had started. He was ready to have it out with Clarice, too, seeing as how it was high time she started acting like a wife and gave him a good fucking, the kind she used to excel at.

THIRTY-THREE

"Luther, get up."

I sat up careful-like, so as not to bang my head on the ceiling and looked down to see B.J. and Cooter. I saw it wasn't no use delaying, so I got down and stood in front of the bars.

"Yes, sir?"

"Me and Cooter need to speak to you."

"'Bout what?"

B.J. looked over at my cellmate, who by this time was pretending real hard not to be awake. "Barry, you know what's good for you, you best be covering up your ears."

Barry obliged by turning to face the wall and putting his pillow over his head. "Can't hear nothin', Sheriff."

"Damn good thing," B.J. said. He looked down at my shirt pocket. "What's the matter with you, Luther? Can't even go to bed without those cigs?"

"Got kinda partial to them, Sheriff. Helps to pass the time."

"Yeah?" Cooter said. "Gimme one."

I handed the man a cigarette through the steel bars and he stuck it in the corner of his mouth but didn't light it.

"Guess you're wondering why we're here, aren't you, boy?" B.J. asked.
I nodded.

"Well, it ain't to congratulate you on your trial's success, that's for damn sure. I figure maybe my last statement this afternoon did you in."

"Yes, sir, maybe so," I said, knowing that wasn't going to be the end of it.

"Come on. We got us some talking to do."

We hustled down to the same persuasion room they used the last time we had us a private talk. I was trussed up again, those handcuffs slip-sliding up and down the wood struts of that familiar chair. B.J. paced the floor, reminding me of Mr. Garner walking around this afternoon. I guess maybe I have that effect on people these days.

"What're we going to do with you, Luther?"

"What you mean, Sheriff?"

Cooter chimed in. "You goddamn *idiot!* First, we tell you to get rid of that fancy-ass lawyer of yours and you don't. Next, we have ourselves a little meeting like this one and it doesn't do any good. You deaf, boy?"

"No, sir."

"Well, you act like it."

B.J. stopped his walking and reared up in front of me. If he didn't have such a big belly it might've been more impressive.

"Men like you don't learn the easy way. It's got to be hard." He stooped over and looked me in the eye. "You like your momma, Luther?"

"'Course I do."

"You don't act like it."

"I do. I said so."

Cooter lit the cigarette and spent some time blowing smoke in my face. After a few of those blue clouds passing my way, I started coughing.

"Not accustomed to smoking, I see," he said.

"Easier when you're the one doing it," I said, finishing off a cough. "Besides, I'm not practiced up yet."

He nodded. "That old mother of yours seems to me to be acting pretty sick lately."

"She's got the gout, bad."

"Do tell," Cooter said. "That all she's got?"

"A little heart trouble, too."

"I hear she's taken to going for walks outside, sometimes late at night. Even if she has to take that walker of hers. Dangerous thing, an old woman out when it's dark. One of these days, she might be out in the middle of the street, someone come up on her real fast, can't stop, and then what you think's gonna happen?"

I didn't say nothing.

"Hear me, boy?" Cooter asked.

B.J. got tired of me not answering his deputy, so he leaned in a little more, steadying himself with a hand on the back of my chair. I could see his belt was cutting into that belly and giving him some breathing trouble.

"What Cooter's saying, dumbass, it that the life of your mother's in your hands." His breath wheezed out on me, it smelling like old hamburgers and sour onions.

"What you want me to do?" I asked.

"What's right. Plead guilty to Mark Reinhardt's murder."

"But—"

"Better listen to the man," Cooter said. "He's getting tired of asking."

By then, Cooter was almost down to the nub on that cigarette. I never seen anyone smoke so fast.

"You saying that if I don't plead guilty, you're going to run my mother down?"

B.J. straightened up to catch his breath. I 'spect he had hell tying his shoes every morning.

"I'm saying it's time for you to admit your crime and save the county any further time and embarrassment."

"But I'm not—"

"All you got to do is go into that courtroom tomorrow, first thing, and tell that city lawyer of yours that you changed your mind, saw the error of your ways, want to do what's right, which is admitting to the murder. I'll talk to Cunningham and see if we can get you a life sentence, though that's short of what trash like you deserve."

"I didn't kill Mark Reinhardt," I said. "I been sayin' that from the first and it's still the truth."

B.J. smiled a little. "Problem is, boy, I don't give a shit if you did it or not. County needs a man to take the blame and you're the one's gonna do it."

"And if I don't, you'll run my mother down?"

"Let's say an unfortunate accident could be avoided."

I tried to sort out what was right and what was wrong, and the two started getting mixed up in my head.

"I need some time to think on it," I said.

"Sure," B.J. said. "You got 'til nine in the morning tomorrow." He turned to Cooter. "Take him back. I gotta be getting on home. It's late and Millie will be wondering where I am. First thing you know she'll be calling out to the Crawler."

Cooter pulled out the brass knuckles and slipped them on. "How about I give him a little help in making up his mind, Sheriff?"

You could see that Cooter was aching to get going, but B.J. considered the idea, then shook his head. "Naw, might look suspicious since we're already in the trial." Then he had himself another take on the situation, me setting there like a trussed-up monkey. "On second thought, a couple probably wouldn't hurt."

◆　◆　◆

On the way back, Cooter fished himself another cigarette out of my pocket.

"Damn glad you've become a smoking man," he said. "Cigs getting pretty expensive these days. Better get you a new pack by tomorrow. I'll be needing another one or two first thing."

Barry didn't even look up when Cooter dumped me back in the cell. I sat there, against the wall, trying to catch my breath.

"'Member what we talked about, Luther," B.J. said. "I don't want us to have this conversation again."

Then they was off, joking and talking like nothing had happened.

"Goddamn," Barry said as he rolled over, "I guess you'll be wanting the bottom again."

"I'd...sure appreciate...it," I said.

"Shit fuck," he said as he climbed out and hustled up to the top. "Be glad when your trial's over and I can get me some goddamn rest for a change."

I rolled over onto the bottom mattress. It smelled like Barry, all covered over in farts and stinky ass sweat. After a while, I asked Barry did he mind doing something else for me.

"What *now?*" he said, pretending he was asleep, but I knew he wasn't since Barry snores like a freight train when he's out and makes me want to stuff a pillow in his nasty mouth every time I hear it.

"I gotta get something to my lawyer," I said.

"So give it to him."

"Can't. I need it delivered from outside."

"Shit, you mean I gotta take another risk for your dumb ass? What's it worth to you?"

"What you want?"

"My bunk back, you piece of shit. You didn't get beat up all the time I could stay on the bottom."

"Okay," I said, turning on my side. "I'll be up there di-rectly."

"When you want this delivery made?"

"Tomorrow."

"How would I get it to him? You expect me to walk through these fucking bars and out the front door, you stupid ass?"

"Get it to Suzie. She'll finish the delivery to Momma, and then on to my lawyer."

"Oh, hell, all right. Get your ass up here. But this is the last time."

I struggled out and fell on the floor, which didn't help my sore ribs any. Barry was down and back in his stinky hole in two shakes, having to step over me, which didn't seem to bother him none.

I managed to get back up top after a while and thought about Momma and what I needed to do and what was best for everybody and I had a hell of a time making up my mind. Barry must've been disturbed by my tossing around, 'cause he offered me some advice.

"You had any sense you'd get some sleep. This time tomorrow you may be a dead man."

Nice to have such encouragement.

THIRTY-FOUR

"Whoa, there," Blackburn said. "A little struggle makes it sexy, but let's not get carried away."

"Leave me *alone!*" Clarice screamed through the fingers covering her mouth. She kept struggling and grabbing at Blackburn's hands.

"Look, you *bitch*. I spent more'n twenty bucks filling you up with booze. Now it's your turn to give back."

"No. *No!*"

"We're going to walk over there to the bed and you're going to take off your panties and we're going to have ourselves a good time, understand me?" He twisted Clarice around to face the bed.

Her eyes widened in the semi-darkness, a fraction of the room visible from the glare of the opened bathroom door. She knew the inevitable was coming. It had happened before, twelve times. But she had been certain that it was over, finally over. He had left that day, years back, cussing under his breath, Gladys bleary-eyed by mid-afternoon from the drinking, her stained fingers dangling a cigarette with a two-inch ash. Later, they'd had it out, Gladys typical and not believing what her daughter was saying, telling Clarice she had ruined another damn good deal for her and never to speak that crazy accusation again.

She had to try, try to stop Anthony, reason with him this time, like the last one. "You can't. Gladys will hear us."

"Gladys? Who the fuck's Gladys?"

"Mother knows what's going on. I told her. She will save me this time. I know she will." Clarice sagged against Blackburn, now a sawdust-filled doll, slack in his arms.

Blackburn managed to reach the bed and drop Clarice's catatonic form on top of the pebbled navy bedspread. "That's my girl. Now let's get those panties off."

"Momma says you don't need panties on when you're sleeping. Need to air your bottom out."

"What?" Blackburn asked, confused, but not enough to stop tugging on her underwear.

"Momma said you'd be staying a while, Anthony. I'm supposed to be nice to you."

"What the hell you talking about?"

Clarice's eyes locked onto the ceiling. "But Momma never said you'd do this to me. I don't think we should be—"

"Listen, you crazy *bitch*. I don't know what you're trying to pull, but it's not going to work."

She drifted down, down into the blackness of the surrounding water, turning, taking her time as she descended, as if a slight current was determined to dance with her. She saw the pale skin of her arms distinct against the liquid background and felt the breath of the thickening fluid brush against the thin hairs on her arms. Silver bubbles of life seeped from her nose, popping out and drifting upwards in slow motion...

Blackburn pulled at her underwear, dragging one corner down. "Jesus, I don't have all fucking night."

All night. She remembered now that he'd said it before, Number Three. Sounding urgent, pissed off, saying it was her fault for making him wait. That night was one of the worst, when he hit her across the face. She made a feeble grab at the side of her panties. "No, please..."

"*Goddammit*," Scott said. He slapped Clarice's face in his frustration. The raw sound reverberated off the thin Sheetrock wall, surprising him by the sound of the force. Well, what the hell did she expect? Leading him on like that and now acting like some kind of fucking lunatic.

Clarice's hand shot to her burning face as tears pooled around her upturned eyes. "No, please don't, Anthony. Not again."

"What do you mean, again?" He got no response, only more tears. Well, that innocent girl trick wouldn't stop him.

Clarice's eyes closed as her mind groped the water again, descending into her past, remembering the months she'd slept only when completely exhausted, drained from trying to stay awake all night. Denise asking her, girl, ain't you getting any sleep, you look worn out all the time. But it hadn't worked. He'd come in whenever he pleased, having at her, forcing himself inside her, sawing away until he finished. She would watch him get up and leave, never saying another word. It was happening again. She could hear Gladys snoring in the room next door. Her mother didn't care. She needed to understand that, come to grips with her situation. Clarice would have to find a way to stop Anthony, on her own. Then she remembered the butcher knife.

Scott had worked Clarice's underwear down to her knees by then, shifting around the lifeless legs. He hadn't experienced a woman behaving quite like this way before, but, hell, they were all different. Maybe old Carl was the kind that wanted to pretend to screw dead women and Clarice was happy to play the part. Then he noticed Clarice's frantic hand moving under the pillow. What the hell was she up to?

That question disappeared, upended by a swift, solid kick to his groin. He moaned in pain, his nuts feeling like they'd been crushed against a concrete wall as he collapsed against the side of the bed and Clarice scrambled away from him.

The butcher knife wasn't where Clarice had left it. Gladys must have moved it. Clarice stumbled over Anthony's writhing form, pulling up her panties as she went, and opened the drawer of the nightstand. Ah, there it was. Her fingers encircled the grip of the pistol and pulled the hand cannon out.

"*Goddamn* you," Blackburn moaned, still facing the wall. He held his testicles, thinking he might throw up.

"Get away, Anthony. I mean it," Clarice said, standing a few feet away. Tears and snot competed to see which one could cover her face. Her hand shook as she held the revolver.

"Oh, fuck me..." he moaned.

"You go on back to bed with Gladys, hear me? Don't you ever come back in my room again. This is the last time. You touch me again and I'll stick this in you all the way to the handle."

Scott squinted back at Clarice, his chin on the bedspread, seeing the end of the pistol barrel making circles in the air. "All you did was lead me on, huh? Get me to buy you drinks and this is how you treat me?"

Remembering his words from before, Clarice began to calm. This time, it had worked. She was getting rid of Anthony forever. The pistol stopped shaking. She was going to be all right.

Recovering enough to stand, Scott leaned against the side of the bed, a hand supporting him as he faced her. The other still grasped his nuts as the anger rose in him. "You're nothing but a fucking bitch."

"Get out, Anthony."

He turned around as he reached for his underwear across the bed. "You're a stupid *whore*."

That's when Clarice knew that it wasn't going to be all right. Anthony would be back for revenge and the next time she might not be able to stop him. She slipped one hand off of the pistol grip and felt her burning cheek. Yes, Anthony had to be stopped. Tonight.

She placed both hands on the weapon and pulled the trigger.

The hollow-point bullet entered Scott's back right of center, making a dime-sized entry hole. Part of the fractured vertebra and most of his liver blew out the big hole in the front, chunks of meat and blood spraying themselves onto the opposite wall as the bullet twisted and expanded through his abdomen, the remains of it slamming into a stud in the house's outer wall. Scott collapsed against the navy bedspread, smearing it with the red goo pumping from his body. He fell onto his back on the floor, and died silhouetted against the white carpet.

Clarice lowered the knife to her side. Anthony would never bother her again.

Thirty-Five

"Sheriff Sanders, you said yesterday that the defendant, Luther Holman, threatened Mark Reinhardt in your presence—"

"Objection, Your Honor," Mr. Garner said. "My client made no such mention of a threat."

"Of course he did," Cunningham said, surprised to see Mr. Garner up his ass so quick.

"According to the testimony of the witness yesterday, Judge, Mr. Holman had stated, and I quote, 'He had evidence that Mark Reinhardt murdered his daughter and if I didn't do something about it he would.' I hardly think that qualifies as a murder threat."

Harder eyeballed the two attorneys, then said, "Sustained. Continue."

I could tell my attorney was kind of unsatisfied by the brevity of the Honorable Judge Harder's remarks since maybe he was expecting some kind of talking-to like you give your kid for falling through the back fence while he was chasing a cat.

"All right, Sheriff. After the defendant stated he was prepared to act on his own behalf—"

"Objection. My client did not say—"

"Sustained."

Cunningham huffed out his next question. "Very well. It seems the defense is intent on semantics this morning. Sheriff, after the death of Mark Reinhardt, whom did you suspect might have committed this crime?"

"Him, Luther Holman," B.J. said, a scowl on his face as he pointed in my direction for the benefit of anyone in the courtroom that might not yet know where I happened to be sitting. 'Course, B.J. right about them was mighty pissed, me having not confessed like I was supposed to 'fore the proceedings got started this morning.

"And what led you to suspect Mr. Holman?"

"Like I said, he came in the office earlier and said he thought Mark Reinhardt was involved in his daughter's death."

Cunningham nodded like this was the first time B.J.'s words had been made clear. "Thank you, Sheriff. Other than the defendant's statement, is there anything *else* that aroused your suspicions?"

The muscles in Mr. Garner's arms were tight. I could see a movement through the sleeves of his suit coat as he placed his hands flat on the table like he was about to jump and run. Anything Cunningham said wrong he was going after. But by now Mr. District Attorney was playing it real careful.

"Yes, sir, there were," B.J. said. "Several things. Not just one."

"Would you please elaborate, Sheriff?"

"We found a shoe print near the side of the Reinhardt walk. Right where the grass won't grow 'cause it don't get enough water. Size twelve from the measurements."

Boing. "Objection. There is no indication that such a print might match my client's shoe or shoe size, nor was such an item introduced as evidence, nor has the supposed shoe print been made available to the defense's experts to examine."

"Sustained. The jury will disregard the witness' last remarks."

Mr. Garner said, "Your Honor, I would like the jury to be—"

"That's enough." Harder said, cutting off Mr. Garner, then turned to Cunningham. "Proceed."

"What else invited your suspicions, Sheriff?"

"Shirley Johnson's description of the pickup seen in the alley. Luther Holman has—"

Boing. "Objection. This would require the sheriff to have intimate knowledge of all of the local vehicles in the county to make a clear judgment that the particular truck in the alley was in fact Mr. Holman's and belonged to none other."

Harder fussed with some papers on his desk before sustaining that remark, too. I was feeling pretty good at this point, what with B.J. getting hammered down. Kinda made my sore ribs feel a little better. Mr. Garner sat down and I do believe I detected a smile tugging at the corner of his mouth.

"Well, Sheriff," Cunningham said, "let's see if there's maybe one thing you could testify to today that's admissible."

That got some snickers started in the audience and you could tell Harder wanted to join in with them. A judge is supposed to be impartial and sit there listening to all that legal goings-on with an open mind, but you can't tell me he don't have influence on what the jury thinks by the way he looks and turns his head. That part don't make it into the court records, but it's there for sure.

B.J.'s bald head nodded away before he spoke, waving the white line across his forehead toward the audience. I'm sure he'd have on his hat right now if his respect for our fine court system hadn't made him take it off.

"After more than ten years in law enforcement, you get a feeling—"

Boing. "Objection…"

I didn't even listen to that argument and turned instead to sneak a quick look at Suzie behind me. Maybe she'd give me some sign that Barry's backdoor operation had been successful, but I followed her look and there was Momma, staring straight ahead, her mouth open a little looking like she was about to say something but nothing was coming out.

"Momma?" I said.

She pitched forward like she was about to get up, then fell out off the bench and hit the floor, hard.

Thirty-Six

Denise, her short, straightened hair shedding the remaining rain onto the shoulders of the red stretch dress, entered the front door of the Night Crawler and scanned for Clarice.

No sign of her. Maybe she was in the bathroom, nasty as it was.

Denise saw Cooter, lounging at the bar, staring at her through those aviator lenses, looking like the damn stupid fool he was. He turned around to grab a yellow package from Mack, the bartender. Nodding her head as she swept by Cooter, Denise quick-stepped back to the restroom.

Inside, Denise scanned the stalls, bending low at the waist in front of the single closed door, her hands on her knees. "Clarice, you in there, girl?"

A slurred return said, "No…hey, could you get me some toilet paper? I'm all out in here."

Denise removed the roll sitting on top of the paper holder of the neighboring stall and handed it under the door.

"Thanks. I'm not feeling so good, you know, me and my boyfriend…"

Leaving the inebriated woman to her reminisces, Denise stopped at the end of the bar. "Hey, you seen Clarice?"

Mack gave her that male once-over look, the kind women hate, waiting a few seconds before saying, "She's already gone."

"But her car's still out there."

"Left with Scott Blackburn. They were over yonder." The bartender nodded across to the far wall. "He was buying her drinks half the night. Looked to me like they were headed home to party."

"Party?" Denise said, not believing what she had heard.

"That's a nice way of putting it."

"When did they leave?"

"Maybe fifteen, twenty minutes ago. Hell, I'm not paid to keep watch on people."

Denise mumbled her thanks, hearing the staccato of her heels across the wooden floor, hurrying to the door again.

Outside, she saw the flick of red taillights as Bobby Green's pickup turned onto the highway, heading back to his motel.

"Shit," she said, realizing she was stranded. She leaned against the door frame, wondering what to do.

Cooter, still sitting at the bar, finished his last beer and watched Denise wander back in, noticing the woman wasn't wearing a bra, seeing her small breasts undulate as she walked, her nipples nudging out like a pair of tiny noses.

"Hey, you got a problem, Denise?" Cooter said.

"I need to make a phone call," she said.

Mack reached under the bar and brought out a black phone, the kind with a round dial that you don't see anymore, and set it down, watching her all of the time with a creepy look.

Denise broke off one of her long nails in the circular hole of the "3." She listened to the phone ring like it was all the way across the street, sounding tinny and metallic, as she sucked on the end of the damaged finger.

No answer.

"Damn," she said, hanging up, then sitting down on a stool and slumping into failure.

"Problems?" Cooter said.

"Yes…no, not a problem."

"Doesn't seem to me you're acting like someone's got no problems. Looks like your friend Clarice left without you."

Denise looked up, staring into the dark aviators, saying, "I'm worried about her, that's all."

Cooter, remembering the story of the tipsy woman leaving with Scott, suspected otherwise. "Need a lift?"

"No, I'll call somebody else—"

He reached out for her arm. "I'll take you home. That would be the nice thing for a gentleman to do, wouldn't it, Mack?"

Mack grunted as he washed the inside of a glass again, watching the two of them with his lidded snake eyes.

Denise said, "That's fine. I'll wait."

"Come on, let's go. How'd it look, me leaving our secretary stranded in the middle of the night at some dingy bar? B.J. would never forgive me." Cooter's hand encircled her upper arm and began to pull.

Looking at the man's hand on her, Denise was thinking instead of how different it was than Bobby's. And how she hated Cooter. "No, I—"

"I said, come *on*. Car's out back." He snatched up the yellow envelope and half-pushed her toward the rear door.

Denise, thinking about the alternative, said, "Okay, sure, I'd 'preciate it. But I need to pick up my car. I left it downtown." She shifted her arm up to release Cooter's grip, pretending to look back as they walked out of the bar, giving her an excuse to avoid being touched again.

◆　◆　◆

Past halfway to Denise's car, Cooter thought about Scott Blackburn making it with Clarice, easy-peasy, and here he was without any nookie tonight. Once inside the cruiser, he'd turned up the air conditioning blower and watched the blast of air make Denise's small nipples punch out even more.

"Cold in here," she said, crossing her arms.

"I like it that way," Cooter said, swiveling down the police radio's volume knob as they drove. "Say, you ever make it with a white man?" he said, sounding casual with the question. He leaned against the driver's door, two fingers of his left hand guiding the steering wheel.

"No, no I haven't. I never wanted—"

"Me, I never had me a Black woman," he said, turning his head toward her. "Yet." He checked the expression on Denise's face. It was one of concealed terror. "Always heard, you go Black, you never go back. Reckon that's so?"

Denise, staring straight ahead, tried to think through her options, one hand now away from her chest and tugging down on the edge of her dress. "I'm sure that's not true," was all she could come up with, the forced laugh behind it dying in her throat.

Cooter slid his right arm across the top of the bench seat of the cruiser. He slowed the car, leaning back in the seat and enjoying the woman's discomfort, feeling his power. "Naw, I think what I heard was right."

Melting into the side door, Denise went mute.

Cooter's free hand slipped off of the seat and clapped itself on Denise's left thigh, halfway to her crotch, and began to move upward.

THIRTY-SEVEN

"*Momma!*"

I was over the railing and cradling her head before Tommy the bailiff could reach me. Momma opened her eyes and gave me an odd look, like she'd never seen me before, then her eyelids drifted closed.

"Momma! You all right?"

"Let her be, boy," Tommy said. "Medics'll be here shortly."

Everyone that could look was looking and talking at the same time about what in the world had happened and can you see and tell me what the people close in there are saying. They managed to pull me off Momma and over to the side, but I was worried sick about her. Her face looked real old and tired, as if life was clinging to her like dew on the grass, ready to slip away soon as the sun come up.

"Bailiff, take Mr. Holman back to his cell," Harder said.

Most of the audience turned and couldn't believe what the judge had said.

"Your Honor!" Mr. Garner said, genu-inely upset. "Under the circumstances, for God's sake let him remain in the courtroom until help has arrived."

Harder had his mouth open to say hell no get him out of here but he got an eye full of the spectators' looks and decided since an election year was coming up maybe he'd better hold up a bit on the hard-ass stuff.

"Very well, but he must remain where he is."

All the heads swiveled back to the show on the floor. Suzie was on her knees next to Momma, holding the back of her head in one hand and patting the limp hand lying on her stomach.

"Give her some air," someone shouted. "Get back."

Harder wandered down from his stage and started giving orders to clear the courtroom. About half of the hangers-on was forced out into the hall, much to their disagreement, while the rest pretended not to hear and hung around the action.

It seemed like an hour 'fore the paramedics come running in. Edwards was the lead man, which didn't make me feel too good, considering he made worst grades than me in biology class. Still, if that's all you got to work with, you better hope he can reach back and remember which end of the patient the oxygen mask goes on.

After a few minutes of breathing in the gas, Momma's eyes flickered open and there was a general sigh of relief among the curious. She moved her arm up to the mask and pulled it aside enough to call my name. There wasn't much strength to it, but I could hear it clear.

"I got to go to her," I said, and wrenched free of Tommy. He didn't try too hard to stop me. I bent down next to Momma's lips to hear 'cause her voice was so weak.

"Baby, I gotta tell them," she whispered. "Tell them how…"

"Hush up," I said. "You got to save your strength."

She raised her head and stared back at me and knitted those old eyebrows. If I'd been ten years old again, I would've run away and hid for an hour or two until she cooled off. "Don't you tell me what to do, Luther Holman!"

"Yes, ma'am," I said, automatic like.

"I need…need…"

Her head fell back and she wheezed some and closed her eyes and the mask got stuck over her face again and after some more breaths she come up to try to talk again, grabbing my arm tight as she went.

"Luther, I have to…"

"What Momma?"

"I..."

I looked over at Suzie and it was like we were front and center in a theater with our life playing out on the stage and us trying to get a jump on the action but held up by straps so strong and so big that you couldn't move an inch.

"Luther, my God," Suzie said, her eyes open and wild looking.

Momma's eyes closed as her head lolled back on the hard terrazzo floor, surrounded by a thousand chips of rock circling it like a speckled halo.

THIRTY-EIGHT

As Carl's pickup rolled to a stop next to the maroon Cadillac parked in front of his darkened house, the man's blood pressure rose. Clarice's Trans Am was missing, and here was a new car, an expensive car, sitting out front. Carl wasn't supposed to be home yet. His temples began to pound as he switched off the engine. *That bitch*, he thought, *that fucking bitch. In my own house, doing it behind my back.* If the rain hadn't delayed him getting home, maybe he'd been there when they showed up. Or maybe they were inside, in the middle of...

A blast went off inside the house, accompanied by a flash that flicked through the air. It was near the back of his house. Near his bedroom.

Wrenching open the driver's door, Carl jumped from the pickup and bounded through the sickly grass. The door was already unlocked, so he rushed inside, forgetting as usual to remove his shoes despite his wife's continual griping about the marks on her white carpet.

What he saw inside the house brought him up short. Clarice stood in the dark bedroom, staring at a jackknifed form on the floor. He saw the pistol, dangling at her side, forgotten.

"Clarice, what the *hell?*" His hand searched for the light switch and flicked it on.

The woman turned to him, not looking much like Clarice at all, but someone else, someone he'd never seen, most of the face covered with wet snot. Her eyes blinkered, and she said, "Who're you?"

Carl glanced at the naked man on the floor. Blood dribbled from the huge hole in his belly. The man's eyes were wide, staring, unbelieving of what had happened. "Who the hell's that?"

"Anthony."

"Anthony? Fuck, Clarice, did you—"

She pointed at the naked form with the tip of the pistol barrel. "He was here again tonight. Gladys was asleep. I told him to stop, that I had my butcher knife. But he wouldn't listen this time. I don't, don't know…"

Putting a greasy hand to his forehead, Carl tried to comprehend what he was seeing and hearing. He took a couple of steps toward the man. "Who…who did you say this is?"

"Anthony. He lives with us now."

Carl stepped over to the body and looked down. The man's semi-hard penis languished against his left leg. "It's Scott Blackburn, Clarice."

"No, it's Anthony."

"I don't know what you're talking about, baby, but that's Scott Blackburn. What the fuck happened here?"

Clarice's façade began to crack. "No, it's…it's…Anthony. He tried to rape me again…"

Carl's face screwed up in confusion. "He did *what?*"

She started to shake, her gun hand banging against her side. "It wasn't my fault. I swear."

"Clarice, *look* at me!" he said, grabbing her shoulders and twisting her around. "Tell me what you did!"

The glaze in Clarice's eyes began to clear. "Me and Denise went out. To have a drink. That's where he was."

"Where? Where did you go?"

"The Night Crawler. Then Denise left with Bobby and then he…" She motioned with the gun toward the dead man, "he bought me a few drinks. Then he drove me home."

"Listen to me. Did Blackburn, did you two…" Carl paused, gathering his cool, "have sex or something?"

"No," she said, crying again. "I told him I couldn't, I was married. He must've come in through the door somehow."

Carl pulled her to him, feeling the heaving of Clarice's chest. "Okay, let me think. We gotta call the police."

"No!" she said, breaking away. "They'll never understand!"

"Shit, Clarice. We can't leave him dead on our fucking floor. I mean…" He stopped, seeing her eyes going back to that funny look.

She said, "Had to do this. You understand, don't you? I had to kill Anthony."

Clarice looked past Carl and focused somewhere else. She looked like some kind of walking dead.

"Look, Clarice, this isn't Anthony. Only Anthony I ever heard of was that one lived with you and your mother a while back. And this isn't him, okay?"

"Yes. Yes, it is," she said, glaring at Carl.

"Give me that gun," he said, reaching for the pistol. Up close, he saw a red hand print flushed across her cheek. Son-of-a-bitch. He'd hit her. Hitting a woman was one of the few things that Carl never did.

Clarice realized now that this new man wanted to take away her protection. Protection against Anthony, who might be only pretending, pretending he'd never touched her again, saying to Gladys about her being a whore and anything happened was her fault. She had to keep the knife. To protect herself. She felt the other man's hand on the handle, trying to take it away.

"No!" she screamed, jumping back until her back hit the bedroom wall. She held the knife up to protect herself.

"Give me the damn gun, Clarice," Carl said, reaching for it.

She shook her head, slinging it side-to-side in a wide arc like a small child. "You get outta of here. I mean. I'll call Momma you don't."

"Okay," he said, backing away, both hands up in mock surrender. "But you've got to help me get Anthony out of here. Okay? Here, put that down and give me a hand."

Clarice's arm began to drop as she considered the request. "You said you were going to call the police."

"Maybe later, okay? Just help me here."

"Well, I...I guess I could..." She stepped away from the wall, the weapon dangling against her side.

"Get his arm, okay, baby? Okay? Come over here. Please. Put the pistol down and grab his arm."

It almost worked. If Carl had delayed another second or two, the handgun would have slipped onto the floor and he would have retrieved it. Then they could have settled what happened tonight, how this mess came to be.

But it didn't work.

Clarice caught the motion, swift and sneaky, and realized all this other man wanted was to remove her protection, make her helpless again.

His hand covered hers as they both struggled for the gun. Carl had never seen her this upset, this strong, crying and screaming at the same time, acting like she was fighting for her life, crazy-like. He forced the pistol back as he pried her fingers off, one at a time.

Another cannon shot echoed inside the Telford house.

Clarice's grip loosened. She oozed down to the floor like a slug of thick strawberry preserves dropping onto a piece of pasty white bread.

THIRTY-NINE

"Aneurism, the doctor said. Nothing anyone could do."

It didn't matter what caused it. My momma was gone.

"There's the matter of the funeral," Mr. Garner said, getting to the practical part. "I've had a conversation with the judge."

"And?"

"Your wife has made most of the arrangements, but she wants to talk with you. If there's no other family to speak of, it can be held tomorrow."

It was two days after losing my momma. According to Mr. Garner, Harder said at first I couldn't attend the funeral, seeing as I was a potential felon, still bound up to be incarcerated until the trial was over on account of no bail being posted and as far as he was concerned no right to see the ceremony. After some negotiating, Mr. Garner got him to agree I could make the service long as I was handcuffed and attended by deputies so I wouldn't make an escape attempt. Still, it pissed off the judge something fierce that the trial was going to take into next week to finish up.

"The trial will be suspended until after the services, provided they are held tomorrow. If it's not, then…"

"Fine with me. I'm her only child still livin.'" I was all numb inside and couldn't think real straight, having gone around walking and talking and breathing in and out as usual but not knowing for sure how or why any of it had come to pass.

"No relatives?"

"None close," I said. "'Course, just the church folk could fill up a whole building. She was highly thought of. Much more, I'm ashamed to say, than me."

Mr. Garner planted a hand on my shoulder. "I'm so sorry, Luther."

"Wonder what else can go wrong?" I said.

◆　◆　◆

The Methodists here know how to hold a funeral, long as you don't count the Black folks. It was as good a one as I've ever seen, full of thanking the Lord about her life and remembering Momma's years on this earth and how she was home with the Lord now and not suffering anymore and that we all needed to be rejoicing and not crying.

That last part, though, I had some trouble with.

Suzie tucked me under her wing and petted me as best she could a man with cuffs on and a deputy on the other side. We got through it, and the cemetery scene, too, with the good Christians saying to me on the way out how hard it was but she was a good woman and lived a long time and stuff like that. I nodded most of the time and spoke little. I figured half of them was thinking what a shame that she birthed a dirty murdering bastard that deserves to die for killing the mayor's kid.

Momma's buried next to Daddy's spot, who is next to my sister Debra Anne. On the other side of Momma is my five feet, then Summer's already laid between me and Suzie's plots. I've always thought it was hard for my little dead daughter to be out there all by herself, not snuggled up to her next of kin yet, but when me and Suzie are both gone she'll have lots of company. I'm beginning to think maybe I'll be in my own spot here pretty soon.

Me and Momma kept planning on getting some decent headstones instead of those cheap ones they put down flush with the ground, the kind have your name and date on 'em and nothing else, no loving something or other, or related to so-and-so, but there seemed to always be a more pressing need for money elsewhere.

Right after the lowering of the casket I was hustled back to jail and searched for contraband and dumped back in my cell. I hung up my suit and eased into the top bunk.

"Sorry about your old lady," Barry said.

"'Preciate that. Hard to lose your mother," I said.

Barry snorted. "Depends on the mother. Mine wasn't nothing special."

I leaned over the edge and looked the man in the face. "How can you say that about your own momma?"

"Maybe you didn't know her, but I did. Besides, Carl was her favorite, all along. Kept comparing me to him, wondering why I couldn't measure up."

Near as I remember, Carl and Barry was both hell on wheels, nothing much either wouldn't do, and their ole mammy was worse. Still, it seemed wrong for a man to criticize his dead mother.

"What makes you think she liked Carl better?" I asked.

"Hell, he got her trailer when she died, didn't he?"

"Yeah, but it wasn't…." I stopped before I finished the remark about the dump they all lived in, but it wasn't soon enough.

"Wasn't what? Good enough? It's as good as that damn piece of shit house you live in."

"I didn't mean to—"

"Hey, *fuck you*, Holman! You and your whole goddamned family. I'll be glad when you're out of here." Barry turned over and faced the wall, putting the pillow over his head.

"I'm sorry, Barry. I never—"

"*Shut the fuck up!* I was like you and on the way to Huntsville, damn if I'd spend my time criticizing another man's house."

Recent experience told me it was no use apologizing again. I turned back and faced the ceiling, counting the cracks for the hundredth time.

The rest of the afternoon I took Barry's advice and spent the time walking around inside my head and thinking about my parents both dead, Daddy gone at fifty of a heart attack and my sister Debra Anne got herself drowned when she was thirteen and me eight. Try as hard as I could to see her face, floating there in front of me, fuzzy-like, it wouldn't never come clear. I wondered if her eyes were blue or brown, imagine that, and no one's left alive to ask.

FORTY

"Cooter, please *stop!*" Denise grabbed his hand with both of hers and was able to arrest the movement of his paw for a few seconds. She thought about her missing underwear, knowing that if Cooter's hand made it up between her legs, stopping him would be impossible.

"Now, now, you want this more'n I do," he said.

He pulled the car to the side of the road, the tires scraping along the curb as they ground to a stop, his left hand juggling around the steering wheel to pull the shift lever into park.

"I *mean* it," she said, using her small hands to try and force his groping mitt back.

He turned, one foot on the brake and the other raising off the floor, both of his hands free now. "Why don't you come on over here and give me a big kiss and let's have ourselves a good time. Like your slutty friend, Clarice, is doing."

"*No!*" she screamed.

"Fuck's the matter with you?" he said, grabbing at her flailing hands as he slid across. "Think you're too good for a white man, huh? We'll see about that."

"Look, Cooter, you let me go or I'll get out right now."

"You're not going anywhere," he said, flush against her now and grabbing for the same door handle. She felt his suffocating presence on her like she was being buried alive.

"You leave me alone," she said, "or I'll tell B.J."

"Yeah? And what would you tell him?"

"How you—"

"Case you forgot, we're close relations, you little bitch."

Denise, frantic now, tried again. "Look, Cooter, maybe we need to think about this later. I mean, I got my period right now. Know what I'm saying?" She felt him ease up.

"Huh?"

"Right in the middle, pretty messy." She managed a short laugh. "You know that boyfriend I had before? Jerome? Said it wouldn't matter to him, but when he tried it..." She shook her head. "He said it was *way* too much for him."

One side of Cooter's lip curled as he started to back away. "Well..."

"Okay, then have at it," she said, trying to control the shaking of her legs as she spread them apart. "I'll take my tampon out. Not like I didn't warn you."

He eyed her for a few seconds, then shifted back to his side of his seat. "Shit," he said.

"Probably a bad idea," she said, closing her legs. "Us working together, you know? How'd it look, you dating a Black woman? What'd your friends say?"

Cooter, the mood gone, grunted and shifted the car back into gear, not talking to her any more. He squealed the tires as the Ford's big block V-8 gunned the car ahead. They drove for a mile in silence.

"What's this?" she said, picking up the yellow envelope from the floor where it had fallen, trying to create a distraction.

"None of your fucking business."

"Feels like maybe money's in here," she said, pressing the bulge in the envelope with her thumbs. "Is this something—"

Cooter snatched the envelope away. "You listen to me, Denise. What happens in our office stays there, hear me? I ever hear of you telling anyone, you'll wish you hadn't."

"Hey, *relax*," she said, pointing. "My car's right up ahead there, middle of the block."

The car's headlights illuminated the back of Denise's Chevy Citation. It was alone along the dark block.

"Thanks for the lift," she said, starting to get out.

Grabbing her departing wrist, Cooter stopped Denise halfway out of the car. "'Member what I told you. I ever hear word of you telling anyone about us... Well, you'll be the first one I come see. And you won't like it, neither."

"Don't be silly," she said, tugging her hand out of his grasp. "You and B.J. got nothing to worry about. Besides," she said, turning and forcing herself to look back inside the vehicle, "I took that bag of pot from you guys the other day, so I'm guilty, too, right? No way I could ever tell, even if I wanted to."

"What did you do with it?" he asked.

"Burned it up in the fireplace."

"Liar," he said.

"God's truth. Thanks again." She turned and hustled her keys out of her purse, almost dropping them in her anxiety. She managed to unlock the door, feeling Cooter's eyes on her rear. The engine hesitated, but started up. She put the gearshift into reverse, bringing on the white backup lights.

Cooter reversed the cruiser, taking his time, giving Denise just enough room to back out, then put his foot on the brake. The headlights of the patrol car wavered on the water settled into the shallow depressions in the dark asphalt, the surface filled with quivering puddles of mercury. He set the manila envelope in his lap and opened the tab, thumbing through the cash, watching the rear of Denise's car get close to his bumper, then the car shot forward and disappeared around the next corner, her driving a little too fast.

It occurred to him then that he'd never seen Denise without a bra on, guessing now she hadn't started out the evening that way, remembering Mack's story about her leaving earlier with the man called Bobby Green.

Left and came back without underwear.

Not likely for a woman on the rag.

He tossed the envelope onto the passenger's side of the wide bench seat. The take was less than he'd expected, so he shifted into figuring out how he could skim some of B.J.'s part and the sheriff not notice. Hard to pull that off, though, B.J. always on top of things like that.

The more he thought about it, what he wanted most was to pay Denise a surprise visit and have himself some of her tight little ass.

Reaching down, he returned the radio's volume back to normal. He waited another minute, giving her time to think she wasn't being followed, then headed down the street. The radio squawked to life, interrupting his planning.

"Come in Unit Three. Unit Three, come in."

Cooter reached for the microphone hanging on the dashboard clip, then pushed the Talk button. "Unit Three."

"Where you been?" the dispatcher asked.

"Tied up," he said.

"Sheriff wants you out at the Telford trailer right away. Been calling you for five minutes."

"I'm busy right now," Cooter said, turning off Main, heading west toward Denise's house. He'd decide later what to do, maybe wait outside, go up to the door, pretend to apologize, then…

"B.J. said get over there soon as you can. Been a murder," the dispatcher added.

Cooter sighed. Denise would have to wait. But maybe not for long.

He switched on the roof lights and turned around in the middle of the street.

159

FORTY-ONE

By now, I'd long since figured out that Mr. Garner's motion to redo the trial all over from the start hadn't worked out. Now it was Monday and time for the judge to do his lecture.

Harder started in. "Though we have discussed the matter of Mr. Holman's mother's death before, I wish to reiterate to the jury that your opinion of the ultimate guilt or innocence of Luther Holman must rest on the testimony and evidence presented at this trial. While it is unfortunate that this woman's death occurred during his trial, any sympathy or pity for Mr. Holman must not alter your deliberations regarding the charge of murder against the defendant. Only what is presented at trial should guide your deliberations. Is this clear to the members of the jury?"

Harder adjusted his reading glasses and gave the twelve good citizens an official scowl. All of 'em nodded like their teacher had give 'em hell for climbing trees at recess.

"Very well. You may proceed, Mr. Cunningham."

"State recalls Sheriff B.J. Sanders."

The sheriff's gut brushed against my arm as he lingered near me, then waddled to the witness stand. I didn't have to see his face to take his meaning. Didn't look like this man was ever going to want to get along with me.

"Sheriff, remember that you're still sworn," Harder said.

"Yes, sir."

Cunningham started in. "Before the trial was interrupted, as I recall you were testifying as to your reason or reasons to suspect the defendant in the death of Mr. Reinhardt. Is that correct?"

"I was trying," B.J. said, "but that attorney of his didn't seem to want to listen."

Cunningham made a big pretense of hiding a smile and said, "Please continue, Sheriff."

"Like I said, the deputy and I thought that—"

Boing. "Objection."

Harder slung off his spectacles. "Mr. Garner, I believe we've plowed this ground before. Can you not allow the witness time to even finish his sentence?"

"Your Honor, it is our contention that the sheriff and his deputy incorrectly and maliciously targeted Mr. Holman as the sole and only suspect in the death of Mark Reinhardt, and that they have persistently refused to consider any other person as capable of committing this crime. Further—"

"Your Honor," Cunningham started in, "the People—"

Harder thumped his fingers on his desk. "Mr. Cunningham, will the State acknowledge that local law enforcement may have had preconceived notions about the most likely suspect?"

"Well, I—"

"And Mr. Garner, will the defense acknowledge that regardless of any preconceived notions of local law enforcement, that they have a right to investigate the case?"

"Yes, but—"

"Then let's move on," Harder said.

Mr. Garner wasn't going that easy. "Your Honor—"

"I *said*, let's move on, counselor."

Seeing he had done about all the good he was going to, Mr. Garner took his seat. He leaned over to me and said, "If the trial doesn't go our way, this may be reversible later on."

I nodded like he'd won a great victory, but as near as I could see it, it didn't do nothing but waste a minute or two.

"Now, Sheriff, would you describe your actions after discovering Mr. Reinhardt?"

"Well, like I said, based on Luther Holman's past threats..." B.J. saw Mr. Garner getting up and changed in mid-sentence, "...or let me say, based on Luther Holman's past statements, we considered him a man we wanted to talk with right away."

"And did you?"

"Yes, sir. The deputy and I went right over to his house."

"And what did you find?"

B.J. had caught on a long time ago about this sing-song routine with Cunningham, so he spit out a sentence or two each time and waited for the next question.

"We found the defendant at home with his wife, Suzie Holman."

"What was he doing?"

"Watching TV, near as we could tell. His wife answered the door."

"Watching TV," Cunningham said, and shook his head. Of course, this was supposed to mean I was a cold-blooded bastard that wasn't no more concerned than nothing about having killed a man a few minutes before.

"Then what happened?"

"We asked could we come in and she said, 'Sure.'"

"How did Suzanne Holman act at this point, Sheriff?"

"Objection. Calls for a conclusion of the witness."

Cunningham shook his head from side to side real slow. "Your Honor, the witness has over twenty years of law enforcement experience to draw on. I hardly think his opinion of Mrs. Holman's nervousness is—"

Harder didn't wait for his to finish. "Overruled." I suspected that the judge had about enough of my attorney objecting to every damn thing said or asked about.

"Please answer the question, Sheriff," Cunningham said.

"She appeared nervous."

"How so?"

"She held her eyes down and was twisting a dish towel in her hands."

"How did Luther Holman act?"

"Like he hadn't done a damn thing."

"Sheriff," Harder said, "I told you before to watch your language."

"Yes, sir. Like he was completely unconcerned."

"Did this surprise you?" Cunningham asked.

"Not a bit."

"Why not?"

"I'd seen him when his daughter died. He's a cold man, one that doesn't show his feelings."

"Objection," Mr. Garner said. "The witness is assuming that Mr. Holman knew of Mark Reinhardt's death and was unemotional about it. The truth is, he knew nothing about the events that had recently transpired."

"Sustained," Harder said. He rubbed his forehead and added, "Confine your remarks to the facts of this case, Sheriff."

"Okay. He didn't act like anything was the matter."

"What happened next?" Cunningham said.

"I asked him where he had been tonight and he said at home. Then I asked did he go out at all and he said no."

"And?"

"I told him there had been a murder. He stood up then and asked about it."

"What did Mrs. Holman do?"

"She went in the kitchen and didn't come out."

"Not even to hear about who was murdered?"

"No, sir."

"Humm," Cunningham said, acting like this was a big surprise to him, but like Mr. Garner told me, a lawyer never asks a question he don't know the answer to already. But I didn't appreciate what they were saying about Suzie, not one damn bit.

B.J. didn't wait for the next question, but started up on his own seeing as how the last remark was more like a pause than a question.

"I asked him did he have a pistol and he said yes, his daddy's, and I said could I see it."

"Did the defendant give you his gun?"

"He opened the drawer on the table beside the sofa and started to get it out when we stopped him. My deputy took it out real careful to avoid disturbing any fingerprints."

"Had the weapon been recently fired?"

"Yes, sir, it had. I could smell powder on it."

"What happened next?"

"I said he better come with us."

FORTY-TWO

As Cooter walked past B.J.'s gleaming Ford LTD, he caressed the fender with his finger. B.J.'s vehicle always looked polished and clean. It should, considering the jail trustees washed it every day. The new vehicle was a reward for the recent takedown of two dopers out on Terry Blackburn's farm. Cooter had done all the hard work that day, including the killings and the arson, but it was B.J. who ended up with the new cruiser. Hardly fucking fair, Cooter thought, glancing back at his own vehicle, the usual B.J. hand-me-down.

Carl, incubating in the backseat of the cruiser, mouthed words through the closed glass window, words that Cooter couldn't quite make out, Cooter guessing it was hotter than two sides of hell inside the enclosed car and not caring a bit. Carl should be used to it by now, him working at the plant and all.

Inside the trailer, the sheriff stood in the Telford bedroom, hands thrust in his back pockets.

"Well?" Cooter asked, surveying the corpses. "Who killed who?"

B.J. studied the scene before replying. "Looks like we got us three possibilities. Carl claims his wife, the one there with her head half blown off, said she shot Blackburn for trying to rape her. Then he claims he tried to take the weapon away from her and she accidental-like got shot in the face."

"I take it that's one," Cooter said, sliding over to have a good look at Scott Blackburn. Bending down, he could see the surprise still reflected in the dead man's face.

"Or two, maybe old Carl busts in on his wife getting dicked by the dead Chevy dealer here. He's furious, takes the gun outta the drawer, and pops one in the lover's back. Then he lets wifey have it next."

"I like that one," Cooter said.

"Or three, someone unknown comes in and shoots them both, maybe for the hell of it, and Carl finds them after."

"How many killings we had this year so far, boss?" Cooter said, already knowing the answer, but wanting to make a point.

B.J. removed his hat and patted the sweat off of his forehead with his forearm. "This makes four. Least ways, four that the public knows about."

"Quite a few for a God-fearing, safe kinda county," Cooter said. "Suspect the jury needs to send a message to the next defendant. That they ain't too happy about so many victims dying around here."

"Suppose so." B.J. replaced the hat, his thumb and index finger sliding along the brim, acting like he was creasing the edge. Cooter knew that habit meant the man was playing for time, thinking, maybe an idea already in his head. "Still, you gotta count those two beaners you shot as whole people to get up to four."

"They had it coming, trying to take over the local dope business." Cooter paused before speaking again. "From what you're saying, I take it we want Door Number Two."

B.J. nodded. "That's the one I like. But it comes with a few problems."

"Like what?"

Pointing to Clarice, B.J. said, "Like the female victim. She's lying there with her undies on and Blackburn there is naked as a jaybird. A suspicious mind could wonder why she's still got her clothes on."

"Maybe they was playing games. You get naked first and then I'll follow. I think Cunningham could sell that. Besides, I can fix that problem right now," Cooter said, bending down.

"Hold on. I said let's think this through."

Cooter folded his arms, impatient, waiting for B.J. to come to a conclusion. Seeing what was left of Clarice made him wonder again about

Denise. He hadn't given up on that nocturnal visit to her house just yet. In his mind, he saw himself on top of Denise, working his cock around inside her. It would be better if she struggled some. He could see himself holding her arms down while she insisted she wanted him to stop. Cooter's tongue ran across his lower lip in anticipation. For now, he needed to get back to the murder discussion.

"Mack said he saw them leave the Crawler tonight, together. Said she was drunk as shit, and before that was in the booth with Scott for a while, laughing her ass off at his stories."

B.J.'s eyes narrowed. "What the hell you doing there tonight? It's a day early."

"Don't you think I know that? But I didn't want to bother old Jack on a Friday. He pissed and moaned a lot, but I got the money in the car."

"How much?"

"One thousand."

"That's all?"

"Jack says times are hard."

"Motherfucker," B.J. said.

Cooter watched the sheriff's eyes to see if he could detect any suspicion there. The customary split was he got thirty percent and B.J. seventy.

"That's it, huh?" B.J. said.

Cooter shook his head. "Call him up. You'll see."

B.J said, "Now that Blackburn is out of the bar-owning business, maybe his partner Reinhardt needs some assistance. You up to replacing poor old Scott?"

"What would I want with a fucking bar?" Cooter said.

"Because, you dumb shit, an owner's take's gotta come to more than we get."

The pair argued for a few more minutes, discussing the pros and cons of ownership versus the steady flow of graft. Lacking a conclusion, they returned to the mess on the floor.

Cooter said, "Come on, let's get on with it."

At that point, the trailer's phone rang. B.J. picked it up.

"Sheriff Sanders here. Denise? What do you...Well, we're here investigating...me and Cooter, that's who. You did? Well, then I got some bad news. Clarice is dead...that's right, you heard me...yeah, I can't believe it either...don't know yet, we're still trying to figure out what happened, but it looks like maybe her husband did. I've got to go. I'll talk to you tomorrow." B.J. hung up.

"*Our* Denise?" Cooter asked.

"Yeah."

"She say anything about me?"

B.J.'s eyes narrowed. "Why'd she do a thing like that?"

"No reason. What'd she want?"

"Don't really know. Once I told her about Clarice being dead for sure, she busted out crying."

"Yeah," Cooter said. "Seems like I 'member she and Clarice were pretty close."

B.J. pointed to the wall. "Blackburn must've been standing by the bed when he got shot in the back. You can see where his guts are sprayed out on the wallpaper over yonder. I suspect you'll find what's left of the bullet inside the wall. But he's in a bad spot if we say he was rooting around inside Clarice. Better he was turned around some, lying on the bed maybe. Still, no way that would work now." B.J.'s mouth tangled into a twisted scowl. Why couldn't this be easier? "He got his underwear tangled up in his feet, so he was either taking them off or putting them on. Which one you figure?"

"Taking them off, of course. About to get himself a hot piece of ass."

"Maybe." B.J. studied some more. "If he was putting them back on, Carl's story fits better. But, of course, we can't use that one."

"Right."

"See, what I think Blackburn was doing was maybe getting dressed, not undressed. He was after some tail and it didn't work out. Maybe she changed her mind. Who the hell knows what a woman thinks, huh?"

Cooter didn't reply.

"But that means either a busted fuck session, or maybe our fine upstanding citizen there's a rapist."

"You think so?" Cooter asked, imagining himself with Denise again and how it might turn out.

B.J. nodded. "I got me an idea. Go get the camera outta my car."

FORTY-THREE

Mr. Garner was doing the leaning routine, like Cunningham, keeping a sideways eye on B.J. like maybe he was about to escape from his temporary prison of spindles and carved railings.

"Now, Sheriff, you testified a minute ago that your deputy, Cooter Sanders, picked up the pistol from the table beside the sofa. Is that correct?"

"That's what I said."

"I know it's what you said, Sheriff. I asked you if that was *correct*."

B.J.'s face flushed. "I don't lie."

"Umm," Mr. Garner said, raising up and sticking one hand in his pocket. Watching lawyers and the way they walk around and hold themselves would have been real fascinating to me if I hadn't had my neck in the noose. Every gesture was made to make the jury think they were the ones to be trusted, the ones with a stranglehold on the right facts, when half the time it seemed to me they was actors playing a part, making up the words as they went.

"Isn't it possible, Sheriff, that Mr. Holman, not Cooter Sanders, picked up the pistol—"

"No."

"...and by picking it up automatically placed his fingerprints on the grip of the weapon?"

"That's not how it happened."

"Tell me, Sheriff, if you were standing near the front door, where was the table?"

"Over there a little." B.J. flicked off a motion with his thick finger.

"And the chair Mr. Holman was in?"

"A little to the left of it."

My attorney made a big show of walking over to the imaginary table and trying to place himself in the right place. After a few missed attempts, B.J. got him redirected to the right spot.

"Here, then?"

"Yeah, that's about right."

"Okay." Mr. Garner sat on the top of our defense table, casual-like, and said, "Mr. Holman puts the recliner's footrest down and stands up," he stood, "...and talks to you and your deputy," he turned toward B.J., "...and you ask about his pistol and he turns to his left," more turning, "...and opens the drawer to get out the pistol. Is that correct?"

"Yes."

"Tell me, Sheriff. How is it that you're so sure Mr. Holman didn't pick the pistol up by its grip? After all, my back is blocking your view."

B.J. was up a stump again, puzzling over how to convince the jury of his version of what happened.

"Well?" Mr. Garner asked.

"I know what happened. Luther started picking up the pistol by the barrel and my deputy stopped him."

"By the barrel?"

"Yes."

"Were his fingerprints found on the barrel?"

"The barrel was smudged from handling."

"Oh? Smudged?"

"The handkerchief Cooter used. It slipped and smudged the fingerprints."

"I see," Mr. Garner said again. "Your Honor, would you have the court reporter re-read Mr. Sander's previous statement about his deputy picking up the pistol?"

"Very well," Harder said. "Mrs. Elliott?"

The reporter worked through her paper tape, staring at it like there was a direct message from aliens about to appear on it. After finding the right spot, she said, "'He opened the drawer on the table beside the sofa and started to get it out when we stopped him. My deputy took it out real careful to avoid disturbing any fingerprints.'"

B.J.'s face got red again.

"Sheriff?" Mr. Garner said.

"What?"

"Did Mr. Holman pick up the pistol or did your deputy do so? Which of those two conflicting statements do you wish to retract?"

"Objection," Cunningham said. "Badgering the witness. Sheriff Sanders is obviously being harassed."

Harder turned to B.J. "State for the record which of the actions described, to your knowledge, did in fact take place."

"My deputy said he picked up the pistol. I'll trust what he said."

Mr. Garner gave B.J. The Square Eye. "If it's alright with you, we won't."

"Objection! Your Honor, defense is—"

"Withdrawn. Did you examine the pistol later to see if any shots have been fired?"

"Yes. Two."

"Two shots?"

"Yes," B.J. said while he shifted his big ass around.

"How many bullets did the medical examiner recover from Mr. Reinhardt?"

"One."

"Where was the other one?"

"We didn't find it."

"Didn't find it?"

"No."

"Where did you look?" Mr. Garner said.

B.J. scowled. "Inside the house."

"Oh? Where in Mark Reinhardt's house?"

"His office. Where he was killed."

"No second bullet, huh?"

"No."

"Sheriff, do you find it odd that a murderer, after shooting Mark Reinhardt in the forehead, would fire off another round *outside* the house as he left?"

B.J. squirmed like the hemorrhoids was eating into him. "I'm sure that didn't happen."

"Or perhaps that a shot was fired elsewhere in the house? Did you check the entire house?"

"As best we could."

"No second bullet, I take it."

"I *told* you before. No."

"I see," Mr. Garner said in that lawyer tone, seeming to collect the thoughts in his head. "Then if my client murdered Mark Reinhardt with a single shot, a single shot that was heard by Shirley Johnson, who previously testified that she heard one, or perhaps two, pistol shots, what do you think happened to the second one? Maybe you weren't that careful in your investigation." This caused some titters from the audience and a smile or two from the jury.

Cunningham was on his feet to object when B.J. blurted out, "This is all a bunch of crap. Luther Holman's gun killed Mark Reinhardt and his fingerprints were on the pistol—"

"I don't mean to interrupt you, Sheriff," Mr. Garner added over Cunningham's talk, "but no legitimate testimony has yet entered into these proceedings that my client's fingerprints were even *on* the murder weapon."

"Order!" Harder started shouting and worked his toy hammer up and down to make the point.

"It will," B.J. said, clenching his ferret teeth together like he was biting through a piece of steel chain. "And then Luther Holman won't be able to lie his way out of this one!"

"Move to strike. Prejudicial," Mr. Garner said, his eyes locked on B.J.'s.

FORTY-FOUR

Carl mouthed off as Cooter searched the interior of the police car for B.J.'s camera.

"Stow it," Cooter said.

"Listen, you *dickhead!*" Carl yelled. "It was an accident, dammit. My wife was being raped by that fucker, you *hear* me!"

"Shut the hell up, Telford," Cooter said as he felt under the passenger side of the long bench seat and found the camera case.

◆ ◆ ◆

Once back inside the house, Cooter handed the camera to B.J.

"First, we take some pictures as it is," B.J. said, snapping away at both bodies. He took shots from a series of angles, framing one, then both, victims. "Okay, now move the bed down some. Make it look like he was more in the middle."

Cooter tugged at the footboard, scooting the stubborn feet across the snowy carpet. The sheriff motioned toward Clarice's body. "Take her drawers off."

Cooter slid the underwear down, revealing the dead woman's crotch to his greedy eyes. "Quite a muff on this one," he said.

"Sling them over yonder, on the bed. Then kick her legs apart."

Cooter did as instructed, nudging the inanimate limbs with his boot.

"That's good." B.J. focused and took three more photos. "Now we've gone from being a victim to a willing participant." He bent down, getting close-ups of Clarice's shattered face. "This ought to impress the jury as it relates to Mr. Telford's violent nature."

"What about Blackburn? You want to leave him like that?"

"Take the underwear off his feet. Put them over on the bed. Next to hers."

"Okay."

"Good," B.J. said, seeing Cooter was finished. "Two lovers caught on the bed, maybe on the floor, in the midst of a passionate embrace. Man stands up to apologize and get dressed and damn if he isn't shot in the back by the jealous husband. The wife rushes to the husband, begging for forgiveness. Bam, the bastard lets her have it, too, right through the eye."

B.J. photographed the bloody wall, the stained bedspread, a close-up of the grouped underwear, taking care to fully record what remained of Clarice's face. Standing up with effort, he took his hat off and mopped the sweat. "Whew. Felt like I had a tourniquet across my gut."

"Maybe you oughtta get a bigger belt," Cooter offered. "Or go on a diet."

B.J. replaced the hat. "Cost a lot of money to get my belly this big. Seem a shame to lose it now."

"What's Carl gonna say about your pictures? Not like he won't know we fooled with things," Cooter said.

"Carl don't matter," B.J. said. "Who's gonna believe a jailbird caught shooting up two people, one of them an upstanding citizen?"

"And the other photos? The real ones?"

"Insurance. Let things simmer down, then we'll pay us a visit to Scott's ole daddy. Let the man know we covered up for his rapist kid. Tell him know we'll be expecting a favor in return, when the time comes."

"And Carl?"

"Carl needs him a good lawyer. Take my car back to the jail. After you lock him up, give Franklin a call. I'll square it with Judge Harder if I need to, but I doubt the judge's got a problem with getting the wheels of justice moving early."

"What're you going to do?"

"Rearrange a few more things if I need to. You know I don't like loose ends. I need some time by myself to think on all this, not miss anything. Then I'll call the ambulance."

"Damn shame," Cooter said, staring down at Clarice's crotch. "I wished I'd had me some of that while it was still warm. Now it's all gone to waste."

FORTY-FIVE

"Hot damn, Mr. Garner, you done good."

"Luther, we had some successes today, but-—"

"No buts, Mr. Garner. You took old B.J.'s story apart."

Mr. Garner put his elbows on the table in the same little office off the main courtroom. He was studying about something real hard. I waited for him to speak his mind.

"Luther, regardless of how I made the sheriff look, the simple fact is that the fingerprint witness is next and he's going to nail you for having held the gun, the same pistol that killed Mark Reinhardt and was found in *your* house with two shots recently fired."

"Like I told you, Mr. Garner," I said, "I picked the gun up by the grip. Cooter asked me could I give it to him."

"Maybe we can overcome the deputy's testimony, but what about the shots fired?"

"What about them?"

"Damn it, Luther. How does a pistol get in your sofa table drawer with two shots were recently fired and you not know about it? Either you've been lying to me or you're guilty as hell. Which one is it?"

I could see Mr. Garner was pretty agitated, since he don't say 'damn' less'n it was special circumstances.

"Well?" he asked. "We don't have much time. Court will reconvene in about five minutes."

I thought up a couple of explanations that might work, but seeing as how we were down to the nut-cutting, as they say, I figured I better tell the truth.

"I wasn't at home part of the night."

"You've told me all along you *were*!"

"Well, me and Suzie were gone for a while. About two hours."

"Why didn't you tell me this before? *Damn* it!" Mr. Garner had his eyebrows clinched together and looked pretty much like a man driving an open convertible just got passed by a truckload of diarrhea cattle.

"That night, when B.J. and Cooter showed up? He asked me where I had been and I didn't want to say, so I said I was home all night. How did I know there was a murder weapon three feet from me?"

"Why didn't you tell him you were out?"

Shaking my head, I said, "We went to see someone I didn't want B.J. to know about."

"Who?"

"Billy Yates."

"Why, dammit?" Mr. Garner asked, impatient to get on with the story and me like a kid with chocolate all over my face and pretending I didn't know where the candy wrappers come from.

"We hadn't heard anything from Billy since that night we was at the Crawler. He'd already told me and Suzie, a week or two 'fore Reinhardt was killed, that he had information on Summer's killer, and could we meet up. But that same night, Cooter caught him talkin' to us and he said afterward he wasn't never goin' to say anything else. Then along comes this phone call. Guess Billy was needing money bad, 'cause it must've took him several years to get over Cooter threatening him. Anyways, me and Suzie went out to see what he had to say about Summer. About the information he said he'd sell us. See if maybe he'd take less'n the thousand he was askin' before."

"What did he say?"

"He said, 'You ask me that again, it's going to cost you another grand.'"

"Why didn't you admit where you and Suzie had gone?" Mr. Garner said.

"We met out in the country, behind an old barn was about to fall down. Nobody seen us, so what's the use of tellin' a jury where we was? They wouldn't believe us. No way."

"Tell me the rest of this story. Please."

"Billy told us that night that for sure the sheriff knew what happened to Summer. And who had done it. But that's all he'd say without the thousand dollars. Said he was risking his neck enough as it was."

Mr. Garner leaned back. "Are you telling me the sheriff is—"

"I'm tellin' you that's what Billy Yates said. Seeing as how you can't ask him yourself 'cause his head ended up about half the size it used to be, you'll have to take my word for it. Besides, you don't think I would tell B.J. I was out solicitin' information connectin' him with my daughter's murder, do you? My bad luck it was the same night that bastard Reinhardt bought the farm." I was fed up with this cross-examination routine and was beginning to wonder if the man believed me at all, but I could also see past that, too, on how he was real disappointed in me right about then.

Mr. Garner thumped his fingers on the desk, thinking his way through the story. "So you met Billy Yates for information the night Clarice was killed, then met him again for the same purpose the night Reindhardt was killed?"

"Guess Billy was bad luck, all the way around." I shrugged, not knowing what else to say.

"I suppose there wasn't anyone at the house with you the night you were arrested?"

"Momma was there a little earlier."

"Why?"

"I told her before about the meetin' we was goin' to have with Billy. I knew he still wanted money and we was tryin' to figure out how to raise some more. See, Momma was on the social security, and after payin' for the medicine each month she's lucky not to be eatin' cat food. But she come up with four hundred and me and Suzie had about three. But it wasn't enough."

"Did you mother stay at your house after you both left?"

"No. She left, too."

"Did she lock the door on her way out?"

"I don't know. She's not around to ask."

"Don't you remember when you came home if the house was locked?"

I thought about that. "Maybe, I don't remember. Half the time I don't lock my doors, not like we've ever had anything stolen, this being a small town—"

"So then anyone could have…" Mr. Garner stopped thumping. "Who, besides yourself, knew that you had a pistol at home?"

"Most people around town got some kind of gun for protection. Wouldn't take a genius to figure out I was normal."

"But they would have to know where it was. Not enough time to search your house and be sure you wouldn't be back…" Mr. Garner looked through me at the wall, working out the details in his head.

"Unless," I said. "Unless you'd been in my house before and knew how long we was goin' to be away."

Mr. Garner gave me a sharp glance. "Why the *hell* didn't you tell me this before?"

"You honestly think anybody's going to believe I was only out of the house a couple hours that night, the same couple hours that somebody took my gun, shot Mark Reinhardt, and then put it back in the drawer 'fore I got home?"

The door opened and Tommy said, "Judge is ready to start back up and doesn't like to be kept waiting. Y'all come on back in."

FORTY-SIX

"My client says you're lying," Bob Franklin said.

"Dammit, Bob, this ain't hard." B.J. said, continuing to pace in front of the lawyer's desk. "What the hell's up with you?"

Franklin's fingers combed through the few remaining strands on the top of his head. His hair had once been thick and black, the one proud display on a body that was otherwise unremarkable. "I'm only saying—"

"Who's the jury gonna believe, huh?"

Leaning back in his cracked leather chair, now almost faded to black with age, Franklin began to shrink. He hoped for a miracle he knew wasn't coming.

"Well, who?" B.J. insisted.

"Okay, look, there's several things." Franklin fished for the statement buried under the foreclosure he had been working on. No need to hurry. Carl Telford was marinating inside a cell in the county jail, sweating it out in the back part with the busted air-conditioner that never seemed to get fixed. "First, Carl says his wife's panties were on her."

"You got the photos. You blind, too?" By now, B.J. had flopped down in one of the cheap arm chairs paying homage to Franklin's desk.

"No, I saw the pictures."

"You accusing me of faking evidence here?" B.J. asked, leaning forward, hoping a little physical intimidation would get this matter resolved.

Franklin soldiered on. "He says you moved the bed. Claims it's not in the right place. Makes it look like they were on the floor or maybe started out on the bed, doing it, when Blackburn got shot. And he tells me there wasn't any underwear on the bed, either."

"He got any witnesses?"

"You know he doesn't."

"Then what're we discussing this for?"

Sensing defeat, Franklin propped his head up on his arm. "What is it you want, B.J.?"

"You got yourself a convicted thief and known liar for a client." The sheriff ticked the points off on his stubby fingers. "On the other hand, I got clear pictures of the scene showing your client murdered those two lovebirds. And statements from his co-workers show he was angry and in a dangerous mood before the crime was committed. Threatened to hit one of 'em, just for delivering a message." The sheriff settled into the chair, satisfied. He started to cross his legs, but failed as the top one slid off of the slick khaki material. "I've already talked with the honorable district attorney. We figure your client's got one chance. Tell Carl to plead guilty and throw himself on the mercy of the court. Get this over and done with."

"No way he's going to do that," Franklin said. "It'll be an automatic death sentence."

"Okay, then not guilty."

"We've got other options here."

"Insanity? That what you're tying to sell me, Bob?"

Franklin remained stoic. "I'm saying it's an option, that's all."

"You know that won't work around here. Besides, it would cost us money to hire expert witnesses on both sides. Might have to raise the good folk's taxes all because of your guilty client. We wouldn't want that, now would we?"

Franklin gazed out of his window, under the dusty blinds, across the street toward the courthouse. From where he sat, he couldn't see the back of the building where the jail was located. "I'll go see if he'd be willing to plead to manslaughter and a lesser sentence."

"Fuck. No." B.J. stood up, knowing now it was over.

"You can't reject an offer! An answer has to come from the district attorney, not the sheriff. There has to be some damn legal procedures followed around here."

"Cunningham will say the same thing. You know he will." B.J. replaced his hat, squaring it, then sliding his thumb and finger across the brim. "See you in court, counselor."

"We'll claim interference, tampering with evidence."

"Go right ahead. See how far you get."

"I need something, something to take him, B.J." Franklin said in a small voice. The man had shrunk down in the last few moments, becoming a supplicant without leverage.

"Okay, how about this? His worthless brother Barry? Got himself arrested last night. Again. Shame, but he had this bag of weed in his car. Now, if Barry gets busted for this with his prior record, well, he'll be doing hard time for a good while."

Franklin shook his head. "There's any deals to be done, you have—"

"Tell ole Carl he's got two choices here. One, he pleads guilty. Two, not. Either way he's convicted. His brother gets off with maybe a misdemeanor and a couple months. Or two, he pleads nutso like I think I'm hearing you say, or says we tricked up the photos, and both those fucking Telfords go down." B.J. smiled across the desk. "Like I said, it's not hard, is it?"

Franklin continued to stare out of the window. "I'll call Cunningham, see what—"

B.J. leaned over, both hands planted in the middle of Franklin's clutter. "Look, asshole, that's the deal. Else maybe we discover a few bags of coke in the side panels of Barry's car."

"You're enjoying yourself, aren't you?"

B.J. said, "Those Telfords, they're nothing but dog shit. Their old sorry-ass mother made her living on her back. Nobody knows who their daddies were. Be doing the county a favor to get rid of at least one of them. Executing your client might cut the county's crime rate in half."

"This isn't right. These men are entitled to—"

"Cut the law school bullshit, Franklin. It's not having any effect on me. I'm sweeping out the trash, and your client's stuck in the broom."

Franklin's look of contempt didn't faze B.J. He leaned forward. "What's the matter? Worried about your win/loss record?"

"No."

"Good, 'cause it's not about to get any better."

"Listen, Cunningham and I need to—"

"Dates for the trail already been set by the judge. You got any problems, take it up with Harder."

The door slammed, rattling the glass in the shrunken wooden frame. Bob Franklin spent the next long minutes gazing across the street, looking at nothing this time.

FORTY-SEVEN

The official ten-minute timeout helped B.J.'s composure, at least at first. Somebody, maybe Cunningham, had calmed him down so he wasn't so pissy this time around.

Even after our last conversation, Mr. Garner did his level best to tear the sheriff a new asshole, or at least lubricate the one he already had. I wouldn't have thought about saying things like that before, but being around the criminal element for the past few months makes you a bit unconcerned for the sufferings of others.

"So we can say that you never considered any other suspects, Sheriff?"

"No need to. We had the murderer."

"Ever wonder if the pistol was removed from Mr. Holman's house, discharged, and then returned in the original table drawer?"

"Of course not."

"Why not?"

"Why would that be? That's a crazy idea," B.J. said.

"Ever check on Mark Reinhardt's background? See if he had dealing with any unsavory characters? See if anyone else had a grudge against him and wanted him dead?"

"No need to. Mark Reinhardt had no enemies."

That remark might've carried some weight with another man, seeing as how it come from a law enforcement official, but the statement caused the jury to shift around a bit. Regardless of who you were, everyone in town knew Mark Reinhardt kept an oversized set of skeletons, enough so it'd take a walk-in closet to hold 'em all and two strong men to wedge the door shut.

"No enemies, Sheriff?"

"None I know of."

"Ever check?"

"I believe I've answered that before. We had the murder weapon and the murderer."

"Are you sure?"

"Of course."

"So, if I understand your testimony, Sheriff, Mark Reinhardt had no enemies, was never in trouble, and, as far as we know, pure as the driven snow."

That last one made even B.J. squirm like his shorts was up in his ass crack, but by now he had his foot in the water pail and had to pretend there was nothing on the end of his leg but a cowboy boot.

"Well, I wouldn't say pure—"

"Oh? Something we should know?"

"No man's perfect. Nothing important, though."

"Says who?" Mr. Garner said, enjoying needling the man.

"Objection. Badgering the witness," Cunningham called out.

"Sustained. Move on, Mr. Garner."

"No further questions."

B.J. stepped down, his big belly giving a shake as his second foot hit the courtroom floor.

Cooter was next up on the witness stand, saying he was only following orders from the sheriff, him only taking tire track photos and impressions, and yes there was a set taken both in the alley behind Reinhardt's house and also in my driveway, but something must've happened to those in the alley, him not exactly able to say what that was. Mr. Garner worked him over good, saying evidence you can't produce isn't of much value and hinted maybe the stuff that got lost ended up being that way on purpose. Then they fought over how Cooter picked up my pistol and did he hold it right, and it went on and on. 'Course, there were lots of objections from Cunningham at the cross-examination, but I couldn't see that Cooter's testimony made one lick of difference.

Then came the fingerprint witness, a Mr. Schick, who it was told spent all his time in the FBI crime lab. We had to sit through an hour of ladling up his smartness, plus a discussion of whirls, ridges, fifteen magic points, and stuff like that, all intended to make him sound like an absolute genius when in come to figuring out whose skin oil ended up on pistols grips. After all that, he got to the meat of his talk.

Cunningham said, "And so, Mr. Schick, based on your twenty-three years of experience in fingerprint analysis, what is your opinion of the fingerprints lifted from the murder weapon?"

"The prints on the grip belonged to Luther Holman."

"The defendant?'

"Yes."

"Are your certain?"

"Yes."

"Thank you, Mr. Schick. Your witness." Cunningham sat down, thinking there was no way this witness could blow up on him like some of the last ones had.

Mr. Garner mosied up to the stand and adopted his familiar good-ole-boy attitude.

"Mr. Schick, how many trials have you testified in, in your career?"

"I don't keep count."

"I see. But about how many? Five, ten, fifteen?"

"Over a hundred."

"A hundred!" Mr. Garner said, all surprised-like.

"Over a hundred," Mr. Schick corrected him.

"My, my. Ever been wrong?"

"About what?"

"About fingerprint identification?"

"No."

"Not ever?"

"No."

Mr. Garner shook his head in disbelief. "Mr. Schick, I'm terribly impressed. All that checking and never an incorrect identification?"

The witness sat there, not saying anything. 'Course, somebody been on the witness stand that much was expecting a steel-jawed trap lurking right under their chair. He wasn't about to put a foot down, so he'd made up his mind to wait Mr. Garner out.

"Mr. Schick?"

"Sir?"

"Never incorrect?"

"I don't sign off on a fingerprint identification unless I'm certain."

"Never even a teensy-weensy bit of doubt in your conclusions?"

"Objection, Your Honor. Counsel is badgering a witness again. Mr. Schick has answered this question several times."

"Sustained."

I watched Mr. Garner go on like nothing had happened. It must be a skill they teach you in law school, saying things are one way when you know they aren't and expecting to get called down. Maybe one time in a hundred it works so you keep at it. I got to thinking that trial lawyers were kinda like thieves who keep checking for unlocked doors, one after the other, and after a while you'll find one and get in.

"How many prints were you able to make comparisons on?"

"Three."

"Three?" Mr. Garner said. "Last I looked, Mr. Holman had four fingers and a thumb."

The witness leaned forward some. "I was able to compare three essentially complete prints."

"Mr. Schick, my understanding is that fingerprint identification is somewhat subjective. That two experts might not identify the same number of points as matching. That instead of double-blind tests it's one person's viewpoint. Could that possibly be correct? Have you ever had a hard time identifying fingerprints?"

Schick saw that fastball coming and was in his stance, ready to swing. "Smudged prints *are* difficult to identify. Without the correct number of points, I put those down as unidentifiable."

"I see. Were there any of those types of prints on the barrel of the murder weapon?"

"Yes, several."

"And you couldn't identify them?"

"No."

"So you chose not to mention them."

"Objection. Leading the witness," Cunningham said.

"Your Honor, I was only asking the State's witness a question. Surely he can testify whether or not he is able to determine if the other prints were made by another person."

"Overruled," Harder said. "But let's not linger on this matter, Mr. Garner."

"Now Mr. Schick, you have testified that you readily identified the fingerprints on the grip of Mr. Holman's pistol, and that three of them were his. I suspect that if you examined the pistols of most of the good citizens of this city, they would *also* have their own fingerprints on their grips." A few nods of understanding come from the jury box. "Were there any unidentifiable fingerprints on the barrel of the same pistol? Yes or no?"

"Yes."

"So you admit there were prints other than Mr. Holman's?"

"Not necessarily," Schick said. "I said there were unidentifiable prints. They could be Mr. Holman's."

"Could they be someone else's?"

"Yes."

"So you admit that more than one person could have touched the pistol barrel?"

"It's possible."

"How much is the state paying you for your testimony, Mr. Schick?"

"I'm being compensated for my time."

"No further questions of this witness," Mr. Garner said over his shoulder as he headed back to our table.

"Your Honor, the State rests," Cunningham said, standing up and buttoning his coat like this was the end of the whole damn thing and why couldn't the jury go ahead right now and declare me guilty and save everyone a whole lotta time.

"Considering the lateness of the hour," Harder said, looking at his watch and sounding far away like a god sitting up on the mountaintop, "we will re-convene at nine-thirty tomorrow morning. Are you prepared to call your witnesses at that time, Mr. Garner?"

"Yes, Your Honor."

"Court is adjourned."

I wondered how in the world we could be quitting so soon, but maybe Harder wanted to spend the rest of the day out fishing. While we were standing up, I leaned over to Mr. Garner and said I wanted to make sure he or Suzie had gotten the stuff I sent him by way of Barry's connections. He gave me a puzzled look and said he didn't know what I was talking about. Then he started going on about how he still had the big city reporter in the audience, writing about the case for the papers, and how that would help our cause, the publicity, but I didn't hear him complete 'cause I was busy wondering what the hell happened to the stuff I sent. I made my mind up to check with Barry first thing.

I saw Suzie as I turned around to leave. She was standing alone, all by herself now, nothing but a little bit of woman. Her eyes was hollowed out and she had this sad look about her, like a cat got kicked every night but still showed up for dinner 'cause that's all it had to look forward to. I realized then I'd been so busy with myself I hadn't realized she'd about had it. I reached out to touch her, but the Tommy the bailiff came by and grabbed my hand and said time to go back.

"Suzie, you all right?" I asked.

"I got to go to work," she said.

Her eyes followed me out the side door. I know because I glanced back three times, the last one as I rounded the door frame and her expression never changed. It was like I was on a troop ship, sailing away to war, the dock and the woman I loved disappearing and nothing I could do to grab it back.

Forty-Eight

"Then the sheriff's a fucking *liar!*" Carl Telford screamed across the table.

Bob Franklin held up a palm, as if the presence of a patch of pallid flesh would stop the spiked words, somehow reflecting them back to the sender and rendering the recipient unharmed.

"Do you *hear* me, *dammit!*" Carl yelled.

"Yes, Carl, I hear fine."

"Then do your damn *job!* How about some justice in this shithole town? Wouldn't that be a first."

Bob waited, sensing that Carl was winding down. After a while more, his client flung himself back into the well-worn chair, resigned now that his fierce defense of the truth was getting him nowhere.

Seeing the man's intense anger ebbing, Bob seized his chance. "Carl, look, I believe you. I think you're telling the truth. I mean it."

Carl's eyes flicked to his lawyer. "Really? No bullshit?"

"No bullshit."

The prisoner sighed, proving his weakening resolve. Bob had seen the sequence many times before: the fierce determination to proclaim your innocence, the intense anger coming from the realization that the truth would not save him, the search for alternatives, and the resignation to the inevitable outcome. Sort of like the stages people go through accepting death. All it took was time and an understanding that there was no way the system would protect you. And Bob hated every time it happened. Hated it and hated himself so much that at times he thought he would do lose his mind, go screaming through town, yelling to everyone about the cruelty of the sham justice he was a part of, pointing out the culprits so they could be thrown into the street for angry mobs to tear apart. But he didn't lose his mind. And the mobs never came. Because this was Douglas County, where social order and public safety mattered much more than misfits receiving a fair trial.

He began again, knowing how it would all end. "Look, Carl, here are the facts as we have them. You were working at the plant that night. Had a run-in with the safety foreman—"

"Fucking Maxwell. What'd that shithead say?"

"In his statement, he says you weren't obeying plant safety standards, and when he confronted you, you yelled at him and threatened him."

"Told him to eat shit. You call that threatening?"

"He remembers it that way."

"Yeah, but..."

"After that, you went to the breakroom, and this other man, Michael Houston, comes along to tell you that the supervisor wants to see you. They've got a couple of witnesses said you hauled off and almost hit him."

"Trying to get the man's attention," Carl said, his finger working the groove at the table's edge. "That's all, damn it."

"Your plant superintendent says you were belligerent."

"What's that mean?"

"It means you wanted to fight."

"Not him, maybe, but those other management bastards, hell, yes. I'd like to kicked the shit outta all of 'em."

"Mr. Simpson says that he sent you home to cool off."

"Yeah, so what?"

"It establishes a pattern of behavior. And a state of mind."

"State of mind?"

"Carl, you've got an anger management problem and when you left the plant that night, you weren't exactly in a good mood."

The groove in the table consumed Carl's attention. The edge of his fingernail attacked the crack, sawing at it with enthusiasm. Franklin could see a red tinge flower at the side of the nail as metal cut into the flesh.

"Carl?"

Carl's eyes refused to recognize his lawyer. "Yeah?"

"Is all of this true?"

"So what if it is? 'Cause a man's having a bad night don't mean he killed his wife."

Bob extracted some additional papers. "Then we come to the part about the sheriff's statement. And the photos."

This time, Carl looked up as the busy finger stopped its punishment. "We've been over this before."

"I know. You insist that the photos were faked."

"They *are!*"

"But we can't prove it."

The silence between them stretched over seconds that seemed to turn into minutes.

After the long pause, Franklin said, "I know you don't want to hear it, but there's the matter of Clarice's situation at the Night Crawler."

"No, I don't want to hear it." Carl returned to the table groove, though by now the pace of cleaning had slowed to a distracted inching down the horizontal slot. "Me and the wife fought some, sure. From time to time. What couple don't? But run around behind my back? No way. Not Clarice."

"What makes you so sure?"

"I know so. That's all. A husband knows."

Bob Franklin watched his client. "The thing, is, Carl, well, we don't have many options here."

"Options?"

"Okay, we've got pleading guilty. Or we can go ahead and maintain your innocence. But there's a third option."

"What's that?" Carl asked.

"Plead temporary insanity."

Carl didn't reply.

"If you don't agree to that approach, then that leaves one of the other two."

Carl's finger stopped and moved to his mouth. Sucking on the bleeding end, he said, "What do you think?"

"The insanity defense is probably our best choice."

"But I wasn't crazy. And I didn't kill my wife on purpose. It was an accident."

Bob turned his head away. Outside the jail stood a thin tree, drifting sideways in the morning rain that lashed the barred window. He waited, facing the window. He hadn't mentioned Barry and the deal that B.J. had offered. If Carl didn't take the deal, then he'd have to square it somehow with B.J. and not end up screwing Barry.

"I'm sorry, Carl, but those facts don't matter right now. My recommendation is insanity."

"That something the D.A. put you up to?"

"No, it's not. The fact is, I was told by the sheriff not to. If you plead that way, it's gonna cost the county serious money for expert witnesses on both sides. They want either guilty or not guilty. Told me so, if you really want to know."

"They don't want me to? You sure about that?"

"Sure as shootin'."

Carl grinned for the first time. "Then I like it."

"It'll take some preparation. You got to get on that witness stand and convince twelve people that you killed you wife while you were insane. Temporarily. We can't bring in any of the other parts of the story, about Clarice being raped or disturbing the scene. And people around here will be a hard sell on insanity. This is your life we're talking about."

"Yeah, I know." Carl's finger returned to the desk edge for some further polishing. "But, to tell the truth, I don't got a chance in hell with the other two options, do I?"

Franklin nodded. "It would be...difficult...to convince a jury of your innocence."

"Let's go your way."

Franklin considered his next remark before speaking. "Another thing I've got to mention, something you need to know. I talked with B.J. He's threatening that if you don't plead guilty, they'll uncover some more evidence on your brother Barry and he'll go to prison."

Carl turned his head, suspicious of his attorney again. "When did he tell you this?"

"After you got arrested."

"And why are you only tellin' me now?"

"I need you to know. In case it affected your decision to plead insanity."

For a few moments, Carl didn't speak. Then he said, "Here's what I want you to do. Tell B.J. I'm pleading guilty—"

"But Carl, we've got—"

"You need to hear me out. Tell B.J. I'll give him what he wants. He'll release Barry, then you tell my brother to get the hell outta Douglas County. Tell him to stay gone a good two, three months. When we go in front of the judge and he asks how I'm pleading, we say insanity."

"You sure about this?" Franklin asked.

"Damn right," Carl said. "I can see their faces now."

"Yeah," Franklin said, a troubled look crossing his face, "Me, too."

FORTY-NINE

B.J. was early. I suspect he didn't want to get home, take off his sheriff costume, and then have to get all re-dressed up to come see me.

"Luther, get on over here."

I was in no hurry to get worked over, so I took my time in climbing down.

"Yes, sir," I said, stopping outside his reach.

He eyed me through the bars. "I oughta kick your ass."

"You want to, nothin's stopping you," I said.

"You're right about that." B.J. caught sight of Barry listening in. "Telford, you know what's good for you, you better..."

Barry did his trademark roll with the pillow over his head.

"I'll be talking to you tomorrow, Barry," B.J. said to Pillow Head. He looked back at me. "That stunt your lawyer pulled today? Giving me hell? I suspect you liked it a lot."

"No, sir."

"Shit, give me a break. I could see a smile come on your fucking face when he was going after me."

"No, sir. No smile. God's truth."

"You think I like being humiliated?"

I started to compliment B.J. on his use of a big word like "humiliated" but I seen ahead of time it was no use. He was working himself into a stew.

"All this...controversy wouldn't have happened if you'd done what I told you."

"Sir?"

"Getting rid of that damn attorney. Fact is, boy, you're going down no matter what he does."

"How you figure?" I asked.

"Let's say I have a person on the jury who's favorable to doing what's right." He smiled at the thought. "I can see the look on your dumb face when they say 'guilty as charged.'"

"No way you could know what the jury's going to decide," I said. "Mr. Garner, he says you can't never tell what a jury will do."

"Yeah? You think so?"

"Yes, I do."

B.J. pulled back from the bars. I expected he'd be unlocking the door next and letting me have it, but he stayed on his side. Tonight there was no Cooter to back him up. Must've been ten-dollar night at the whorehouse.

"You think on what I said. And Barry, don't act like you can't hear me. I'll be seeing you tomorrow, when Luther here is in the courtroom."

Barry half turned over and said, "About what? I ain't done nothin'."

"Hell you haven't. You been smuggling out your pretty boy's messages, that's what."

"I never—"

"Shut your lying mouth," B.J. said. "Don't you insult my intelligence, you piece of shit. Jake gave you up after he got caught with that message to Luther's wife. You two think you're smarter than me? Truth is you're both just a couple of dumb pricks."

My heart went cold, 'cause that meant sending stuff out was impossible.

"Luther, I'll deal with later. No sense damaging the merchandise tonight, so close to the end. Besides, Cooter'd miss his part of the fun. We got a little more time. But you," he said, pointing his baton at Barry, "Tomorrow, like I promised. And you, Holman, you ever tell anyone what happens inside this jail, your wife'll wish you hadn't."

After B.J. left, Barry spent the next twenty minutes cussing me and everything connected to me. Crazy to get involved, he said. He'd known better, but now it's The Explanation again, like he hadn't had it enough times already.

I said I was sorry, but Barry didn't pay no attention and brought up the trailer remark from last night and what a fucker I was and proceeded to bitch and piss and moan for another hour. After a time, he wore himself out and went to sleep, still mumbling. Jailbirds got nothing but time to waste and sleep's the one thing they're good at.

I spent a few hours turning over B.J.'s remarks about the verdict being already in, and him knowing for sure which way the jury would fall. B.J. could drop by their house, ask to speak in private, mention a few old debts, maybe something got covered up before, and sure enough when the weak ones was having trouble making up their minds, along comes the sheriff to remind them of their civic responsibility to get rid of the criminal elements in their midst. One thing this town's not known for is independent thinking.

I could see it working out how the sheriff wanted, slick as snot, me dying for killing Mark Reinhardt, and no way in hell to ever prove what really happened.

FIFTY

Bob Franklin watched Carl Telford's trial proceed like an assembly line in reverse. Instead of putting Carl together, the legal proceedings were taking the man apart, piece-by-piece. It hadn't mattered that Franklin had managed to find a psychologist to testify that Carl was clinically insane when Clarice was killed. The so-called expert fell apart under the close questioning of Cunningham and left the jury wondering how the man ever got a license. Cunningham's expert, on the other hand, was the model of polished composure and clinical certainty. No, of course not, Carl Telford was not insane, just very angry, and Franklin saw half of the jury nodding with the remark.

The rest of the defense wasn't holding up, either. Cunningham delivered a damaging blow by painting Blackburn as a single man accepting the invitation of a horny housewife, accidentally becoming the victim of an enraged husband. The sole chance of success for their strategy now hinged on a convincing presentation of Carl's passionate reason for killing his wife, a reason that the same man continued in private to protest had never existed.

After two days of testimony, it was now Carl's turn on the stand. Despite the preparation and encouragement of his attorney, Carl seemed shaky at best when he took his oath to tell the truth.

"Mr. Telford, can you tell the jury what happened the night that your wife died?" Franklin said.

Carl nodded, but failed to start the story. Off to the side, Franklin heard B.J.'s faint snicker.

Harder hammered his gavel, giving the sheriff a sharp look, and then turned to Carl. "Mr. Telford, your attorney asked you a question."

Carl nodded, and started in. The part about the run-in he had with his co-workers went well enough. However, he floundered when telling the story of him arriving at home and finding Clarice with Scott Blackburn.

"When I come in the room, I saw 'em both. Together, having sex," Carl said.

Franklin nodded. "Were they naked?"

"Clarice had on her bra, but Blackburn as naked."

"And where were they, Carl?"

"On the bed. He was on top of her."

"And they were having sex?"

"Near as I could tell."

"Go on."

"Clarice looked around the side of Blackburn and saw me and yelled out my name. Blackburn turned part-way around and just stared at me. Looked like he'd seen that expression on another man's face before."

Cunningham objected and Harder instructed the jury to disregard the remark as there was no proof Mr. Blackburn had ever been in this situation before and Mr. Telford was not in a position to offer expert opinion of Mr. Blackburn's state of mind. Several members of the jury rolled their eyes.

"Did Mr. Blackburn say anything to you?"

Carl nodded.

Allowing himself a smile, Franklin nodded back. This was going according to plan. Maybe it would work. "Please continue, Carl."

"Well, I asked him what the hell did he think he was doing and Blackburn didn't say nothin'. Clarice was raising up on her elbows by then and said it was all a mistake."

"And how did you feel about that statement?"

"I was crazy jealous, going out of my mind."

"How did you handle that change in your personality?"

"I went to the night stand and got out our gun."

"And what type of pistol was it?"

"A 0.44 magnum."

"Then what happened?"

"I told Blackburn to get the hell up and he yelled back at me. Used some bad cusswords."

"What exactly did he say?"

"He told me to, to…"

"Go ahead, say it out loud."

"He told me to fuck myself and that I was a sorry piece of shit."

This revelation stirred the crowd, which required a further admonishment by Harder, but Franklin could tell that, despite the lie, the jury was buying most of it. Scott Blackburn's bad behavior was not unknown, or at least had been suspected by many of the good citizens of the county.

"I see. Then what?"

"Like I said, I was crazy jealous by then. I told him to get off her and he told me again to fuck myself and then turned back around. Like what I said didn't mean nothing and he was intent on goin' about his business. I raised the pistol and told him again and instead he kept on cussing me, so I shot him."

"In the back?"

"Yes."

"One shot or several?"

"Just one."

Nodding, Franklin hoped that the jury would see the point and not think Carl had unloaded his entire collection of ammunition into the dead man. Of course, this had been covered earlier by the pathologist, but it didn't hurt to remind the twelve. Still, it might backfire and indicate that Carl wasn't *that* crazy if one bullet was enough to satisfy him.

"That seems cowardly, Carl. Shooting a man in the back."

"He was looking around before, right at me, like I said. Not like he didn't see me. Not like I snuck up on him."

"Did the shot kill Mr. Blackburn immediately?"

"He fell off my wife and died right there."

"I see. And what about Clarice?"

"She jumped up and started screaming at me 'bout what I'd done."

"She was very excited, then?"

"Well, hell, I'd killed the man was having sex with her."

"What did she say next?"

Carl's breath rattled out of his chest. "I don't remember exactly, but something like what the hell did I think I was doing. Stuff like that. She kept screaming her head off. Didn't act like anything I said made any difference."

"And how did you respond?"

Carl turned his head down toward the floor, unwilling at first to continue with the fabricated story.

"Carl?"

"Yeah?"

"What did you say to Clarice?"

"Something I'll always regret."

"What was it?"

Carl, in a low voice, said, "Shut the fuck up or I'll shoot you in the face."

The jury stirred. Men frowned and women raised their hands to their mouth. They'd all heard this kind of talk before, of course, but some of them only in the movies, and the very idea of someone admitting to talking to his wife that way, and in public no less.

Franklin expected the reaction and moved to mitigate the damage. "Is that how you usually talk to your wife, Carl?"

"'Course not. I never cussed her direct before. Never, not once. People around here might think we weren't the best sort, but we had our own rules. Lines we never crossed. I never hit her, neither. Like I said, I must've been crazy to be actin' that way, outta my mind. I...I didn't know what I was doing." He held his head, rotating it inside of a cupped hand.

"Carl, I know this is difficult, but please finish your story."

Carl raised his head and swallowed, the picture of remorse. He might not be telling the truth, but it was clear to everyone present how anguished the man was over what had happened. "I told her again to shut up and she didn't and I don't know why, but I pulled the trigger and killed my poor wife."

At that point he started sobbing, and not a few of the audience members looked away in a diluted effort to avoid adding to the man's public humiliation.

"Carl? Mr. Telford?" Franklin asked after an appropriate length of silence.

"Yes," he said, raising his head and displaying the thin line of wetness glistening on both of his gaunt cheeks.

"Do you believe, really believe, that you were insane at the time you shot Mr. Blackburn and Clarice Telford?"

"The thing I believe is that I'll burn in hell forever for killing such a precious thing as my Clarice." He stopped, considering the original question. "I'd have to be out-of-my-mind crazy to kill her. I know that for sure."

Franklin nodded. "No further questions, Your Honor." This had gone better than he had hoped. For once, he felt he had a chance to get one of his clients off. His analysis of the situation had been vindicated. The insanity plea was going to work.

But then the district attorney arose and said, "Your Honor, I have a few questions for Mr. Telford."

Fifty-One

"The defense calls as its first witness Richard Reinhardt."

The audience mumbling turned into a swell as they realized that Mark Reinhardt's father was being called to testify by the wrong lawyer.

"Your Honor," Cunningham said, "This is most irregular." I noticed, though, he didn't say it couldn't happen.

Calling Mark's daddy was part of Mr. Garner's strategy. He said what we needed was to prove that Mark Reinhardt had plenty of bad side and that anybody could have killed the man, not just me.

"If it please the Court," Mr. Garner said. "The defense wishes to examine the character and reputation of the victim. Who better to set the record straight than Mark Reinhardt's own father?"

Harder knew Mr. Garner was up to no good. After some cautioning stuff he told my attorney to get on with it but the judge was ready to jerk him back.

Reinhardt slunk down the center aisle and give me the same look the sheriff did and if looks was poison there wouldn't be no reason to go on with the trial 'cause I'd been dead inside of fifteen seconds.

Once Reinhardt got sworn in and seated, Mr. Garner says, "Mr. Reinhardt, did you talk to your son the night of December sixteenth of last year?"

"Yes, I did."

"And what did your conversation consist of?"

"I got a call from my son, about 9:40. He was concerned about a strange vehicle parked in the alley and I suggested he call the police."

"Did he say he would?"

Reinhardt's head sagged down. "If only he had."

Reading from some notes, Mr. Garner said, "Mr. Reinhardt, you testified in your deposition that your son told you that he looked out of his back window and saw a dark-colored vehicle parked in the alley behind his house. Is that correct?"

"Yes."

"How high is the fence in the back of your son's house?"

Reinhardt looked startled. "How in the world would I know that?"

Mr. Garner picked up a photograph from our table and held it up for Reinhardt to see.

"Is this the back of your son's property, showing his fence?"

Reinhardt nodded. "Yes, it is."

"And how high would you say this fence is?"

Cunningham objected, saying the witness had no reason to be guessing about the height of some fence that wasn't even on his property and Mr. Garner said okay but they had measured the fence and it was eight feet high and after a bit everyone agreed that it was that high, seeing as how the photograph showed the investigator holding up a tape measure and the picture ended up being the next exhibit.

"Mr. Reinhardt, do you know how tall a pickup truck is?"

"No, I don't," Reinhardt said.

"Would it surprise you to know that most standard trucks, especially the one the defendant drives, are only a little over six feet off the ground?"

The district attorney starting griping again and there was another tussle, Mr. Garner saying he'd be happy if they all adjourned to my house and measured my truck, since that's the one was suspected of being in the alley, or he could produce official dimensioned drawings showing how tall the truck was, but after talk simmered down, Mr. Garner had won out and got back to working on the old man.

"My question is, Mr. Reinhardt, if your son's fence was eight feet high and most pickup trucks are only six feet or so tall, then how do you expect your son could see a vehicle parked in the alley, behind an eight foot tall fence, while inside his house, looking out a rear window?"

"I have no idea. Maybe his house is high enough off the ground. All I know is what he said on the phone."

"Do you think maybe he went out the back and looked down the alley?"

Cunningham started in with, "Objection, Your Honor—"

"Sustained," Harder said before the district attorney could finish. "Mr. Garner, I warned you before—"

"Withdrawn." Mr. Garner went back to his notes. "Shirley Johnson testified that after she heard what she took for a gunshot, she looked out the window within a few seconds and saw no vehicle parked in the alley. How do you account for that?"

Before Reinhardt could offer an explanation, Cunningham objected about conclusions from the witness and before you know it Mr. Garner and Cunningham were in front of the judge and Mr. Garner was getting taken to the woodshed. You couldn't hear what was said, but you could see the look on Harder's face, and it wasn't one he kept back for his favorite grandkids. No way Harder was going to let my attorney work over a prominent citizen like that.

Mr. Garner paused on the way back to the witness stand and looked over to the jury, trying to catch their eye and let them know he'd been shut off by the judge without cause.

"Mr. Reinhardt, did your son ever get into any trouble with the law?"

"None that I know of. He was raised to be a good citizen."

Mr. Garner thought about that for a bit 'fore he replied, "Any arrests or convictions?"

"I don't know of any," the old man said, determined to protect his family's dignity, assuming you believed there was any of it left.

"Mr. Reinhardt, would it surprise you to know that your son has a record with the state authorities?"

Reinhardt glared at Mr. Garner. "I don't believe it."

"Your Honor, I would like to introduce Mark Reinhardt's State of Texas arrest record, if it pleases the court."

There was another huddle at Harder's roost after that but they let it in 'cause it had to do with the victim's prior criminal history, meaning that maybe I wasn't the only person coulda had a grudge against the man. Next, Reinhardt had to sit there and read off some of the charges against his son, concerning speeding, driving under the influence, some controlled substance deal, soliciting a prostitute, and several others. Funny, but all the charges was outside the county. Most had been dismissed, but a few stuck.

"So, Mr. Reinhardt, based on your son's arrest record, which you said you have no previous knowledge of, do you have any reservations about your earlier statements regarding your son's behavior?"

"Absolutely not. My son might've done a few things a little out of line, maybe one or two of them foolish, but all men do. You can't hold that against 'em."

"Oh?" Mr. Garner said, "We can't?"

Before Reinhardt could answer, Mr. Garner said he'd had enough of the old man and let Cunningham have a go at him.

Leaning on the witness stand rail, Cunningham looked like his favorite puppy had ended up under the wheels of a semi. "Mr. Reinhardt, we were all sorry, so sorry, to hear about the terrible murder of your son. It was a shock to the entire community."

"Objection. The district attorney is making a speech and forgetting to ask a question," Mr. Garner said.

Cunningham gave a slow nod. "I apologize, Your Honor, for expressing my personal feelings. Now, Mr. Reinhardt, how did you hear about this heinous crime?"

"The sheriff's office called late that night and said that there had been something serious happened at Mark's house..." Richard Reinhardt stopped talking, remembering that night, how it happened. I've seen that same look on Suzie's face once, and I almost felt sorry for him, but then those few seconds was over with.

"Mr. Reinhardt?" Cunningham said, waiting the right amount of time before asking again.

The old man snapped out of his reverie and took up talking. "I arrived at his house about 11:00 that night. The sheriff had roped off the front driveway with that yellow tape they use and naturally I was extremely concerned."

Cunningham had wandered off a little from Reinhardt, but now took up a position beside him, close enough to act like he was real attentive but not block the view from the jury box. Cunningham nodded while Mr. Reinhardt paused for a breath, it being pretty blamed obvious that it was painful for the old man to recollect that night's activities.

"I went on in and Sheriff Sanders was there, along with Cooter—"

"That would be Deputy Jeremiah Sanders?"

"Yes. Anyway, that's when they told me my boy was dead." Mr. Reinhardt stopped talking and dropped his head again. "I lost him nine days before Christmas." Then the old man started crying a little and you could see the jury was feeling real sorry for him right off. Being a parent that's lost a child myself, I could almost sympathize, except when I consider all the man's son done during his sorry-ass life, I wonder how he ever lived as long as he did.

"I'm sorry, Mr. Reinhardt, the jury needs to hear your story. Do you think you can go on?"

Reinhardt nodded yes, then said, "They said Mark had been shot once in the middle of the forehead. And that he was dead."

"Did your son have any enemies you know of?"

"No, *sir!*"

"Can you think of anyone that might want to kill him?"

"Only one. That's him sitting over there," and he pointed right at me, and the jury, except for Mrs. Murphy who was about out again, swiveled their heads toward me and gave me a hard look.

"Let the record show the witness is indicating Luther Holman," Cunningham said, and then added, "Why would you think that, Mr. Reinhardt?"

"He thought my son did something that's impossible. And the bastard killed him for it anyway."

Mr. Garner jumped up and objected, which was sustained and the jury was told to disregard that last remark, meaning that Mr. Reinhardt shouldn't have said what he did out loud in court, but he'd already done it and now they was all supposed to pretend they hadn't heard it but you can't take back words already floated out there in the air where anyone that's got ears knows what they were. Cunningham sat down and Reinhardt was dismissed. I couldn't see that this part had done me much good at all.

Once Reinhardt was gone, Mr. Garner said, "Defense calls Muriel Kirkland."

Fifty-Two

"Mr. Telford, are you sorry you killed your wife?"

Carl nodded at Cunningham, confused at first about the question. "I done said I was. Didn't you hear me?"

The remark was meant as a question, but the tone came across as defiant and Cunningham moved to seize the opportunity. "Yes, I heard you say a great many things, Mr. Telford. A great many things."

"So what's your question?" Carl asked.

"You said you were sorry about killing your wife. What about Mr. Blackburn?"

The question surprised Carl. "Well, I..."

"You're not sure, then? Whether it was okay to kill Mr. Blackburn?"

"No, that's not it. It's...well, it seems to me..."

Franklin was objecting, but the judge let the prosecutor press on.

"Answer the question, Mr. Telford," Harder ordered.

"No, it's not right to kill people."

"Yet you killed two human beings in the span of a few seconds."

"Like I said, I was out of my head."

"That mean you can kill anyone you want, as long as you claim you were insane?"

Harder gaveled Franklin's objection and instructed the witness again to answer.

Carl waited a few seconds. "Look, that hadn't never happened to me before. I couldn't handle it all at once. That's why I did what I did. Not like I'd go around town shooting people."

"Okay, Carl, let's say you're telling the truth, that you were overwhelmed, overwhelmed enough to do things you would never do otherwise. Would that be a fair statement of what you are claiming?" Cunningham appeared lost in deep thought as if he was considering the matter for the first time.

"Yeah, that's right." Carl nodded, seeing an easy escape from the difficult question.

"You walked into your bedroom and saw a man making love to your wife?"

"Yes."

"Could you tell who he was?"

"Not at first. Not until he turned around."

"So he was facing the other direction?"

"Like I said, he was on top of Clarice."

Cunningham turned away from Carl to reenact the position of Scott Blackburn. "Pardon me for saying this, but if I was Mr. Blackburn, making love to your wife, would this be the view you would have had of my back."

"That's about right."

Franklin saw it coming, but he couldn't think of an objection.

"How was your wife positioned, Mr. Telford?"

"Well, Blackburn was between her legs. You know, facing her."

Cunningham addressed the twelve persons on his left. "Ladies and gentlemen of the jury, please forgive me for this indelicate line of questioning. I am only seeking to—"

"Objection!" Franklin yelled, hoping the stop the demonstration. "The district attorney is—"

Harder nodded. "Sustained. The district attorney will confine his remarks to the bench and his questions to the witness."

"Yes, Your Honor. I apologize. Very sorry." Cunningham repositioned himself. "If I was Mr. Blackburn, Carl, was I about this same distance away from you when you walked into the room?"

"About."

212

"What was the first thing you said when you entered the room?"

Carl paused, then said, "I said get the hell off my wife."

Cunningham nodded while pursing his lips. "Yes. Then what did Mr. Blackburn say?"

Rising again, Franklin said, "Your Honor, the conversation between Mr. Telford and Mr. Blackburn has already been related to us."

"If it please the Court, I only want to make sure in my mind exactly what happened. I don't think the jury would mind one more run-through."

Several of the jurors nodded their approval. Harder scowled, then said, "Overruled. But let's get on with it."

"Yes, Your Honor. Carl, please tell us what Mr. Blackburn said."

Carl reflected on the question, trying to remember for certain what he had made up the last time he went through the proposed questioning with Franklin. "He said, 'Who the hell are you?' Yeah, that's right. That's what he said."

"Then might he have assumed you were someone who just happened by?"

"No, no way he could have thought that. He knew who I was."

"He did?"

"Sure he did."

"Are you certain?"

"Hell, yes, I am."

Harder interrupted. "That'll be enough of the profanity in my courtroom, Mr. Telford. Confine your remarks to the questions asked, and if there weren't any curse words spoken then, I don't want to hear them now."

"Okay. All right," Carl said and leaned back, rubbing the tops of his thighs with his sweaty hands.

Cunningham said, "I'd like the defendant's previous testimony about confronting Mr. Blackburn repeated, Your Honor."

Mrs. Elliott did her search and said, "'I told Blackburn to get the hell up and he yelled back at me. Used some bad cusswords.'"

"So which is it, Carl? Did you tell Mr. Blackburn that Clarice was your wife, or did you only cuss him out?"

Carl, confused now, said, "I...I'm sure I told him she was my wife."

"Certain this time?"

"Yes."

Cunningham said, "Isn't it possible that you're mistaken again, and that the man you killed might not even have known you were Clarice's husband, and yet you still blew a hole through him?"

"Well, I think I told him she was—"

"Since the autopsy on Clarice Telford failed to indicate the presence of semen in her vagina, do you wish to change your testimony about them having sex, Mr. Telford?"

"No...I mean, I don't know. Maybe he wasn't done yet."

Cunningham pressed forward. "If Mr. Blackburn turned in your direction, as you say, does that mean he turned at his waist, swiveled his torso?"

"His what?" Carl asked.

"The top of his body. Did he turn at the waist so he could face you?"

"Yeah."

"And then you shot him."

"No, not at that moment. Like I told Mr. Franklin earlier, I told him to get off of Clarice and he told me to go screw myself."

"And then you shot him?"

"Yes. After he said that, when he turned his back. What he said, it meant that he had no decency, none at all. He was only there for one reason. To have sex with my wife." Carl nodded at his own words. "I think a lotta married men would've had enough by then. Besides, he didn't seem scared of what I was saying one bit. Acted like all he wanted was to get back to what he was doing."

"Where did you shoot Mr. Blackburn?"

"In the middle of the back. Kinda to the left side."

"Left? The autopsy proved the bullet entered the right-hand side of Mr. Blackburn's back."

"Oh…yeah, I meant right."

"Here?" Cunningham asked, turning part way around and pointing to a spot on his back.

"Yeah, about there."

"So you're sure now where you shot him?"

Carl's face darkened. "I said I was."

"And the bullet penetrated completely through Mr. Blackburn's body and ended up embedded in the wall?"

"That's where the sheriff found it."

"Must've been a pretty big bullet, Mr. Telford."

"It was a hollow point."

"Oh?"

Carl nodded. "Mushrooms on impact."

"I see," Cunningham said. "And why did you have that kind of ammunition in your pistol?"

"Somebody comes by to rob my house, try and shoot me, I want stopping power, no fooling around."

"Then this bullet must've made a pretty big mess as it exited out Mr. Blackburn front."

"Yeah, I guess so."

"From the autopsy photos and the remains of Mr. Blackburn's liver on the wall of your bedroom, I'd say—"

"Objection," Franklin said. "Prosecution is trying to sway the jury by dwelling on the violence of the crime. Mr. Telford has admitted to the murder. It's not like he deliberately took time out to search for special ammunition."

Harder considered the matter for a few seconds. "Overruled. I'll allow it."

Cunningham continued, "Can we at least say that there was a significant spray of blood from Mr. Blackburn's fatal wound? Confirmed from the crime scene photos of the bedroom wall?"

"Sure."

"Then answer me one question, Mr. Telford."

"What's that?"

"If Mr. Blackburn was on top of your wife, and sitting up, and you shot him through the back, tell me how it is that forensics found that Clarice Telford had no blood on her body belonging to Scott Blackburn?"

FIFTY-THREE

Mr. Garner and Cunningham spent quite a time at Harder's bench arguing over what Mr. Garner later said Cunningham called the "appropriateness" of Muriel Kirkland and whether she had any "special knowledge" about Mark Reinhardt. Then Harder says okay he'll let her give testimony, but watch it and he'd jerk the deal if things didn't go right.

Mr. Garner was primed and I could see Muriel didn't have no idea what he was fishing for. From the looks of her knees, an army of ants was up her white pants and she was working at them real hard, her thighs banging something fierce to smash the little fellers into eternity. She also had a wad of tissue in her lap that she was torturing up pretty good. I could see the tissue wasn't the thin kind like we have to use at the school, since the administration's too cheap to buy anything that you could blow your nose on and not leave a hole in the middle. But Muriel had her a good brand that wouldn't come apart without some effort. Must've been two-ply.

"Miss Kirkland, may I call you Muriel?"

"Sure," Muriel says and readjusts herself to get a better angle on the ants.

"Are you nervous, Muriel?"

"Very. I never done this before," she said, and glanced over at the jury box like she had her head in the noose and them all ready to pull the lever, jiffy-quick.

"Nothing for you to worry about. All you have to do is tell the truth, Muriel. You do remember the oath you swore?" Mr. Garner was rubbing the handrail again.

"Yes. Yes, sir."

"Tell me, Muriel. Do you know the defendant, Luther Holman?"

"Sure. His wife Suzie works with me down at the diner."

"And what's your opinion of him?"

"Objection," Cunningham says. "There is no purpose to this line of questioning. The State asks that this witness be excused."

"Mr. Garner?" Harder said, ready to send Muriel packing.

"If you'll give me some latitude, Your Honor, this 'line of questioning' will become clear in a moment."

Harder thought it over and decided a couple more questions might be okay. "Stick to the subject, Mr. Garner."

"Yes, sir. Now, Muriel, what was your opinion of Mr. Holman?"

"I always figured him for a decent man. He's good to his wife, that's for sure."

"Were you surprised when he was charged with Mark Reinhardt's murder?"

Cunningham had enough by that time and was buttoning up his coat while he was standing. I figure he's real practiced up since he does the button thing ever time he gets up. "Your Honor—"

Harder glared down at Mr. Garner. "Counselor, I warned you about this."

"If it please the court, if you will allow me one more question?"

"One more," Harder said.

"Muriel, did Mark Reinhardt ever mention his connection with drug dealers while you two were having sex?"

People started looking around like a blaze had come up in the courtroom and they had all forgot to check out where the exits were. Cunningham and Harder was stunned for a couple of seconds. Muriel's knees weren't moving any more.

Mr. Garner pretended to be confused and cupped his ear. "I'm sorry. I didn't get your answer."

You could hear the clock ticking off the seconds while it was dead silent. "Muriel?" he said.

'Fore she could answer, Harder called the two lawyers over and they had another pow-wow. Harder's face was colored up a bit and I noticed over my shoulder that Mark's daddy's face was flushed out like an air hose had been stuck up his butt and his insides was up to about two hundred pounds.

After a bit, Harder said, "Miss Kirkland, please answer the question."

"Yes," she said in a tiny voice.

Mr. Garner said to the judge, "Your Honor, in light of this answer may I continue with this line of questioning?"

Harder nodded.

"How long were you intimate with Mark Reinhardt, Muriel?"

She looked down at her lap a while before answering. "A few times."

"Two, three, four?" Mr. Garner asked.

"Maybe a dozen."

You could tell from the rumble that the audience was a bit surprised that the fancy son of the mayor would lower himself to poke a second-class citizen of Muriel's caliber, but you never know what kind of bun a busy wiener might be slipping into.

"A dozen? So you knew Mr. Reinhardt well?"

"I wouldn't say that. He was a hard man to get to know."

"Did he discuss any of his relationships with criminal elements with you?"

"Once. We'd been over to Beaumont and were kinda drunk and ended up spending the night. He said he had 'connections.' Could get me anything I needed to feel good. The good stuff, as much and as hard as I wanted."

"Your Honor," Cunningham piped up. "Surely the court doesn't put any credence in the off-hand statements of a person who was admittedly under the influence of alcohol. I see no reason to continue besmirching the reputation of a dead man who can't defend himself."

"Mr. Garner?" Harder said.

"Muriel, do you think he was serious or only making a casual offer?"

"Oh, he meant it. Gave me the names of a couple dealers. Said tell them he sent me and I'd get top quality stuff."

"Did you?"

"What?"

"Go see these people?"

"Of course not. I don't do drugs. But he acted like others he ran with wanted—"

"Objection," Cunningham said. "Call for speculation on the part of the witness."

"Sustained," Harder said, looking like he was tired of the whole thing.

Mr. Garner said, "Did you continue to see Mark Reinhardt after that?"

"The next time was he came in the diner, he whispered to me he wanted us to go out again and I told him no."

"When was that?" Mr. Garner asked.

"A few days after we'd been to Beaumont. He came in the diner late, after the regular crowd. We were getting ready to close up and there were only a couple of customers still there. Me and Suzie were waitressing. I went over to his booth and told him I didn't want to run with him no more."

"Why not?"

"Well, it was a personal thing."

"Oh?" Mr. Garner asked.

"He was, uh, a little too rough," Muriel said, ducking her head.

"I see. And what did Mr. Reinhardt say when you told him you didn't want to see him any more?"

"He was upset. Grabbed my arm and called me some names."

"Did he leave after that?"

"He hung around instead, waiting for his food. Suzie was serving him that night instead of me 'cause it was her side of the restaurant. She was taking him his silverware and accidentally dropped a knife on the side of his hand. It cut him a little, but she had a handkerchief in her pocket and tended to it real quick. It didn't bleed much at all. A scratch, really."

"And?" Mr. Garner prompted.

"Well, he said some things I can't repeat," Muriel said.

"Why not?"

"Because of the language he used."

"Oh? And what was that language?"

Muriel looked at Harder to see if she had to answer and Cunningham got to objecting and Mr. Garner said he believed that the words spoken were material to this case and Harder agreed to let her answer.

"What language did he use, Muriel?"

"He said, he said…" Muriel was busy knotting up the tissue with her hands. "He said she was a fucking bitch and no wonder her damn daughter was dead as clumsy and stupid as she was." Muriel paused a few seconds. Nobody in the courtroom made a sound. "I never heard anyone be so mean in all my life. After that, I came over and told him he needed to leave and I couldn't believe a man would talk that way to a woman who'd lost her child. Then he got up and left. That was the last time I ever had anything to do with Mark Reinhardt."

It's a good thing Suzie never told me that story or I'd have killed the bastard then, but the jury didn't know I never heard it, and you could see it dawning on a few of them that this gave me one more reason to murder the mayor's kid. It didn't look to me like this helped me out one bit, unless you figure the man needed killing to start with.

FIFTY-FOUR

"You think this was some kinda record?" Carl asked.

"What do you mean?" Franklin said.

"Forty minutes to get convicted on two counts of murder. I mean, shit, you'd hope they'd at least spent the night talking about it."

"I had this one case," Franklin said, "where they were out only ten."

"Guilty or not?" Carl asked.

"Guilty."

"We never had a chance, did we?"

Carl Telford and Bob Franklin sat in a small room in the back of the jail. It was a hot afternoon, the day after the jury trial.

"I thought we did. For a while. I should have been better prepared for that question about the blood. Caught me by surprise." Franklin paused, his trademark distant glaze overcoming his face. "Should have expected it. I'm sorry."

"Hell, after hearing Cunningham's closing argument *I* would've voted to convict me. Looking back, I figure I was done for from the start. Just a matter of time. No way that jury was going to let me walk, no matter what my defense was. But forty minutes? Shit."

"You never know with juries."

"I bet they took the vote in the first five minutes, tops, then sat around and shot the shit for the next thirty-five to keep it from looking bad. You see the way they looked at me after the verdict was read and when you had them polled, one by one? Like I was a damn rabid dog needing to be put down."

"Remember, Carl, we get an automatic review at the Court of Appeals. Then there's the Texas Supreme Court, and—"

"What I remember most is Denise, on that stand, tellin' about what she and Clarice was doing that night, before I got home. Having a few laughs, a few drinks. Said she'd never known Clarice to go after another man. Never. You know, that's the only part of this bunch of shit I think was right, goddamn right. Clarice wouldn't screw that fuck Blackburn. I *know* she wouldn't. He was trying to rape her, goddammit, like I told Sanders and that piece of shit Cooter. I still can't figure out why she was acting so crazy. Like a fucking zombie or something." Carl gazed through the glass window at the deputy outside. "How much time we got left?"

"Five minutes or so."

"Funny how your life disappears." Carl snapped his fingers. "You're alive one day and dead the next. Because you came home a few minutes late. I'd a been there when they pulled up, none of this would of happened. Still, if there's any good come of this, it's that Blackburn's dead and not out raping some other woman."

"Carl, we *will* appeal. There's lots of time…"

"To do what?"

"Have a higher court reconsider your case, that's what. Maybe pursue that idea that the evidence was faked."

"And how about me saying all that lyin' shit on the witness stand? That it was made up by me and my lawyer? That we decided no way I could get off tellin' the truth? How about that, Mr. Public Defender?"

"Carl, I know it will be difficult, but like I said, but I'll see if we can find a procedural error we can appeal on and—"

"No appeal, counselor."

"What?"

"I said, *no appeal*. I deserve to die for killing my wife. What's the shortest time on Death Row? What's the record?"

"Nine months. Give or take."

Carl shook his head. "Sounds good to me, get it over and done with."

"But her death was an accident!"

"Doesn't matter. I killed her. It's my fault she's dead. Simple as that."

"Carl," Franklin pleaded, "give this some time. You'll see it's better if we—"

"Mind's made up. Sorry you don't get to charge the county for a shit load more legal paperwork."

"Don't start with me, Carl. I tried my best."

"Your best, huh? Everybody in town knows the sheriff owns you. What kinda defense would I *expect* to get? How many times you won against Cunningham? How many times?"

Franklin sighed. "I don't have the statistics at hand."

"Maybe you should look them up, lawyer-man. I bet it's not one outta *ten*. Maybe one outta a *hundred*. Unless you're defending somebody that's a butt buddy of the sheriff. In that kinda case, my guess is that your record's pretty good."

Franklin flushed at the accusation. "Now hold on—"

"Tellin' me you were on my side and you'd like to see their faces when I pleaded being crazy. Shit. I bet you told them all about it. You like being their lap dog? Huh, Bob? You and Cunningham and Sanders work out that insanity defense bullshit all by yourselves, or did the judge help, too?"

Franklin attempted to control his anger. "That's not true. Carl, can't you see? Now that we've lost the case, all you—"

"Always been that a man without means can't get a fair trial in this county. And that you're a big part of that problem."

"That's a damn lie."

Carl stared at his lawyer. "It's goddamned true, and right now, I can't stand the smell of you. I'm ready to go. Where's the deputy?"

Fifty-Five

"How you think the day went, Mr. Garner?"

"I'd say about perfect."

The attorney reared back in his chair, lifting the front legs off the floor, a real satisfied look on his face. It was the first time I seen Mr. Garner sorta happy since this thing first started. We was stuck again in that small office, the day all over now, us having ourselves an end-of-day recap. I got to see Suzie for a few minutes after the trial adjourned and she had perked up, too. Mr. Garner nodded to her and said everything was first rate, then he give her one of his funny looks.

"Sounds like a pretty powerful statement," I said.

"Let's recount what happened." Mr. Garner started up, knocking the events off with his fingers like they was balsa wood sticks and he was breaking each one with a snap. "We started off with Mark Reinhardt's father. He did everything he could to convince the jury his son was an innocent lamb led to the slaughter, but you saw how well that went over."

"Can't imagine anyone in town believing Mark Reinhardt was a poor innocent soul to start with."

"Then Cooter admitted he couldn't find any photos or impressions from the alley, so they can't prove your pickup was there. Next, we had Muriel, who testified about her affair with Reinhardt and that he was mixed up with the criminal element. She even managed to get that part in about Suzie accidentally cutting him with a knife and how he reacted. I can imagine how you felt when Suzie told you about what he said to her."

"She didn't," I said.

"Didn't what?"

"Tell me what he said. Only about nicking his hand. If'n I'd heard what he said to her…" My hands was grabbing at each other like they were Mark Reinhardt's neck.

"Well," Mr. Garner said, giving himself time to clear his throat and not let on about the look on my face, "then the trooper was next. He shot plenty of holes in the innocent victim theory with those state arrests. Especially that one for narcotics possession." Mr. Garner shook his head. "His testimony about the state thinking of taking over the prior investigation since the sheriff had failed to produce any results was very damaging. Still, if Mark Reinhardt was as big a drug dealer as I think he was, I can't imagine why the autopsy didn't show any evidence of him taking drugs himself."

"One thing you got to know," I said. "Richard Reinhardt paid for Dr. Matthews' medical school."

Mr. Garner's eyebrows shot up. "You're kidding?"

"Nope. The Matthews was family friends of the Reinhardts, and when the doc wanted to go to med school, Richard Reinhardt offered to pay for it on two conditions."

"Which were?"

"That he stayed within a hundred miles of here after he got out. And whatever kind of doctor he became, all the Reinhardts would get treated, if they had that particular condition, for free."

A smile wandered over the attorney's mouth. "Looks like he fooled them. Not much a pathologist can do for people still breathing."

"That's where you're wrong," I said. "Plenty he can do come autopsy time."

Mr. Garner sat back in his chair and considered what I had said. "Maybe I should get an order to dig Reinhardt up. Have another forensics examination done."

"No problem. All you got to do is get Harder to sign the order."

Nodding his head, Mr. Garner said, "I hear you. Still, I don't think that issue is too significant. Besides, tomorrow we're throwing them a curve."

"What's that?"

"The manager of the Night Crawler. He's going to testify."

"Jack Roberts? No way."

"I've subpoenaed him. He'll have to testify under oath. If he starts lying, I'll tear his testimony to pieces. He doesn't show up, I'll get the state troopers after his ass."

I could see from the look on Mr. Garner's face that he'd been in this situation before and come out on top. I said, "This is a small town, Mr. Garner. Everybody knows everybody else's business. Least, most of it. Jack Roberts' got to live here with B.J. and Cooter after you done gone back to Austin."

"Are you saying he'll lie?"

"Like a thirteen-year-old boy been caught with his hand down his pants."

The grin came again. "Sounds like personal experience speaking."

"Maybe," I said, and laughed a little at the memory of it.

"Listen, Luther, we're getting into the final part of this case. I didn't want to seem too optimistic right now, but I'm telling you now that, absent a big surprise, I think we've got a good chance."

"How you figure?" I asked. I couldn't believe this was all about to get settled, and without me getting convicted in the bargain.

"Remember, we don't have to prove you didn't kill Reinhardt. All we have to do is establish reasonable doubt. And Mark Reinhardt's past gave a lot of others reason to kill him."

"You sure this is going to work?" Mr. Garner had said this before, how you bring up all sorts of ideas about how somebody besides the accused could have reason and ability to kill the victim. After a while, if the attorney's done his job right, the jury's not sure the man next to 'em didn't do it. "I know what you said at the first about doubt, listened to every word of it, but I'm here to tell you that *these* twelve people are gonna need lots of doubt, not a little bit. They couldn't show their faces in town otherwise."

Mr. Garner nodded. "The biggest problem we have is the murder weapon in your house. Still…" He had another thought right about then. "Tomorrow I think you'll be pleased with how things go. Besides, I've got a surprise for the judge."

"What?"

"The Texas attorney general will be here."

"Why for?"

"Our organization has done a lot of complaining to them about the fairness of the criminal trials in small counties where the accused has a public defender. They're also getting heat from that newspaper reporter from Dallas. So the state boys want to make a political appearance, assure the electorate they care about justice. I know you haven't seen the articles in the papers, but the people in the state capitol sure as hell have."

Tommy came in and said I had to go back now, and with that, Mr. Garner's pep talk was over. I swear I was walking on air back to my cell. I couldn't wait to share some good news with Barry, but he didn't seem too interested.

I got down and pulled on his sleeve and begged him to hear me out. When he turned over, I seen why he was reluctant. He had one eye closed, turning somewhere between black and purple, and a string of blood coming out the right side of his nose.

"Barry," I says, "What happened to you?"

"Payback for passing notes," he said. "Kind of like in school, except the principal here's got a bigger switch. Lucky Jake got rid of that other thing and only got caught with the note."

"I'll tell Mr. Garner tomorrow," I said. "He'll fix this."

Barry's open eye rolled. "You stupid shit, you don't ever get it, do you? There ain't no fixin' this like there ain't no chance you're not going to die for that Reinhardt murder. Besides, tonight you're on suicide watch."

"What's that mean?"

"Their words were, 'You're depressed. Suspected of trying to kill yourself.'"

228

"Why'd I want to do that? I had me a good day in court."

Barry sighed. "I could give a shit. The story is you're upset with how the trial's going, so they say, and are about to be 'overcome with remorse' for your dirty deed."

"Bullshit. Nobody'll believe that."

"B.J. and Cooter be comin' around tonight to make sure you don't hurt yourself. Take away your sheets and belt so you can't manage a do-it-yourself-er." Barry rolled back to face the wall. "Unless they take care of you themselves. All I gotta do is keep my mouth shut and I'm out thirty days early."

"How are they going to explain that shiner?" I asked.

"Don't you remember?" he mumbled. "You did it. I tried to calm you down and then you hit me. That's what gets 'em in the picture. Protecting me."

"I got to get word out to Mr. Garner," I said.

"Who's gonna carry it out for you? Superman or Batman?"

FIFTY-SIX

"You need to get this thing behind you, go on to more pleasant opportunities. Carl doesn't want an appeal and I do believe that's the first thing I've ever heard him say I agree with," B.J. said.

"Give me time. I'll convince him otherwise," Bob Franklin said.

"You know, Bob, I'm real disappointed in you."

"Oh, should I be ashamed?" came the sarcastic reply.

"We had a deal. No insanity plea, 'member? Guilty or not guilty were your options. You forget that part?"

"No, I didn't forget."

B.J. put his boots up on Franklin's desk, rocking the insteps into the edge of the finish on the old desk. "Then why the fuck did you let Carl pull that stunt about changing how he would plead?"

"I felt it was in the best interest of my client. He agreed. That's why."

"Best interest, my ass," B.J. said.

"Look, despite what you and the rest of the county might think of me, my job is to defend my client to the best of my ability. Sorry it didn't match your idea of kangaroo justice."

"Oooh, the lawyer suddenly gets a conscience?"

"Go to hell," Franklin said, and turned to face the window.

B.J. emitted what passed for a half-hearted sigh. "Me, I thought about burning that brother of Carl's like I said I would, after he finally snuck back into town. Then I thought, what the hell, Barry'll do it to himself. Only a matter of time and I'll have me another shot at him. Besides, I'm a fair-minded man, Bob. Let past mistakes stay in the past, time to move on." B.J.

shook his head. "You know, I hear there used to be some money waiting for you back at the office."

"What for?" Franklin asked.

"Taking care of that last scrape for Reinhardt."

"Yeah, well, I'll rush right down there and collect."

"No need. I confiscated it to help pay the county back for those expensive expert witnesses." Folding his arms, B.J. said, "Sorry to have to tell you that, Bob, 'cause I know you need the extra money."

"Thanks for your thoughtful consideration," Franklin said, still facing the window.

"Wouldn't want your whore going without a new coat, what with winter coming on and all."

Swiveling around, Franklin said, "What the *hell* are you—"

"Folks tell me that wife of yours puts a lot of store in showing off at the church suppers. They say that pe-can pie of Sharon's is a real wonder. Wouldn't want her suffering on your account, having to stop coming to the Wednesday night affairs 'cause she was too embarrassed. On account of all the faithful knowing her hubby's been dicking a stripper."

"You're lying, you bastard!"

"Oh, I got the pictures to prove it. Nice size prints, too, considering they were taken with that little bitty camera in the ceiling of your love nest. Took some work to get it all set up, too. Shame you keep on renting the same room every time." B.J. shook his head. "Real careless of you, Bob. But you always were predictable."

Franklin's eyes dropped to his desk.

B.J. leaned forward. "I'll remind you that your job is to work within the system. With the people that are trying to help you, counselor. That way, both you and the stripper can keep a-coming." B.J.'s mouth opened from its pucker as he laughed at his own joke.

Franklin remained quiet.

"Shame you didn't ever take her to a nicer place. I mean, that shitty old motel north of Houston? The Shangri-La? Come on, even *you* can do better than that. Hell, maybe I'll send Sharon a copy of the one with the bitch on top, for her scrapbook? Same position Sam Blackburn was in when he got shot by your client."

"Go to hell."

B.J. grasped the doorknob on his way out. "I'll take that for a no. You change your mind, let me know. Cooter said to tell you he was impressed, though. Didn't think you had that much stamina. Lasting an entire weekend, slopping around in that big ole loose pussy all day long." The sheriff paused, remembering a further duty. "Election's a while away, but it's none too soon to plan. I'm thinking lots of yards signs this time." B.J. swept his hand through the air. "My name at the top, then 'Integrity, Honesty, Experience'. Red letters on some kind of blue background, wavy like the flag. Yeah, that would be nice. Be stopping by soon, Bob, since I feel sure you'll be interested in making a substantial contribution to the re-election effort."

FIFTY-SEVEN

I heard the sound of B.J.'s and Cooter's boots on the concrete floor for what seemed like ten minutes 'fore their mugs appeared at the cell door.

"Hear we've had some kind of disturbance in the jail," B.J. said.

"Yeah, a violent confrontation," Cooter added.

"No trouble," I said from the top bunk. "No trouble at all."

Cooter looked at B.J. and shook his head. "Dumb bastard doesn't get it, does he?"

"'Fraid not. Come on down here, boy. We got ourselves some talking to do."

"I'm not goin' nowhere with you two," I said.

"Oh, you're going all right," B.J. said. "Either with two legs that work or two that's broken."

I saw it wasn't no use postponing my punishment, so I headed down the ladder. B.J. made me turn around in the cell and put my back against the bars so he could cuff me.

B.J. said, "Deputy Sanders, I believe this inmate has assaulted his cellmate."

"Yeah. You can tell from that one over there that they been at it. He's hurt pretty bad."

"Who you reckon could have done it?" B.J. said.

"Must've been our boy here, Mr. Luther Holman. I hear he's up for capital murder and must've got carried away."

"So he is. So he is. Come on, boy," B.J. said, opening the cell door.

"Reckon his cellmate's awake?" Cooter asked.

"I doubt it," B.J. said. "He's beat up pretty good. How about that, Barry? You awake?"

"No, sir," Barry said. "I'm so sore and tired out I'm fast asleep."

"Good thing, Telford."

They pushed me out in front, prodding me along with their nightsticks like a cow into the squeeze chute right before the bolt gets shot in its brain, and afterward slung on a hoist and carved up. We ended up same as before, me handcuffed to both the rails of that same damn chair bolted to the floor and the two of them hovering around me. I pulled on the rails hard as I could, trying when I was doing it to not let them see me, but the wood was solid as ever.

"Luther, you disappoint me," B.J. said.

"Why's that?" I said.

"This was all going to be simple. You threatened to take care of Mark Reinhardt, out of some completely crazy idea that he raped and murdered your daughter. When we wouldn't act on your little fantasy, you took the law in your own hands and shot the man. Bob Franklin, alas, fails to get you off. You go to Huntsville and wait on Death Row. A few years later, your appeals exhausted, you die while Richard Reinhardt, me, Cooter, and your poor little wife get to watch. Simple as that."

"Sorry I messed up your plan," I said. "But I told you I didn't kill—"

B.J. stuck his head in my face. "I told you last time it don't matter if you did it or not. You been sniffing floor cleaner so long you can't hear me, boy?"

"I can hear fine," I said.

"No, I don't think so. We told you several times to dump that fancy lawyer. And we told you what was going to happen to that old mother of yours if you didn't. Lucky for you she died on her own."

"You wouldn't have run over her in the street like you said. That's murder. You'd get caught."

Cooter let out a laugh. "You moron, we're the law here. Lots more than you have learned *that* simple lesson."

"Oh?" I said. "Like who?"

"Your roomie for one. Other people in town know we mean business when we make a request. You can't seem to get that through your thick head."

"You're right," B.J. said. "His head's so thick he can't hear too well. We might oughta open him up a little. Let in some air."

"This is the part I like the best," Cooter said, and pulled an ice pick out of his back pocket.

"What are you doin'?" I said, but I had already figured out what was coming up.

"Gonna help you hear better, boy. You should thank us."

Cooter walked around the back of me. I twisted my head to stop him from trying to stick me, but he stood off and laughed. Then he reached around and quick-like snatched a cigarette out of the pack in my pocket.

"Worried, Luther?" he asked as he lit the match and watched the sweat wet my forehead.

"Sure am," I said.

"Most people smoke after taking care of business. I prefer before. Steadies my nerves. And believe you me, you're gonna appreciate a steady hand."

Cooter smoked along for a minute or two and didn't say a word. B.J. watched him like he was a circus clown and you didn't know what kinda crazy thing he was going to do next to entertain the audience, making it all up as he went.

"Not bad," Cooter said, dropping the filter to the floor and crushing it with his boot. "I prefer Marlboros, but I'm much obliged at you letting me have one of yours."

"You're welcome," I said. "Can I get back to my cell now?"

"Not yet," Cooter said, nodding to B.J., who took me in a headlock from behind and wrenched my left ear up to the light.

Cooter took his time easing over, tossing the ice pick end-over-end and catching the shaft in his palm. "You remind me of that brother of Barry's. Now what was his name..."

"Hurry this up, dammit," B.J. said. "I can't hold him forever."

"What about Carl?" I asked, pulling like hell to get my head away. The wood cracked a bit, but the brackets holding the legs to the floor was strong as ever.

"He was a lot like you. Stubborn. Proud. Unable to accept things the way they had to be. But he got over it, didn't he B.J.?"

"Yeah."

Bending over, Cooter touched the tip of the pick to my earlobe. I felt the point go into my skin. "'Member when you were a kid and had an earache? Maybe had to go to the doctor and have that eardrum lanced? Can you feel the pain of it? Even now?"

I had a bad ear as a kid 'cause of going swimming in dirty ponds. Doc Mayfield punctured my eardrum one afternoon after I had been lying in bed for a couple of days, the throbbing of it by then so loud I was sure you coulda heard it across the street. Right after that needle went through my eardrum and the pus squirted out, I figure the whole waiting room could hear me screaming.

"You gotta be still," Cooter said. "This is delicate work. A miss and I might tear something down there. Then you'd be deaf on this side. Permanent."

The steel point slid by the lobe and entered the ear hole, working further down inside, stopping at times to press against the sides of the little tube.

"Feel that?" Cooter asked. "Nothing like it. Like somebody's pulling your guts out through your mouth." He nodded to B.J. "You can let him go now. If he moves, he's done for."

The sheriff let go of my head and stepped back. I could see him watching Cooter, fascinated by it all.

"Ear canal's not very long," Cooter said, "About an inch. Short stab is all it'll take."

I froze, not knowing what to do.

"You could save yourself some discomfort," B.J. said.

"How?" I asked, my head still turned at a crazy angle. Cooter kept working the point around inside, pushing it deeper, a little bit at a time, as I tried real hard to concentrate.

"Confess," he said.

"To what?"

B.J sighed. "To killing Mark Reinhardt, dumbass. You do it tomorrow. Tell your lawyer you want to take the stand and do what's right. This trial's taken way too long. A couple days would've been plenty. Now we hear the attorney general's going to be here tomorrow, snooping around, maybe stirring shit up. What better time for you to admit to what you done in open court?"

"Or what? You'll stab me in the ear?"

"That's for starters," Cooter said. "How about you get to hang yourself next?"

"Nobody'd believe it! My lawyer—"

"There you go again. Not listening," B.J. said as Cooter turned the shaft of the ice pick, pushing it in a little further in, teasing me with it. "Barry understands the situation. He'll swear you beat him up and then killed yourself."

"It'll never work," I said.

"It *will* work," B.J. said. "Before and now."

"With who?" I asked, trying to not think about the steel point deep in my ear.

"You're being a smart ass. I don't like smartasses," Cooter said, and drove the end straight through my eardrum.

FIFTY-EIGHT

Denise, nervous, sat outside of the security cubicle, waiting for the guard to bring the Death Row prisoner in. Maybe she should reconsider her visit, she thought, but, no, there were things that needed asking.

"Why're you here?" Carl asked after being seated.

"Things I had to know," Denise said, hearing her voice sound a bit higher than normal, the thud of her heart pounding in her ears.

"Yeah? Like what?"

Denise leaned forward. Time to get this over with. Arranging to talk to a Death Row inmate at the Ellis Unit wasn't the easiest thing to do if you weren't family.

"I got to know…" she began.

"Curious, huh? Can't wait for the formal execution? Had to get some details early?" Carl glanced to his side, studying the guard watching them both.

"That's not it."

"Then I suspect you're wasting my time. See, I don't have a lot of it left and I kind of watch it careful, you know." Carl made a face. "I got the theatre to go to tonight and as I recall the charity auction's tomorrow. Have to check my appointments with my social secretary." He punched the air with his finger as his head nodded in agreement. "Here I got a nice cozy cell all to myself. Even get to watch a little TV. Don't even have regular prison number here, only special Death Row numbers. Right 'fore I get killed, they'll even let my buddies say goodbye. Yeah, it's pretty nice in here. Real special."

Carl pressed on as Denise stared at him. "Be in this wonderful place for a couple more weeks, then they get to watch me die from a few squirts of the good stuff dripping in my vein. Average time it takes to get killed in here is ten years. But I got myself on the accelerated plan, seeing as how I refused all but the mandatory appeal. I been here nine months, almost, and I'm ready, way ready. Maybe you could come down? Sheriff might plan a caravan of interested local citizens."

"Why'd you do it, Carl? Why'd you kill Clarice?"

"You forgot the trial already? I thought it was pretty clear. Remember? You were one of those testified against me."

"Yes," she said, looking down at the tabletop. "I remember."

"So?"

"I've had time to think this through. About the things that were said at the trial. And I got some issues, some confusion in my head, about it all."

"Then you're the only one in Douglas County that does," Carl said. "I think even that fucking lawyer of mine was sure I done it."

"What you mean 'Sure you done it'? You said you did, right there in court."

"So what else we going to talk about?"

Denise's eyes narrowed. "You telling me now you didn't kill my best friend?"

"No, I killed her. Sure as shootin'." He laughed off his joke. "Sure as shootin'."

"Carl, I need to hear it from you, why you killed her. You two had your arguments, she said. Lots of times, but nothing like that. I have to believe deep down you always loved her. Loved her a lot. And she loved you, too."

Carl's features softened. "You're right about that. Not that it matters now."

"Then I don't see how…"

The convicted man's face grew tight. "You work in the fucking sheriff's office. You hear shit all the time about people in love killing each other. Why're you wasting my time?"

"Sorry."

"Now we're getting somewhere. You got nothing else to say, I'm going back to my cozy room at the Waldorf. Getting close to dinner time. Maybe we're having the lobster, or maybe tonight's the sal-mon fi-let. Got to get the schedule out and see."

Denise stared at Carl, trying to read his face, but failed. Disappointed, she nodded. "Okay, I'll leave you alone. Sorry I bothered you."

"Tell all the upstanding citizens back home I said 'hi', will you? Know they'll be glad to hear from me."

"I just know…" she began.

"Know what?"

"The day you sat on that witness stand and told about killing Clarice. That there was something not being told right."

"What makes you say that?" Carl said, turning his head to the side as he gave her a look.

"Because. What you said about cussing her. I never believed it."

"You and the jurors got a lot in common, then. They didn't believe me, neither."

"Carl, I…"

"Look, you need to go on back home now. Doesn't matter anymore what really happened. All the people that county got their own version of events all fixed up in their heads. And it don't matter what story I told on that stand. I was a dead man come hell or high water."

Denise stayed in her chair, mute.

"What're you looking at?" Carl asked, returning her stare.

"The man I don't believe ever, ever, intended to kill my best friend, no matter what he said in court."

Carl glanced down to the flat surface and started his finger along the edge, working his flesh against the hard surface. "You, uh…" He paused. "You mean to say that you…uh…really want to know what happened?"

"That's what I came here for."

Carl gave his head a slight shake. "I never figured out why she went crazy that way, over Blackburn. She was weird looking, when I found her, right after she shot him. Didn't even call him by his right name, and I know she knew who he was. She'd come home with him, from the bar."

"What are you talking about?" Denise said. "Clarice shot Blackburn?"

"Kept calling him Anthony. Hell, only Anthony I heard her talk of was that man, you know, Clarice said stayed a while with her and Gladys, back years ago."

◆　◆　◆

"Denise, why'd you take Friday off? Where'd you go?" B.J. asked.

She decided she couldn't lie to B.J. Maybe he already knew. "Huntsville."

B.J. leaned back in his new oversized leather chair, the one several of the local citizens had presented to him as a special gift for his efforts in combatting serious crime in Douglas County. The ceremony was last week, and his butt had already formed a customized depression in the padded seat.

"Why?" he said.

"To talk to Carl Telford."

"Carl won't be with us much longer."

"I know."

B.J. regarded the woman across the desk. "There some personal reason you went to see the man?"

Denis nodded. "I went to ask him why did he shoot Clarice."

"Damn, Denise, that all got covered at the trial. Weren't you listening?"

"I listened. But I wanted to hear him say it himself. To my face."

B.J. watched the thumb of his right hand make a slow circle on the pad of his index finger as it massaged the swirls together, him considering what Denise had really been up to but wasn't telling him. "So, you satisfied now? Did he own up to his mistakes, or not?"

"He did."

"All right then. You better get back to work. Paperwork's piling up in there. You know how Cooter hates to deal with paperwork."

She said, "Not just yet."

The finger movement stopped. "Oh?"

"Carl said some things that troubled me, B.J."

The sheriff sat up and stared at his secretary, his meaty arms straight on top of the chair sides as his paws gripped the ends. "Such as?"

"Such as the fact that he says he didn't kill Clarice the way he said he did at the trial."

"Meaning he lied on the stand?"

"That's right."

"So he admits to being a liar? And that confession makes you think he's telling the truth now? Jesus, Denise, listen to yourself."

"A feeling I got. From the way he told it all to me."

B.J. chuckled. "No offense, but it's a good thing the damn justice system doesn't run on your 'feelings.'"

"He said it was all an accident. That Scott Blackburn had tried to rape his wife, that Clarice went kinda crazy, because of some past experiences, and shot Blackburn, and that he, meaning Carl, accidentally shot her while he was trying to take the gun away from her."

"Well now, isn't that a new, convenient *and* convoluted story to explain away the fact he murdered his wife."

Denise looked straight at the sheriff. "He said he told you that story, the night he was arrested."

Feeling his face beginning to flush, B.J. waved his hand to the side. "What the hell makes you think any lying Telford would stick to one story about what happened, Denise? Hell, the man started out telling us he was pleading guilty and then went for insanity. You only heard the last version he felt like making up. He'd had another week 'fore you came in, he'd have him another."

"I don't think Carl deserves to die, even though he said all along he'd wouldn't fight it. I think mainly he feels he wants death for killing Clarice." She stopped, considering what to say next, then continued on, almost in a whisper. "Did he really tell you the story about Clarice killing Scott, and him accidentally shooting her that night?"

B.J. rubbed his chin with a free hand. The other one tightened against the chair arm. "I think it's time you got back to work, Denise. Time you quit interrogating your boss about things aren't none of your business. You hear me, missy?"

"He says you moved the furniture. Faked photographs after you were in the house. Things like that."

B.J. jumped up and exploded. "Then why didn't his damn lawyer take that up in court? Huh? Maybe because they couldn't prove it because it's all *bullshit* and you're too damn *dumb* to understand it?"

"Did you do that or not?" Denise said, her voice low and cautious.

Coming from behind his desk, B.J. rounded the side and stopped close at Denise's side. She looked up to see the flush deepening down his neck, a sure sign the man was about to lose control.

"I suggest you take a couple *more* days off," he said. "This time without pay. Get your head outta your *ass*, before you come back to work, else you're not *coming* back. I make myself clear?"

Denise both heard and felt the heavy breathing beside her. There were a number of things she wanted to say, to ask, but she controlled the impulse, trying to think through her options.

"I said, do I make myself *clear?*" he repeated.

"Yes, sir."

B.J. relaxed, but not much, adding a hand to the side of the desk to steady his thick form. "You remember when you came to me needing a job, saying you had to make some money and get that boyfriend of yours off your back? Huh? You remember that?"

"Yes, sir."

"Good, 'cause I sure as hell do. Me and Cooter went to see your Mr. Jerome, told him the department didn't appreciate a low-life motherfucker like him sniffing around one of our employees and it was time he quit. And you didn't seem to mind that after we explained the situation, after he got his arm set in the emergency room, that he never bothered you again. Huh? You telling me now that you *minded* us taking care of your problem?"

Denise's head dropped. "No, sir."

"What I'm hearing here, Denise, is that you got some selective ideas about law enforcement. That as long as you benefit, you're okay with what happens, but when it doesn't go your way—"

"No, sir, that's not it, I—"

"And you seem to have also forgotten about that bag of marijuana me and Cooter let you take home, right before Clarice got killed, and the fact that you two probably got high that same night smoking joints and maybe that's half the reason she went nuts and killed the mayor's kid."

Raising her head, Denise said, "So *Clarice* killed Scott. Carl must've told you that and—"

"Doesn't matter what *you* think happened in that house that night. A jury found otherwise."

Denise's eyes widened. "Carl was telling me the truth! Why did he make that other one up unless, unless…"

"*Shut up!*" B.J. said.

Denise quietened, a thousand thoughts chasing themselves through her head.

"You telling me you didn't smoke any weed with Clarice that night?"

"No, well, she had a couple of joints, but I—"

"You wonder why that didn't come out in court, in the autopsy report?"

"No. Not at the time."

"Because it got taken care of, to keep from embarrassing you."

Denise was thinking maybe it had more to do with the court finding out about her getting the weed from the sheriff. "But that might've helped

Carl's case if his lawyer would've known that she smoked it. You know, maybe another reason she was acting funny…"

B.J. sighed. "I don't think you're hearing me, Denise. I don't think so at all. See, decent society depends on a series of implied obligations between people, contracts made between the citizens about how they're going to live together in peace and harmony. Not only in good times, but the bad, too."

"You telling me I need to keep quiet?"

"Maybe what you need to do is get the *hell* out of this office. Or maybe you could quit work and go live with that new honey of yours, that Bobby Green fella? Think he makes enough to keep you in nail polish?"

Denise, feeling a little desperate now, said, "I need this job, B.J."

"Yeah, don't we all." With that, he returned to his chair. Denise saw now that his earlier redness was receding. He was pleased, believing he had won again.

"You see," he said, "what we got here is what I like to call a 'zone of protection.' People inside the zone, they get along just fine. Things turn out all right. People outside the zone, they have problems. Lots of problems. Believe me, you don't want to be outside the zone, Denise."

"No, sir."

"Go home for a couple of days. Hell, I might even pay you. *If* you straighten up afterward. Then…" he said, his voice tightening, "when you come back, I don't want to hear you *ever* second-guessing me or this office again. *Hear me?*"

"Yes, sir."

"'Cause there are things, Denise, that need to stay in this office. Things that you might have heard, or maybe *thought* you had heard, that *will* stay here. Things that if I ever hear told around town I might think they came from you. That would end up being unfortunate for you. *Very* unfortunate. I make myself clear?"

"Okay."

"What did you say?"

"Yes, sir."

"Me and you are going to have us an understanding or you're gonna wish you'd never worked in this department and you're not gonna work in this county ever again." B.J. paused for a deep breath. "Not *anywhere*, hear me? Now you get the *hell* outta here. You've put me in a bad mood and I don't *like* being in a bad mood."

Denise rose and left. The shock of what had been said, the truth about the night Clarice died, spreading through her mind like a wild grass fire.

What she had to do was find Bobby Green. Together, they'd decide what to do.

FIFTY-NINE

The blood oozed out of my ear while the headache lingered on.

"Nice, clean shot, I'd say," Cooter said, backing away now, still throwing and catching the ice pick while he admired his handiwork.

"Yeah," B.J. said. "Luther, you should see what happens to some of 'em. Jerk around at the last second and end up with their whole eardrum wrapped around the end of the point. Messy business. Now, where were we?"

"Luther here's gonna confess tomorrow," Cooter said.

B.J. nodded. "You been quite a problem for us, boy. Now, I gotta get on home. The missus will be wondering what's taking so long. 'Fore you know it, she'll think I'm catting around like Cooter here."

Cooter grinned at the compliment and stuck the ice pick in his back pocket.

"See, we're having ourselves a little trouble with the evidence situation at your trial," B.J. said. "Looks like right now we've got too many loose ends."

"So fakin' evidence didn't work out the way you hoped?" I said.

Cooter slapped me across the face, but I heard it on only one side of my head.

"You fucking little shit, I…" B.J. stopped a minute, getting his official voice back. "Better I say this before I change my mind. Thing is, we got it squared with Cunningham that if you'll plead guilty to manslaughter tomorrow, all this 'persuasion' we've been forced to use will go away."

"Manslaughter?"

"That's right."

"But…what…" I wasn't sure what was going on.

"Here's how it'll work. You tell Garner first thing you want to see if you can plead to a lesser crime. That you're really guilty and that you've remembered that manslaughter doesn't carry the death penalty."

"He'll never believe that."

"He will if you're convincing enough."

"And if I don't?" I said. "Be too late to pretend I hung myself."

"We got other ways of putting the pressure on. Besides, if this doesn't go as planned, we can always work up a noose tomorrow," Cooter said. He moved beside me and leaned down. I could feel his stinking breath on my neck. "That cute little wife of yours? Suzie?"

"What about her?" I asked, feeling the dread rise up in my throat like a sour chili pepper.

"Looks to me like she'd be a nice piece of pie."

My arms strained against the handcuffs and the hardwood rails, but it wasn't no use. B.J. watched Cooter with a gentle surprise, like he never quit being amazed at what the man could come up with.

"You ever did that I'd…"

"Stow it, Holman," B.J. said. "You can't threaten us. You're in jail, 'member?"

"Maybe," I said, "Maybe if people knew the way you run this county…"

"Think you're special?" B.J. asked. "You're nobody. Shit under our shoes. Me and Cooter do what's necessary to protect the peace in this county. The people here don't ask any questions, which means we don't have to explain how it all gets handled."

"Who else you done this to?" I asked.

"Barry's brother Carl? One that shot his skanky wife, Clarice?"

"So?"

"After he was arrested, Carl told us he'd plead guilty if we'd let his stupid brother go. Next thing we know, Barry's run off and Carl's changed his mind and pled insanity. Thought he fucked us good."

"Why're you tellin' me this?" I asked.

B.J. bent over. "We end up with a deal tonight, don't try the same kind of shit. Even if you decide to go on with this 'I'm innocent' crap, we got a hole card on the jury. A guaranteed vote for our side, and a persuasive one I'd say. So even if you don't get convicted this time around, and there's a hung jury, Cunningham will re-try you and the next time you'll be found guilty."

"Must've been you two that took care of Billy Yates, then," I said.

"Old Billy," B.J. said. "He was useful in his day. Problem was, Billy saw the drug business changing, other people coming in and taking over with Mark Reinhardt out of the way. That Billy, always shooting his mouth off when he should've been quiet. Well, we had to make an example of him. Get it through his thick skull that *we* run this town, and are not about to let some pieces of shit like him and his buddies move in on our territory." B.J. slammed his fist into his palm. "And he did have a thick skull. Took three good shots of a hammer to cave it in."

"Franklin in on this, too?"

"Let's say that Bob sometimes has to be persuaded. You'd think by now it'd be on automatic. Your representation was going about perfect until that Garner bastard came along."

"And Harder? Cunningham?"

B.J. shook his head. "Judge believes he's doing what's right, getting the bad people off the street in a hurry. He needs to help the process along with his rulings, that's okay with him. But he considers the drug trade dirty money. Cunningham wants his conviction stats to look good so he can run for higher office. We bring him a solid case, no holes, no surprises, he does the rest. That's what your case was supposed to be. Neat and clean. Until you and Garner fucked it up."

"What makes you think I won't tell on you two?" I asked.

"Insurance," Cooter said.

"What you mean?"

Cooter bent down again. "That wife of yours, Suzie? You confess, we'll let her be. You don't…" He put his head down close to mine. "Mark, he preferred them real young. Always did. Couldn't get enough of little girls. All he had to do was make him a trip down to Mexico and get 'em whenever he wanted, served up fresh. But sometimes he couldn't wait. Like with your daughter." Cooter shook his head, whispering now. "Ain't it ironic? Tomorrow, you get to confess to killing the man that did your daughter. Me, I prefer the more mature kind, with some hair on their pussy. Like that Suzie of yours." His tongue came out in a nasty move as he opened his ugly mouth. "Man, I can taste her pussy now." He reached in my pocket for another cigarette. "More I think about it, the better that sounds…"

I guess this was where I was supposed to say okay and agree to what they wanted. But the thought of that bastard with his hands on my wife, and the idea of what that piece of shit Reinhardt did to our little girl, the next thing I know, the rails on that chair was in splinters all over the floor and I was on top of Cooter, choking the life outta the damn bastard, seeing death in his eyes heading toward him like a freight train running a hundred miles an hour.

If it hadn't been for B.J.'s nightstick, I would've finished the job.

◆　◆　◆

I woke up on the floor of my cell, feeling like I'd been rolled down a hill inside a barrel. Everything hurt so bad I couldn't stand up. I don't know how long I laid there before I managed to work my way up the ladder to the top bunk.

Barry said, "Goddamn, man. What'd you say to them?"

"Plenty," I said, and reached over to fish in my pocket to see if my cigarettes was still there. They was, but crushed together some. The effort hurt more than I expected.

"You shouldn't rile them up so," Barry said. "Go with the flow. It'll turn out the same anyway."

I took a few breaths 'fore I could continue. "Maybe so, but there's a story I gotta tell you. About what really happened to Carl."

SIXTY

Two months after the State of Texas executed Carl for the double murder of Clarice Telford and Scott Blackburn, B.J. and Cooter paid the previous owner of Blackburn Chevrolet a visit.

Terry had his feet up on the desk, it being a slow Tuesday morning at the car lot and not much action, despite the ritual ass-chewing he'd given his salesmen that morning. Now they were busy working their client lists, telephoning and begging for business that down deep they knew depended more on the local economy than their own individual persuasiveness about the unbelievable pleasure a person would have from owning a new vehicle. Terry knew it, too, but this was part of the routine in the car business. Kicking ass and taking names. Or, as he told them in the sales meeting, you do it right, selling cars was like clubbing baby seals on the beach.

The officers stopped at Betty Morrison's desk and asked to see the boss.

"We didn't lose any cars last night, did we?" she asked.

"No. A private matter to discuss with Terry, that's all," B.J. said.

"Okay, I'll see if he's busy," Betty said. She rose and headed for the corner office.

"Busy, my ass," Cooter said. "Fucking off's what he's doing. Saw him through his office glass with his feet up on his damn desk when we drove up."

"Now, now," B.J. said. "Let's not spoil the mood."

Cooter paced until Betty returned in a few minutes. "Terry said he'd see you now."

B.J. touched his hat brim. "Ma'am," he said as he walked past her desk. Cooter slouched after him, an envelope squeezed tight enough in his hand that the yellow paper was starting to crinkle from the sweat.

"Sheriff, Cooter. How you boys been doing?" Terry said as he stood to shake their hands. "Here, take a load off," he said, pointing to the arm chairs in front of his desk.

"Thanks," B.J. said, "'Preciate you seeing us on short notice."

"Nothing's too good for our public servants. What can I do you for?"

"How're things going these days?" B.J. asked.

"Difficult. You know, I'd given the dealership to Scott, and he was handling it fine. Now, with him gone, I've had to... Well, you know..." Blackburn's voice drifted off.

"Sorry to hear that. But there's something personal we need to discuss with you," B.J. said, having difficulty fitting his big butt between the arms of one of the chairs guarding Blackburn's desk. B.J. nodded toward Cooter, who was shutting the office door before he sat down.

Betty's neck craned to almost horizontal as the edge of the door moved across her line of vision and cut her off from the conversation.

"Is it serious?" Blackburn said.

"Depends," B.J. said. He paused for a few seconds, watching the time interval building tension in the man's face. "Not to bring up bad memories, Terry, but we run across something we thought we might need to show you."

"It's about Scott, isn't it?" Blackburn said.

"Yeah, it is. Found some photos in the office file. About your son and what happened."

"I saw all the pictures before the trial." Blackburn sighed. "Don't ever want to see 'em again. I want to try and get past this now that Telford's dead."

"I completely understand," B.J. said, "but these here I don't believe you've seen before."

"Doesn't matter."

"Oh, I think you need to take a look."

Cooter handed the envelope to the sheriff. B.J. opened the clasp, extracted a number of letter-sized color photos, and laid them on the desk. He waited for Blackburn to pick them up.

"Why?" Blackburn asked.

"You see, there was some confusion that night at the crime scene. Confusion about how to interpret exactly what happened."

Terry Blackburn stared at the sheriff. "I don't see there's any *confusion*. That bastard shot my son in the back. And only for taking that tart of a wife home. She was drunk, remember? Probably forced herself on him. What was the man to do, huh? Every time I think about it—"

B.J. held up a hand to cut him off. "I'm with you, Terry. That's what makes this so hard." The sheriff offered a sad smile and continued to settle into the arm chair, the back of his pants now hitting bottom.

"I don't understand." But Blackburn's petulant attitude was slipping, worry now replacing his original dismissal.

"What we got here is the photos that didn't make it into evidence at the trial. Photos that call into the question the particular motives of your son."

"What're you saying?" Blackburn said, concern obvious on his face.

"A person might interpret these different from what the official investigation did. One could even say that maybe your son was intent on having forcible sex with Mrs. Telford. Sex that could be called rape."

"What the *hell*? Listen, you two get outta my office—"

"Simmer down, Terry. Be best if you hold up right now and listen to what I've got to say," B.J. said.

After B.J. finished describing the actual events of the night his son was killed, Terry Blackburn had nothing at all to say.

"See, none of that needed to come out at the trial," B.J. said, leaning forward. "'Cause, really, all you got is speculation as to who did what. Now if the jury bought the idea that your son had improper designs on Mrs. Telford, and that her husband came home after she'd already killed Scott, then I figure things would be a lot different now. Who knows? Maybe some women around town might've come forward 'bout their previous experiences with Scott. Experiences we couldn't have hushed up this time around." He smiled, knowing that, as always, he would receive the expected response from the man who now stared at him across the desk.

"You mean that Carl..." Blackburn said.

"Oh, don't shed any tears over that bastard. Telfords cost this county lots of trouble and money over the years. He hadn't got the death penalty for this, he'd been in prison for something else soon enough."

"But, I mean, putting a man to death if..."

Cooter said, "Telfords are all pieces of shit. Only a matter of time before the law caught up with Carl again."

Blackburn's index finger removed the moisture from his forehead. "Why're you telling me this now?"

"Well, here's how I see it. One, your kid was a rapist. If Carl Telford got off for accidentally killing his old lady, he sues you for all you got. Maybe you lose the dealership and your farm property, too. Carl ends up a rich drunk and 'fore long he loses it all. Now, who's the better for that? Or, two, Carl gets put to death by the state and the overall crime rate in the county goes way down. Which one would you chose?"

"I don't know." Blackburn began. "I..."

"Remember a year or so ago, you had that problem with those Mexicans cooking meth in your old farmhouse?"

"So?"

B.J. nodded, acting sympathetic. "Lots of rural folks've have problems with that kind of thing. Old houses out in the country get taken over by drug dealers. Hell, I know of a property owner next county over got sued by the druggies for personal injury. Man had to sell the land to pay the legal bills. Not right what the law can do to a man's property. Not right at all."

Blackburn nodded. "Yeah, okay, I see your point. But those two Spanish men out on mother's old place? Fortunately—"

"Fortunate for you, *we* was there," Cooter said.

B.J. broke in. "What my deputy is trying to say, Terry, is that if those two had of been arrested and booked into jail, there might have been some ugly…repercussions, as they say. For several people in town, that is."

"Why's that?"

B.J. sighed. "They claimed they were tied in with some important people here, people with names you'd recognize, and that they'd trade that information for getting off."

"That's right," Cooter said. "Wanted to bargain."

"Way I see it," B.J. said, "It's kinda like the Carl deal. Give those low-lifes time to blab their accusations all over the place, some people might take to believing there's some truth to what they're saying. And that wouldn't be a good thing, seeing as they were likely a bunch of liars to start with."

Terry Blackburn's head hung low over the desk as his shaky hand paged through the photos in front of him.

B.J. thought back to the two men outside the farm house, on their knees in the powdered dust of the narrow drive, begging for their lives in rusty English, how they'd promised to give up the money man of the operation in return for leniency. After they'd listened to the Mexicans' pleas, Cooter shot the first one where he knelt, the man's body falling to the side, dead in an instant. The other man jumped and ran away like a crazed deer. Cooter halted him with a shouted promise not to shoot if he'd stop, he only needed one witness, not two, but when the man turned around Cooter plugged him through the chest at twenty yards. The druggie folded up like a kite hitting a tree.

Cooter found two handguns in the house. It was a simple matter to fire off a full magazine of rounds from each pistol and then leave the discharged weapons clamped in the hands of the dead men. B.J. knew the county judge wouldn't be too happy about the damage to his cruiser, but the bullet holes through the windshield, door, and engine block of the patrol car added some needed realism when you're ambushed by outlaw drug dealers.

Besides, B.J. was in the mood for a new patrol car, taxpayer funded. He'd take the new vehicle and let Cooter have his current one.

Most of the seizure consisted of a few kilos of meth and cocaine and a small marijuana stash, but what mattered to Cooter was finding the cash. After a thorough search, the stack of bills turned up under a soiled mattress. B.J. insisted they split the find at the usual preferential ratio, though Cooter complained some that he should get half, seeing as, hell, he did all the actual killings. B.J., thinking now about the proposed split, had Cooter to bag up the drugs and put them in the trunk of the damaged cruiser for safekeeping. After Cooter lugged the body of number one back inside the house and set the structure on fire, B.J. relented and agreed to the suggested arrangement. Cooter got fifty percent due to his dedicated professional handling of the situation. The dope stash, B.J. figured, he'd either give back to Reinhardt, *gratis*, or maybe he'd sell it to him instead. He'd have to think on what would be the best arrangement long-term. Like the flow of jail contraband, illegal drugs had their purpose in keeping the lid on things in Douglas County. Too little available, and people could get out of hand. Too much, and the citizens would notice. B.J.'s mission was to get the amount just right.

By the time they radioed the fracas in, the old house was within minutes of a ruin and the volunteer firemen got to make a show of dampening the ashes. The haste of the firemen also eliminated any traces of incriminating evidence.

The county paper carried their photos above the fold in the Thursday edition, B.J. and Cooter looking grim in front of the smoking hulk of the house, with the title, "Sheriff And Deputy Survive Drug Dealers' Murder Attempt," and went on about how one of the crazed men had set fire to the house right before he died. Commendations were given by the county judge in a special ceremony. Both celebrated Deputy Jeremiah Sanders' crack shooting ability, seeing as how he managed to kill the first one by shooting through the edge of a window behind where the villain had been holed up, firing away at the officers. The other criminal, unwilling to die inside of the burning house, was shot after he ran out the back door, still firing and refusing to give up. The locals talked up the heroic actions of law enforcement, and how lucky they were to have such dedicated personnel on the force. Everyone seemed pleased. Everyone, that is, except for the dead men, Mark Reinhardt, who lost his cash and now had to find two new drug runners, and Terry Blackburn, who was out a place well suited for stacking up cattle feed out of the weather.

B.J. didn't see as how the fact that he and Cooter had deliberately destroyed Blackburn's house needed to be revealed, since it wasn't material to their present discussion. Besides, he needed to finish the matter with the car dealer.

"See, Terry, we feel like we did you a favor here, withholding this evidence and all, and we'd appreciate it if you'd acknowledge that."

"Yeah, sure," Blackburn said, still stunned. He dropped the last of the glossy photos back on his desk.

B.J. reached over and restacked the pages with a sharp whack on the desk, then reinserted them into the envelope. "This'll stay between us, you understand."

"Thanks. I…"

"One of these days we'll need a favor in return, Terry," B.J. said. "Nothing you'd be ashamed of doing, only involve what you need to do. As a decent citizen. Maybe on a jury where we needed help convicting someone who's a danger to society."

"Okay, sure, if that's all there is."

"Not quite." Cooter said, leaning forward. "There's the matter of the money."

Sixty-One

"Luther, are you ready for today? Should be a good one for our side. We have some new witnesses, in addition to the evidence we presented about Reinhardt and his…"

I stared at Mr. Garner, knowing my eyes were dulled out from pain and lack of sleep and the thought of what I was about to do.

"What's the matter?" he said, certain something was wrong.

"I've changed my mind," I said. "About the whole thing."

"What do you mean?" Mr. Garner's head slid sideways, his eyes not moving off of me.

"I want to change my plea to manslaughter. I've decided to confess."

"The hell you have!" Those washed-out blue eyes bored into me, the mind behind them unable to believe the words it was hearing. "Tell me what's happened! Did they get to you last night?"

"Time to come clean." I saw Cooter staring at me through the glass window, nodding his head. "I want the jury to hear what really happened."

"Luther, this is insane!"

"I want it recorded here so it can be played back in court. For everybody to hear."

With a side motion of my hand, I removed a bit of plastic and metal from my jumpsuit pocket, palmed it, covering it as I slid it across the table to Mr. Garner. "Later, maybe you'll understand."

He was smart enough not to ask a question and slipped it into his coat slick as I ever seen it done.

"Has the prosecution offered you a deal they didn't tell me about? Confession for a lesser sentence? By God, I'm your attorney. I have to know. This is illegal if—"

"No, nothin' like that," I said.

"Luther, don't give up hope. We've got a good chance of winning this case. Please, give this a chance!"

"I doubt it. Not in this town. Always someone on the jury that won't believe me."

"What makes you so sure?"

"Feelin' I happened to have. A good, strong feelin'."

Mr. Garner drummed his fingers for a while, then said, "If you insist on changing your plea, I'll call Cunningham and see what we can work out. But I'll only do it if you can convince me why in the hell you now have this idea in your head."

"I want to confess. That's all."

Mr. Garner said, "Something has happened. Tell me what it is."

He was pretty upset. I wanted to think it was because he believed in me.

"Nothin' to tell," I said.

He rolled around what I'd said inside his head for a while. Biting down on his lip, he come to a conclusion. "We'll need a witness to the recording."

"Cooter's in that room over there. Have him come hear it."

Mr. Garner got up slow, looking like the wind was all gone from his insides. Shaking his head, he walked over in front of the glass and motioned for Cooter to come in.

Entering all casual-like, Cooter said, "Problem?"

"We need to record some testimony, Deputy. And we need a witness. However, I need to know two things first."

"What's that?" Cooter said, suspicious right up front.

"My client here, against my advice, wishes to record his confession, to be played back in court today. You can be the witness to it. I will ask if you mind being recorded on this tape, and so state that you have no objection. Is there any problem with that?"

"No, guess not."

"Yes or no?"

The slewing of Cooter's mouth indicated he was getting pissed off. "No."

"All right." Mr. Garner opened his briefcase and pulled out his silver tape recorder. He scrounged a tape package from the corner of it, unwrapped the plastic, and stuck the clean tape in the machine. "One other thing, Deputy. I must have your promise that this is will be the one and only copy of this statement. Otherwise, we will withdraw this tape we are about to offer and refuse to acknowledge its authenticity. Understand?"

Cooter eyed the attorney, then turned toward the control room separated from us by the thick glass. Cooter turned his head to the side and the man inside reached over and made an arm motion.

Cooter turned back to us, not even a bit embarrassed at showing what he'd been up to all along. "Let's get on with it. Court'll be starting up in a few minutes."

Mr. Garner said, "Are you sure this is what you want, Luther?"

"Yes, sir."

Mr. Garner moved his hand over to his side. "Let me make sure the tape is rewound."

We all waited while the tape whirled away and after a time it stopped. Then he put his hand over the recorder, turning it as he punched the button. "Deputy, state your name, official position, and the fact that you have consented to this recording after I start the tape. Do you understand me?"

"Hell, yes. I'm not stupid, Mr. Fancy-Ass Attorney," Cooter said.

Mr. Garner nodded toward the window. "And no other recording."

Cooter glanced over to the control room. "No," he said.

The tape started up. Cooter leaned over the table and said, "My name is Jeremiah Sanders, Deputy Sheriff of Douglas County. I consent to this recording of my voice." He raised up after Mr. Garner pushed the Stop button. "That good enough for you, Mr. Lawyer?"

My attorney repeated the same procedure. "My name is Garner, attorney for Luther Holman, and I am a witness that both Luther Holman and Deputy Jeremiah Sanders have agreed that this voice recording may be made." After turning off the tape again, Mr. Garner said, "That'll do fine, Cooter. Now Luther, are you certain you want to do this? I say again we have a damn good chance of winning this case. I consider changing your plea ill-advised."

"I heard you," I said. "It doesn't matter anymore."

Mr. Garner fidgeted in his chair. A couple of times he opened his mouth to argue, but no words came out. Then he said, "All right. If you insist."

"I do," I said.

Standing the recorder on its side, Mr. Garner said, "This puts the microphone at the top, where the sound will be better. Sit up and speak in a normal voice." His thumb passed over the switch as he nodded to me.

"My name is Luther Holman. I am accused of killing Mark Reinhardt this past December sixteenth. Up 'til now, I have denied any part of his murder. Now, I want to confess."

I don't know how long I talked, but it seemed like less than a minute. I described how I thought Reinhardt had raped and murdered my daughter, but I had no proof. Still, it was in my head that the man was guilty and I was determined to take matters into my own hands. I told how I said to Suzie I was going out for a few minutes, then parked in the alley behind his house, slipped inside, and shot Reinhardt in the head with my daddy's gun. How I returned home, put the pistol back in the table by my chair when my wife wasn't looking. Not expecting the police to arrive so soon, I didn't think about hiding the weapon. Then come the part about B.J. and Cooter showing up at my door and I didn't have time to plan an alibi.

I told the whole thing.

Finished, I sat back in my chair, exhausted by it all.

Mr. Garner worked the switch again and we sat in silence. Cooter was the first to speak.

"Happened like we figured. I knew you was lying all along."

"Luther…"

"Don't ask, Mr. Garner," I said. "Don't ask."

Mr. Garner looked real old now, a deflated balloon with holes in it so it couldn't be blown up again. His client had turned tail on him and confessed to a murder. Taking the tape out of the recorder, Mr. Garner started to put it in his pocket. "I'll keep this until the trial starts," he said.

Cooter leaned over and grabbed Mr. Garner's arm. "The hell you will. I don't get that right now, there's no deal. I'm not about to let you change that tape between now and court."

"You don't trust me?" Mr. Garner said.

"Not one damn bit."

"This is our evidence, to be presented in open court. You can't have it."

"I give that to Cunningham or there's no deal," Cooter said.

"Are you saying you speak for the district attorney?" Mr. Garner said.

"He'll do what we say."

"How do I know you won't alter this tape? I don't trust you, either," Mr. Garner said.

"No tape, no deal." Cooter stood up straight and crossed his arms.

Mr. Garner tapped the cartridge on the surface of the desk. "I'll need some masking tape and nail polish. And a plastic bag."

"What the hell for?"

"Get it. You'll see." Mr. Garner laid the tape on the table. It was small, less than half the size of a business card, and it would end my life.

Before Cooter left, he said, "Leave that in the middle of the table. So my man in there can see there's no switcheroo."

◆　◆　◆

Cooter returned, dropping the items on the table.

"Good thing Denise was working today. She's always petting her nails. Otherwise, you'd be shit outta luck."

Mr. Garner wrapped the masking tape backwards around the small cartridge several times, taking care not to touch the surface of the magnetic tape where it had run through the machine. Finished, he dabbed several drops of polish on each side of the tape and blew on it until it hardened. Then he put the cartridge into the clear plastic bag and taped that shut and marked it with polish, too.

"You can only use this if the district attorney agrees to play it in public, in the courtroom. My tape recorder has output jacks so it can be hooked up to the sound system." He held the bag up to Cooter, who made a swipe at grabbing it. Mr. Garner floated it away from him. "If I see any evidence, any evidence *whatsoever*, that this tape has been removed or touched in any way, or tampered with, the deal is off. Understand me? We'll claim in court that this was all a fabrication and that the statement was coerced."

"Give it to me," Cooter said, reaching out again.

Mr. Garner laid it in his hands. Cooter had a look like he'd found a certified gold mine with the first swing of his pick. "Fifteen minutes to trial time, boys. Luther, I suggest you spend it practicing getting down on your knees and praying to God that the judge don't give you twenty years."

"You better remember what we've agreed to," I said.

"No problema, seen-yor," Cooter said with a wide grin.

The deputy left the room in a big hurry. I sat back, weak as a kitten.

Mr. Garner folded his hands on the table. "What did he promise you? Did it have anything to do with your family? With Suzie?"

I didn't say a word.

"Luther, you've always talked a blue streak since I met you. Now you've got the most important thing I can think of to tell me and you've nothing to say?"

I looked at the tabletop, remembering the early morning visit from both B.J. and Cooter, how they'd reminded me what was going to happen to Suzie if I didn't cooperate. I couldn't let another person in my life come to harm, even if it meant I'd have to go to prison for it.

As far as I could see, it was all over.

SIXTY-TWO

Terry Blackburn seemed confused. "What money?"

"Money we got coming from *you*," Cooter said.

"I don't..." Blackburn began.

"Perhaps I can clear this up," B.J. said, shifting some in the chair to change position, but the arms held him as tight as before. "What we have here is a financial problem."

Blackburn frowned at the sheriff. "We do?"

"See, taking care of problems costs money, and you know, with the salary the county pays... Let's say we often find ourselves short at the end of the month."

Blackburn was enough of a businessman to see a bribery request coming from way off. "So you two are asking me for money. 'Cause of what you told me about my son."

B.J. said, "Consider it a goodwill gesture in support of loyal law enforcement. A contribution for services rendered."

Rising from behind his desk, Blackburn said, "Okay, I'll get the checkbook from Alice. We'll code it as after-hours security services."

Cooter said, "We don't want a fucking check."

B.J added, "What my indelicate partner is trying to say is that cash is what we prefer."

Arms akimbo, Blackburn stared at the pair for a few seconds before sitting back down. "I could get you a few hundred. I've got some spare cash here in the office."

"A few hundred won't do, neither," Cooter said.

Blackburn's eyes narrowed. "Then how much you boys want?"

B.J. glanced at Cooter before replying. "Seeing as how we were able to save your family's reputation once again, and avoided any public embarrassment about this, and the matter of the drug dealers out on you farm, we feel that ten thousand would be appropriate."

"Ten *thousand!*"

"For the both of us. Not individually, of course."

Blackburn sputtered before he replied. "I don't have that kind of cash."

B.J. stared the man down. "Maybe you could give us part of the funds you pay those twenty-four wetbacks with. You know, the illegals that work on your farms and hide out in your rat-infested bunkhouses at night? Last we heard, your monthly cash payroll is a lot more'n what we're asking for. Or, you could sell of few of those unbranded cattle you seem to have from time to time. You know, the ones deep in the middle of the old Hawthorne place, inside that line of trees makes it near impossible to see into from the fence row?"

Blackburn sat mute.

"Drop it off at the office when you get a chance. Or I could send Cooter here by to collect it. You know, come by and ask Betty did she have the money ready."

"No, that…that's okay. I'll deliver it."

"Fine," B.J. said, pushing against the chair arms to heave his bulk out of the tight space. "Sorry to be the bearer of bad news, Terry, but you know how it goes." He tossed the envelope over. "You can keep the photos. We can make you more copies. If you need them." B.J. touched the edge of his hat. "Mr. Blackburn, a pleasure doing business with you. Come on, Cooter, I'm sure there's a few crooks out there we ain't caught yet."

After the officers left, Betty hustled in and asked what in the world did they want, to which a pale Terry Blackburn replied, "Nothing. Social visit. I've got to make a run to the bank."

♦ ♦ ♦

Denise Jones was finishing a second coat of lavender nail polish, which matched the shade of her short-sleeved tee and the thin lines in her dark gray pin-striped slacks, when the owner of Blackburn Chevrolet presented himself in front of her desk with a taped-up package tucked under his arm.

"Can I help you, Mr. Blackburn?" she asked.

"No, I, uh, is the sheriff in?"

"No, sir, he's out right now."

"How about Cooter?"

"They're together, as usual," she said with a faint smile. "You need to talk to them? I can radio and maybe have 'em come on back in if it's important."

"No, I..."

"Tell you what," she said, glancing at her watch. "I expect B.J. and Cooter are down at the drugstore on Commerce. It's about their coffee time. You can probably catch them there."

Blackburn shifted on his feet. "I, uh, I'd prefer to leave this here."

Denise continued staring at the man, sensing his rising discomfort.

"Tell you what. Can you give this to B.J., Denise?"

"Sure thing."

"I mean, give it directly to the sheriff. Nobody else."

"Must be real important," she said. "You don't have anybody's kidney in there, do you?"

"Of *course* not! What the *hell's* the matter with you?"

"I was only kidding, Mr. Blackburn. I didn't mean to upset you."

"I'm *not* upset."

"Sir?"

He thrust the package into her waiting hands. "See that B.J. gets this. And don't leave it out on the desk, either."

"Yes, sir. I'll put it here on the floor beside me and give it to him the minute he comes in."

"Well, I guess that'll work." He hesitated. "Sorry, I mean, look, I gotta go."

"Bye," Denise said to Terry Blackburn's back.

After her visitor had been gone for a sufficient time, Denise rose, locked the front door, and placed a "Back in 10 Minutes" sign on it. She went to the rear copy room, where she could hear B.J.'s car pull up and still allow herself maybe half a minute to repair the package. After examining the box, she decided to cut the tape and reseal it back so B.J. wouldn't notice. She slit open the side of the box, took out the cash, and started counting as fast as she could.

◆ ◆ ◆

Their coffee break over with, the sheriff and his deputy entered through the back of the office. Denise sat with her left hand outstretched, taking her time painting on the third coat of polish.

"What's up, Denise?" B.J. asked.

"Nothing much," she replied. "Reports are typed and on your desk. Cooter's, too. Been pretty quiet today."

"Damn, Denise, I'd say you're the most efficient secretary we've ever had. How could I do without you?"

She blew on the wet polish to harden it. "I sure I can't imagine."

Cooter gave Denise a glance and a mumbled thanks as he hoofed off to his office. She and the deputy had been distant since their episode the night of Clarice's death. She hadn't yet told B.J. about the incident, but Cooter knew she could at any time. B.J. had remarked to her about their common change in attitude toward each other, but she'd dismissed it as nothing important and he had failed to inquire as to the real cause.

As B.J. passed by her desk, she said, "Oh, Mr. Blackburn did come by after lunch and gave me this for you." She reached down, avoiding touching the package with her fingers by pressing her palms against the sides, not willing to scratch her still-drying nails. "He said give it to you soon as you came in."

B.J. eyed the package. "He say what was in it?"

"Naw. I asked him did he have a kidney or something in there and he said no, like it pissed him off."

"You open it?"

Denise pushed the package into B.J.'s overstuffed arms. "Nope. Should I have?"

"You done good," he said, then headed into his office and closed the door.

Denise pulled her appointment book from the front drawer. It held the meeting schedule of the sheriff, seeing as how he didn't trust computer datebooks. She thumbed through to the back, where she kept shorthand notes and wrote the amount of the Blackburn bribe in a code she had worked out. Better to keep it where they wouldn't suspect it, Bobby had told her. Right in front of their noses.

"Yeah," she said, holding out the painted nails for a thorough examination and subsequent admiration, "you done good, girl."

SIXTY-THREE

I scanned the courtroom and saw the familiar faces crowding the room, all geared up for another round of the spectacle. It was a Wednesday and the room was full, standing room only. Some of 'em must've taken the day off from work, maybe begging off with how the fish they ate went bad or their kid was sick and needed tending to.

Near the back was that big-city reporter, scribbling some notes. After a little looking, I spied the Austin man, too, looking all cool and easy in his nice suit.

Suzie sat right behind me, as usual. Her usual waitress outfit was replaced with one of her Sunday go-to-meeting dresses she got cheap at the half-price store. The blue color was a bit lighter than when she bought it, it having its share of hard times with the laundry detergent, the one she insists on using 'cause it smells good, even after I tell her there's others not so harsh. Her face was plain, no makeup, eyes kinda red and sad. Her hair needed a dye job bad.

To me, she was the most beautiful thing I'd ever seen.

"Hey, baby," I said. "You workin' today?"

"No need to go in." she said. "I got fired yesterday."

"What for?"

"Delbert said too much time away from work. Needed a waitress he could rely on."

"Why that son—"

"Oh, save it, honey. I was tired of that job. I'll get another. Besides, looks to me like you should be out of this place in a few days, right?" She gave me a little smile.

I wanted to say something to her, something about what happened yesterday night and this morning. But I couldn't. "Yeah," I said. "In a few days. Sure."

"What's the matter?" she asked.

"Nothing. Everything's fine."

"No, it's not."

About that time Mr. Garner returned to the table. He'd been having a con-flab with Cunningham and the judge and the trial was twenty minutes late starting up.

"Luther, are you ready for this?" he said in a low voice.

"Yeah. Ready to get it over with."

"How about we present the rest of the defense witnesses? Pursue our side of the case a little further before you decide to change your plea."

"No," I said, "Time to end it."

"If you're sure that's what you want."

Suzie must've heard some of what I was whispering to Mr. Garner. "Luther, what have you done?"

"Only what I had to," I said as I turned around.

Tears sprung up in her eyes. "Luther, my God, tell me what's going on!"

"Sorry, baby."

She lunged and caught my sleeve. "Luther, you *hear me?* What've you got us into?"

I pulled away, watching her fingers slide away from the pinch she had on my coat. I had to turn my head to keep her eyes from changing my mind.

Mr. Garner studied on us both, and said, "The judge indicates he will consider your testimony before he sentences you. Cunningham said he'd recommend ten years. But there's no guarantee the judge will go along. I don't trust them. I still think we have a chance, a good chance here, if you'll stick with the plan."

"No," I said.

"Luther, you listen to me," Suzie murmured in a hard tone, behind my back. "Don't you dare—"

The court was called to order and Harder asked Mr. Garner to call his first witness of the day.

"Defense calls Luther Holman to the stand."

The crowd stirred around some. Story is the defendant's not supposed to testify until the end, and only if they think that can help the case. Mr. Garner says many a man's been ruined trying to defend his actions, so that approach is best left as a last resort. Otherwise, you're supposed to sit still and act like the trial was all a big mistake.

I rose and walked to the stand and got sworn in.

"Mr. Holman," Mr. Garner said, standing in front of me all formal-like, "were you involved with the death of Mark Reinhardt?"

"I'd like," I said, "that a tape could be played instead of me talking up here. It makes the situation clear."

"Your Honor, the defense wishes to enter as the next exhibit a tape that was recorded at the county jail."

"Mr. Cunningham?" Harder asked.

Cunningham stood and buttoned his coat. "Your Honor, only Deputy Sanders and the witness, along with Mr. Garner, have been privy to the statements on this tape. The prosecution would prefer to examine the recording in private prior to it being played in public."

"Mr. Garner?"

"The defense understands the concerns of Mr. Cunningham, but we are reluctant to let the tape out of our hands without proper control."

"Oh?" said Harder.

"Considering the situation, we prefer that this tape be played without any chance of editing or tampering."

Cunningham started in, all puffed up about a challenge to his integrity. "Your Honor, how dare the defense suggest—"

Harder cut him off. "Mr. Cunningham, we've covered this already in chambers. Will you consent to the entering of this tape into evidence and to its playing in this trial? As I understand the offer that the defense has made, this tape will only be made available as an exhibit if it is not opened prior to it being played in open court. Is this agreeable or not? Otherwise, the tape will be withdrawn by the defense."

Cunningham looked at me disgusted-like, and then over to Mr. Garner. He was weighing the chances that I might not admit to the killing good enough to suit him. As it stood, he had me down cold if he'd just agree to play my confession.

"Very well. Play the tape."

"Your Honor," Mr. Garner said, "may I examine the tape and make sure it has not been altered?"

"Proceed."

By this time, the crowd was sure something important was up, but hadn't a clue what.

Mr. Garner opened the bag and checked over the nail polish seals, then nodded and said he was satisfied this was the same tape. The bailiff had rigged up some cables to tie the attorney's little recorder into the sound system of the courtroom, so all Mr. Garner had to do was pop the tape into the machine and it would all be over with.

"Mr. Holman, are you certain that you want this tape played?" he said, kind of like the words you say to a man who has one foot on a bridge and the other dangling in the air and all he needs is a little push.

"Yes, sir, I do."

He pushed a button and opened the door where the tape went into the recorder, then made a show of unwinding the masking tape from the cartridge. Satisfied, he put the masking tape in his pocket and popped the cartridge into the machine. Such a little thing, too, about to end a man's life.

"Okay. I'm pushing Play."

The tape started up at the first with me and Cooter giving the okay to record, but what come next surprised most everyone there, 'cept for Mr. Garner, who stood there looking like a cat with little yellow feathers sticking outta its mouth.

Sixty-Four

B.J.'s wife opened the door to find her husband's secretary, along with a man she didn't know, standing on her front porch. "Denise? My, it's awful late…"

"Yes, I know, Millie, but I need to speak with B.J. It's important."

Mildred Sanders hesitated, then opened the door. "Sorry, please come in. I was taking a nap 'fore bedtime. My manners must've been asleep, too. Been a hectic day. Who's your friend?"

"Bobby Green, Mrs. Sanders."

Bobby took of his cap, dwarfed now in his big hands. "Pleased to meet you, ma'am."

"My, you're a big fella," Mildred said, looking Bobby up and down, then turned to Denise. "You know, B.J. said that the trial yesterday ended up quite a mess, what with that Holman boy—"

"We need to see B.J. That's all. If we can," Denise said.

Mildred shook her head. "Well, alright. He's back in his study. Been there all night."

"Thanks."

Bobby trailed Denise down the hall, his shoulders almost touching the walls as the trio threaded their way to the back of the house.

B.J. was enthroned behind a large mahogany desk which covered most of the floor space in the converted bedroom. A wall-to-wall bookcase sported photographs of B.J. shaking hands with important people. A rag-tag collection of books and a set of antique encyclopedias finished filling up the shelves. B.J. looked up as they entered.

"Well, well. Miss Jones and her boyfriend. Seems like everyone wants to see me lately."

Denise raised an eyebrow. "Oh?"

"You missed the county judge. He was here about an hour ago."

"What did he want?"

"Let me say he wasn't very complimentary about how his county looked on the national news."

Mildred's voice called from behind Bobby's back. "You two please sit down. Can I get you anything to drink? Coffee?"

"That's okay," B.J. said. "They aren't staying long."

A casual frown crossed Mildred's face. "B.J., they're our guests."

His eyes flicking between the two, B.J. nodded in a practiced, official way. "You're right, Millie. Either of you care for something to wet your whistle?"

Denise turned back to Mildred. "Thanks, but no. B.J.'s right. We won't be here long."

"Well, okay. Nice to see you Denise. And pleased to meet you, Mr. Green. If y'all don't mind, I'm going to bed. Need my beauty rest." She smiled. "As if that would make any difference."

"Now, Millie, you're plenty beautiful already," B.J. offered without expression. He watched the pair in his doorway the way a treed cat appraises the pack of dogs baying for its hide.

Mildred snickered. "Oh, he does go on about me. Wish it was the truth. Well, goodnight, then. See them out, will you B.J.?"

"Will do."

The footsteps on the wood-floored hallway died away as Mildred retreated to the far corner of the house. After they heard the bedroom door close, B.J. spoke.

"Like Millie says, where're my manners? You two have a seat."

Denise picked a small armchair. Bobby had difficulty fitting into the recliner.

"Nice of you to come by and offer up support for your boss," B.J. said.

"I wanted you to know," Denise said, "I'm resigning as your secretary. Effective tonight."

"Sorry to see you go, Denise. You've been helpful to the department. And in case you've forgotten, there's a few things—"

"You once told me if I left your office I wouldn't work in this county again. Well, me and Bobby are leaving town, so I guess it doesn't matter."

"Bobby ever going to make an honest woman of you, Denise?"

Bobby leaned forward, looking like the entire chair had pulled itself closer to the desk. "I don't 'preciate that remark, Sheriff. Denise and I are getting married next week."

"Well, well." B.J. leaned back and looked at the ceiling. "I guess congratulations are in order. Sure you shouldn't maybe reconsider that decision, Bobby?"

"No, sir," Bobby said.

Denise was calm. "The main reason we're here, B.J., is to let you know ahead of time about tomorrow."

"Got a nice surprise for me?"

"It's been a long time coming."

"Millie's been wanting a deck built out back, and I been too busy serving the public interest to find time to build it myself. Maybe that's your surprise, your Mr. Green here helping out the poor sheriff?"

"Not hardly."

"And thanks for the damn two weeks notice, Denise. Real fine of you to give me plenty of time to find someone else."

Denise stared at the sheriff. "You won't need a replacement."

"That so?" B.J. said.

"Bobby?"

Bobby Green rose up out of the recliner and covered up the front of B.J.'s desk. "Fact is, Sheriff, besides being a carpenter, I happen to be an undercover agent for the DEA." Bobby pulled a leather fold-over from his pocket and flashed his badge to B.J.

"Wonderful," the sheriff said.

"Expect to be arrested tomorrow morning and headed out for federal arraignment in Houston by the afternoon."

"For what, might I ask?"

"Money-laundering, racketeering, destroying evidence, extortion, to name some. I was you, I'd call me a lawyer tonight. You and a few other upstanding citizens of this county are going to have a hell of a day tomorrow. And I'm not counting the state charges. Murder comes to mind, from what you admitted to on the tape. I hear the state boys'll be after you near about the same time."

The padded chair squeaked under the sheriff's weight. "I'm sure I don't know what you might mean."

Bobby edged closer. "This county's been on the federal radar for a while, Mr. Sanders. Lots of dirty money flowing through here. Drugs, cattle rustling, bribery, illegal aliens, you name it. Be hard for you to make a real case you weren't involved in it all, up to your neck."

"And how do you fit in, Denise? You federal, too?"

"No. I spent most of my time writing down who came into the office and what did they bribe you with."

B.J. nodded. "Should've known those manners of Mr. Green here were fake. All that 'yes, sir, no, sir, I'm-here-to-take-Denise-to-lunch' bullshit. Bet you two enjoyed yourself."

Denise rose and stood next to Bobby. "I wanted you to hear it from us. Before tomorrow."

"Expect me to worry about it all night?"

"Got some agents watching all around your house tonight," Bobby said. "Be difficult for you to decide on a vacation all of a sudden. There's a shit storm a-coming, Sheriff, and you're square in the middle."

"You two get the hell out of my house."

"I'll see your fat ass in court," Denise said, "And I'll be thinking about my friend Clarice, and how you covered up what really happened."

"Listen, you little *bitch*, you ever—"

Bobby made a more toward B.J., but Denise grabbed is arm. "Save it, baby. He'll get his in spades. B.J., call it payback if you want. The least I could do for my dead friend."

◆   ◆   ◆

After locking the front door, B.J. turned off most of the lights and scanned the street through the darkened window. Bobby's truck stopped beside a late-model Impala parked at the curb, B.J. watching the occupants of both vehicles have a conversation. He supposed there was a car in the alley, too, behind the fence.

B.J. always prided himself on being a practical man. As such, he returned to his desk and took out a piece of paper. Listing potential legal problems in one column and their alibis in another, he filled the page in less than a minute. Cooter would be the first one to fall, him giving up his boss right off for promises of leniency. The rest of the involved citizenry would go down right behind him, on their knees, pleading for mercy. Full immersion in Bobby Green's promised debacle was a case of when, not if. He knew the reality of life in prison, the monotony, always looking over your shoulder, fights in the showers, shivs maybe slicing through your ribs in the exercise yard, no more pussy while attending the sheriffs' conventions, and the food...Jesus, the food. Even the county jail grub would've been better if B.J. hadn't taken his ten percent off the top of the no-bid contract.

B.J. thought back on his conversation with Mark Reinhardt about Summer Holman's murder. He didn't have any real evidence that Reinhardt either killed the girl or was even involved, but B.J. acted like he did, if only to watch the man's response, and offered to divert the investigation for a fee. The resultant mid-five-figure bribe all went into his pocket, since Cooter was merely a nervous bystander at the meeting. Still, B.J. wasn't entirely sure Reinhardt was guilty, though the man paid off like he was. Well, it didn't matter now what actually happened. The girl's rape and murder ended up stirring up the entire mess that Bobby Green was now promising.

He removed The Book from his locked safe. The Book listed years of cons, deals, and bribes in a meticulous, chronological order. B.J. wasn't sure why he has always kept such strict notes, except that it was difficult to recall the specific points of so many deals.

The pages went through the department-furnished shredder five at a time.

The letter to Millie took more time to compose. *Sorry about the problems I've caused…Provided a little something for you, saving what little I could…Don't believe what they say about me, it's all lies…Better this way, my dear, save you the pain of an unfair prosecution…Your loving husband, B.J.* It also described the location of the clandestine house they owned in Florida, the off-shore bank accounts, the mutual funds under unidentifiable business names, the hidden trust drawn up by the Houston attorney for free in lieu of an embarrassing DUI arrest. All of it. Pray to God she could keep her mouth shut and not show it to the feds first thing. Maybe, just maybe, she wouldn't fuck things up.

He made his way back to the master bedroom. Mildred snored away, ear plugs and eye mask fitted snugly in place, oblivious to the true consequences of life. He slipped the note into her handbag, hoping the full search of the house wouldn't find the slim paper stuffed behind her credit cards, the ones she was used to pulling out with impunity for whatever she saw she liked. He often wondered if she ever once considered how they could handle their lifestyle on a public official's salary.

Their long time together had always gone this way, he knew. He fixed the troublesome things, told her where they would live and how much to spend in local stores. The rest of the things she wanted were purchased out of town, in the big cities, where no one knew them. She trusted him completely. He imagined her lost without him, her bovine confusion, disbelief at the charges, her inept attempts to defend him, no sensible replies offered to questions of how she could have expected a poorly-paid local law officer to afford a large house outfitted with a slew of expensive furnishings.

It was not an encouraging vision.

Returning to his study, he removed the trophy Browning over-under twelve gauge and rubbed his fat thumb along the checkering on the stock and then down the fine engraving decorating both barrels and the receiver. This hand-crafted specimen was given to him by the sheriff's organization in recognition of two decades of selfless dedication to the citizens of Douglas County and the Great State of Texas.

B.J. broke the weapon open, inserted two number five buckshot shells, and snapped it closed, marveling at the weapon's balance.

After removing his right cowboy boot and sock, B.J. found he had to lean forward more than was comfortable to get the business end of the shotgun tight in his mouth. Doc Mayfield, the old bastard, told B.J. last month that he was a real shitty patient and would be lucky to see sixty at this rate, considering how much weight he carried around with those high blood pressure and cholesterol chasers. B.J. had considered how much he would suffer from cutting back on the chicken-fried steak, cream gravy, bacon and buttermilk biscuits, and resolved to keep right on eating. The doc was right. He wouldn't see sixty. But this was better than losing all of his money to expensive lawyers and either getting whacked in the death chamber or spending the rest of his life in jail being corn-holed by somebody like Bobby Green.

He lifted his fat leg by the ankle, with an extended hand, barely high enough to catch his big toe in the front of the trigger guard. It was a struggle, but he managed to hold steady for a few seconds. One fast downward motion would catch both triggers at once. One, of course, would do the job, but he didn't want the chance of a misfire. He might lose his courage to try again.

Mildred slept through the huge blast but awakened after the agents broke down her front door and roused her from her sleepy reverie.

"You boys want some coffee?" they remembered her saying right before she led them, unsuspecting, into the blood-splattered study.

SIXTY-FIVE

"Come on, Luther. They're waiting."

Mr. Garner latched on to my arm and guided me out through the jail. Along the way, I passed some Texas Rangers that of late had taken over the temporary running of the jail, except for Gene, who had been appointed acting sheriff.

The front doors opened into the sunshine and a passel of reporters and hangers-on, all anticipating their chance to gawk at today's freak show. A stack of microphones taped together adorned the podium. TV trucks, their satellite dishes extended up so high it looked like the vans would topple over any minute, crowded the street.

"Shit," I said. "I don't want this."

"You earned it," Mr. Garner said. "Don't worry. I'll go first."

Mr. Garner stopped in front of the microphones, me standing a bit behind, and amid a bunch of pushy people shouting questions, he began to speak. I wasn't listening too close because I was searching the crowd for Suzie, who maybe I couldn't see 'cause she was so short and covered up by the others. Mr. Garner went on a while about the work of his legal bunch helping out the poor people of Texas that don't have proper representation and how the accused could often be railroaded into bad pleas and prison time for crimes they didn't commit and wasn't it all a big shame, and likely it happened a lot in places like this, least near as they could figure.

He give out grandstanding after a bit and a few of them reporters took to asking silly questions. After answering some, he turned to me. I'd been trying to hide, hoping to skate through this deal without saying a word. But then he added, "How about we hear from Mr. Holman?"

I was pushed forward into flashing cameras.

"Mr. Holman, could you tell us if you are going to sue the country for false arrest and torture?" said a bleached blonde near the front.

"I don't reckon so."

"But you were beaten and abused while in jail, and your family threatened with murder and rape by local law enforcement."

"I know. What's done is done. The people that did this, did it without most of the people in Douglas County knowing. Citizens made the mistake of trusting people in office to do what's right. I hope the guilty here will be punished. That's all."

Another one of them, I take it not important enough to get their microphone up on the stand like the rest, was holding out his own. "Mr. Holman, what are your plans for the future?"

"I don't know just yet. Right now, all I want to do is find my wife."

About that time, I seen Suzie getting out of the truck. She must've had a hard time parking because of the crowd. "Can I go now?" I asked Mr. Garner.

"You're a free man. Go on."

We met in the parking lot at a dead run and I grabbed her up and turned her around, almost squeezing the life out of her.

"Luther, are you glad to see me?" she asked with a big smile and two small arms tight around my neck.

"You are the best damn thing I ever seen," I said. She'd re-dyed her hair brown, her real color, finally getting rid of that blonde holdover. It looked real good on her, too, considering that slow wave in the front. She had on some new clothes, navy blue slacks and a starched white blouse with some kind of necklace, and high heels to boot.

"What did you go and do to yourself?" I asked once I set her back down.

She took her hand and pushed on the side of her hair, slow-like, the way women do when you comment about how they look, like they never thought anyone would pay attention but of course they was dying to hear a comment. "Had it done at Gina's. She gave me a perm, on the house. You like it?"

"Love it."

"Bought this outfit at Bascomb's yesterday. How do I look?" She turned all the way around, taking her time.

"Good enough to eat," I said.

Suzie glanced at the group of people about to break up. Mr. Garner was through with the second round of questions and a couple of the reporters had spied us enjoying ourselves. They were making a bee-line for us, along with some photographers.

"Wonder if we can get away?" she said.

"Probably not. Besides, I sure need to say thanks to Mr. Garner again."

We wound our way back, Suzie trailing behind, holding on to my hand tight, as we dodged questions and people. Mr. Garner still had couple of hangers-on standing around and we stayed back 'til he was done. He spied us outta the corner of his eye and walked over.

He stuck out his hand. "Luther, it's been a pleasure."

"Same here," I said, shaking his hand. My other mitt was wrapped around Suzie and wasn't about to let go. "Without you, I'd be on the way to Huntsville."

He nodded. "Possibly. Well, this case certainly got a lot of publicity at the end."

"Mr. Garner, why me? Why this trial? And why you do this kind of work?"

"Lots of questions, Luther."

"Call me Edward," I said.

"Edward?"

"My middle name, remember? I kept Luther out of respect for Momma. But it's time now to call myself what *I* like, now that Momma's passed on. Edward's what I prefer, if that's okay."

"Let's sit down and I'll tell you the story." He motioned to a bench near the front door.

By then, the crowd had wandered off, the show over. There were stories to write, video to send, friends to gossip with. The curious had their fill of us. It was time to find someone else's scabs to pick at.

◆　◆　◆

After we was all by ourselves, Mr. Garner gave us the lowdown on his career.

"I started out as an assistant district attorney, the way a lot of lawyers do that are making a career of criminal law. It's a revolving door, with most attorneys leaving in a short while to enter private practice and defend the same type of people they were previously hired to prosecute. I lasted eight years, then the prospect of all that money got to me. Representation of wealthy criminals can be very lucrative."

I nodded. "Look, I know we never talked about a fee. Me and Suzie, we can—"

He held up his hand. "The Defense Fund has all of this covered."

"But Mr. Garner…"

"How about this?" he said. "We'll call it even if you'll agree to call me Malcolm." He smiled. "My mother liked it. She thought it was a good, solid name."

"Know where you're comin' from," I said.

"Mr. Garner," Suzie said, "we can't expect—"

"The bill's paid, Mrs. Holman. Knowing that Luther…Edward…didn't go to jail for a crime that he didn't commit is repayment enough." He paused and give me a look. "I *am* right about that, aren't I?"

"Yes, sir, you're right."

"Hardest part, for me, is knowing who and what to believe, if an innocent life's in your hands. It's not supposed to matter. A client's entitled

286

to your best effort, guilty or not, but it was always important to me, deep down. I believed you, Edward, from the first. An instinct I have."

"So I guess once you made a lot of money off of your rich clients, your conscience got to botherin' you, right?" I said.

"Something like that." He looked embarrassed.

Right away I saw I stuck my foot in my mouth. "Sorry," I said. "I didn't mean to..."

"Let's say I arrived at this point in my life from a circuitous path. Some of the twists and turns were a little painful."

"Malcolm, how'd you pull if off?" Suzie asked. "The tape and everything?"

"Reminds me. I've got a present for Mr. Garner," I said. I pulled out a battered cigarette pack and handed it to him. "Returnin' this. It's not in as good a condition as it started out, but it still works."

The pack was wrapped with rubber bands to help keep it from falling out of my shirt pocket. He tore the paper down the side of the pack, showing the side of the tiny tape recorder. Across the top were short lengths of filters cut off and glued together and to the package with rubber cement to make the top look like a gen-u-ine store-bought pack.

I said, "I kept a few real cigarettes stuck down the side of it, where you tear the paper off, in case I needed to give them away. Besides, it let the sound in better. Turned it on by pushin' on the side of my pocket, acting like I was scratchin'."

"Ingenious," he said.

"But how did you get it in the jail?" Suzie said.

"Mr. Garner brought it in with his briefcase, along with another regular recorder. All the people coming into the jail get their stuff searched. They inspected his briefcase but stopped when they saw the first recorder. The other was hid inside a hollowed-out law book, along with a couple of spare tapes, like in the movies. After he got it in, he knocked his briefcase off the table and in the pickin' up process I hid 'em in my jumpsuit."

"Seems like you're guilty of something," Suzie said to Mr. Garner.

"They'll assume Edward obtained it though the regular jail smuggling avenues."

"But the tape Edward made? What happened to the one that you told me had his confession on it? How did you manage that?"

"Simple," he said. "Edward gave me the one with B.J.'s and Cooter's voices on it, the one where they tried to intimidate him into confessing. He expected me to listen to it later. He didn't tell me what was on it, but I knew right away it had to be important because he was changing his plea. I took a fresh tape out of my briefcase, then switched it with the used one. I made a show of rewinding the 'new' tape. Cooter forgot a new tape doesn't need to be rewound. Then I insisted on putting the deputy's okay on the first part of the tape. Made him even more certain that it was genuine. Then I switched the tape off and never recorded another word."

"But I saw you," I said. "Saw you turn on the switch."

"No, you thought you did. I turned the recorder around to my side, so the tape would be away from Cooter and he couldn't see it wasn't running. You didn't notice it either. Fortunately, the prosecution fell for our trick of not playing it back before court reconvened."

"So what they had all along, in that plastic bag with all of the special polish and tape, was a blank?"

"That's right," he said. "And when it came time to play it in court, I switched them again."

"We didn't hear all of the tape played out in court," Suzie said, "since the trial was sort of interrupted by all the yelling."

"I only had a few minutes between the time Edward gave me his real tape in the jail and the time the trial started," Mr. Garner said. "I listened to the first part of it and knew what I had in my hands. My investigator made several quick copies. One went to the state's attorney general and a few others were reserved for the news media."

"How did you do that?" I asked. "The switch? Back and forth? I was sittin' there and didn't see any funny business."

"Worked my way through college doing magic shows for kids," Mr. Garner shrugged. "I always wanted to use it when it really mattered." He reached into his pocket and pulled out a coin, letting it sit there in his open palm. He closed his hand, made a movement with his other one, and opened the first hand again. No coin. It'd disappeared right in front of us.

I shook my head in admiration. "'Course, there were two tapes. The one before got held up."

"Oh?" Mr. Garner said.

"We had us a previous meeting in the jail. They threatened to kill Momma that time. I sent the tape out with Barry and a guy named Jake. Jake got caught with the note but managed to ditch the tape. I figured after that there wasn't much of a chance of you ever hearing the real story. Good thing I was wrong."

Mr. Garner shook his head. "This place is a real mess. I have to go interview your cellmate next."

"Barry?"

"He's not as charitable as you are. Wants to clean out the county. Seems he doesn't like getting beat up, and besides, he's holding a grudge about Carl getting the death penalty for killing Clarice. Part of it's based on what you heard. And there's also a lot of new evidence that's only now turning up."

"I suspect it'll take more'n an off-hand statement to prove B.J. and Cooter are guilty," I said.

"I've had the investigator look into the crime scene evidence. He came across this close-up photo of Clarice's face. No makeup."

"So?"

Mr. Garner smiled. "Denise says she had on a lot of makeup from earlier. They had it done together at the store. What woman, intending to have sex with her lover, takes off her makeup first?"

Suzie nodded first.

"And there's clearly an outline of a man's handprint on her face. She'd been slapped, hard. Carl maintained at the trial that he absolutely never hit

Clarice, but the jury didn't believe him. Likely that print matches the hand of the man who died with her, but that's impossible to prove now. I've got another person, though, one that claims to have heard from Carl firsthand about what really happened."

"Who's that?" Suzie asked.

"Denise Jones. She visited Carl in prison right before he was put to death, and he told her what really happened, the truth this time. Besides, now we have a surprise eyewitness. Your buddy Cooter's spilling his guts to the authorities, saying it was all the sheriff's idea to make it look like Carl was the murderer. Said B.J. concealed evidence and manipulated the crime scene, that he had to go along. He claims to have photographs in the trailer before it was changed up."

"So did Carl kill Clarice or not?" Suzie asked.

"Looks like it might have been an accident, or maybe a fight that went bad. In any event, Carl probably didn't kill Scott Blackburn. We think now it's likely that Clarice did, while he was trying to rape her."

"Okay," I said. "A mistrial they called it. I understand that word means my trial's over with for now. But they could try come at me again, whenever they wanted."

"They could," Mr. Garner said, "but they won't. Not with all of the publicity about you being tortured by local law enforcement. Not with all the faked evidence. No D.A. would ever take that mess on. We presented enough at trial to indicate a strong possibility that the Reinhardt killing could've been drug related. You're finished with this, Edward. For good."

"But if we keep livin' here, what about B.J.? Not like he'll sit still for this. He'll be out to get me for sure."

"Haven't you heard?" Suzie said.

"Heard what?"

Mr. Garner raised an eyebrow. "B.J. Sanders committed suicide last night. Stuck the business end of a shotgun into his mouth and managed to pull both triggers with his toe."

"But why..."

"Turns out the feds have had him and Cooter under investigation for several years. A man by the name of Bobby Green, along with Denise, got enough evidence for an indictment. It was to be served today. Denise was Clarice Telford's best friend. Carl convinced her that Clarice's death was an accident after all. It became her full-time duty to her dead friend to record the numerous misdeeds of Sheriff B.J. Sanders and company. Anyway, the federal agents started serving warrants today. It was all over the national news, cameras everywhere and lots of publicity. Some rather prominent persons around here are in a lot of trouble right about now."

"What about Cooter? What'll happen to him?" I said.

"He's hoping for some leniency. Basically, the man's a coward if he doesn't have a badge to back him up." Mr. Garner smiled. "He also knows what happens to ex-lawmen in prison."

"One other thing," I said. "The recording. Was it legal?"

"Cooter should have kept his mouth shut. The sheriff, of course, won't be getting a chance to agree. You agreed to the recording, so it's technically legal. However, the tape's probably not admissible as evidence in court, but it's in the hands of everyone now. The news media played parts of it last night."

"Will you get in trouble for any of this?"

"Mix up with tapes is all I can say. Sorry, but I forgot to turn on the switch one time." He smiled. "Doubtful that trick will ever work again. Well, I've got a new client to go see. I hope you both have a wonderful life." He turned to Suzie. "And whoever killed Mark Reinhardt probably did this town a favor. One of these days, perhaps you can put the tragedy of your daughter behind you."

Suzie said, "Thank you, Mr. Garner. You saved an innocent man's life. God bless you." She gave him a peck on the cheek, which seemed from how his old face brightened up, her kiss done him some real good.

"I had a daughter once," he said. "She died about your age. Cancer." His old blue eyes got wet around the edges. "Every time I looked at you, I couldn't help but think of her. I hope I didn't ever offend."

"Does it get better?" Suzie said, the start of tears showing in her eyes as they shifted back and forth between his. "Losing a child?"

He swallowed. "Different. Bearable. Because it has to. That's part of what attracted me to this case. You two had lost a daughter that you shouldn't have and I felt..." He stopped, collecting himself. "Kristine always wanted me to be a public defender, helping out the defenseless, but I was too busy raking in the fees." He fingered one of his gold cufflinks, the ones with the black squares with the fancy gold "K" in the middle. "She gave me these. She said, 'Daddy, wear them when you decide to help out people that have nowhere else to turn to.' I wear them all of the time now. They remind me..." He stopped. "Maybe somehow..."

Suzie put her arm around Mr. Garner. "Believe me, Kristine knows."

He gave her a big hug and a grateful look and stuck out his hand toward me. "Edward, it's been a pleasure."

I grasped his hand. "Thank you for my life. We'll never forget you."

Malcolm nodded down at my wife as her hand unwound from his shoulder. "And, Suzie, thank you, too. What you said about Kristine means a lot to me."

She give him a bright big smile and said, "I prefer Suzanne. Long as my husband's renaming himself, I might as well, too."

"Better go on in before we all start bawling. Edward. Suzanne." He nodded his head each time he spoke our new names, then headed back into the jail.

SIXTY-SIX

We stood at the family plot, Suzanne holding hard around my waist with both hands stitched together. All of the Holmans was laid out in front of us like celery bundles in the supermarket, from my sister on down to our little lost daughter. The day was still hot, but the birds, maybe the same ones I heard outside the jail, was here, too, singing to us from the trees. I watched as a light breeze stirred them and they rode it out on the branches. It's peaceful here, and quiet, which is expected, I guess, considering the residents here don't make much of a fuss. It's a nice place, too, to grab some time to yourself, to breathe in the air and think about things bigger than yourself, and about those you've loved and lost.

"You think we're both going to hell?" Suzanne asked.

"Why you askin' me?" I said.

"I'm serious. I want to see my daughter again. If we're in hell and she's up in heaven, it's not likely we'll cross paths."

"I don't know," I said. "Murderin' a man's bad business."

Suzanne stared at the graves. "If ever someone had it coming, it was Mark Reinhardt."

"The Good Book says an eye for an eye. Could be our way out."

"It also says 'Justice is mine, sayeth the Lord.'"

I didn't see that we were as deep into it as my wife did. "Maybe if Momma explains herself to God, we can skate by, too," I said.

Suzanne pressed her head against me. "Maybe."

"You never told me exactly how it happened. I got arrested before I knew the real truth."

"Momma told me she was sure that now you knew that Reinhardt killed Summer, there'd be no stopping you. She figured you couldn't last more than a day or two and then he'd be dead."

"She was right," I said, moving my hand up and down my little wife's back.

"After we left, she got your daddy's pistol out of the drawer and headed for Reinhardt's house. She said all she wanted was his confession. Momma parked her Buick down behind his fence, so Shirley was mistaken about seeing your truck the night Reinhardt was killed."

"Mr. Garner said nothing was more inaccurate but carries more weight with a jury than eyewitness testimony. Memory's sometimes a hard thing to pin down." I thought again about my sister and her real eye color and wondered again which option was the right one. "When I parked in the alley before, checking out the house, that's when Shirley seen the truck. Guess she assumed it was there again."

Suzanne nodded. "Momma said she walked right up to the front door, that was when her gout wasn't bothering her so much, and told Reinhardt she had some information he needed. Curious about it, he let her in. Next thing you know she's telling him we got evidence we can use in the future, that DNA test, to prove what he did, so he'd better get ready to pay the price for his bad deeds. Next thing, she said he's threatening her right back. Then your momma pulls out the pistol and points it at him and says write out a confession. He told her she's a stupid old bitch and won't shoot him. So she fires one into the ceiling to let him know she means business—"

"The wood ceiling," I said. "That's why they didn't find it."

"They never looked very hard," Suzanne said. "Anyway, she didn't exactly tell me what he said about our family, just that if you'd been there, you'd torn his head off. Then he told her he owned the law and would have her jailed for attempted murder. She said he had to pay for his sins sooner or later. That's when she decided the sooner was going to win out and let him have it. Right between the eyes."

"I can see it happening," I said. "Like I was there."

"She left out the back, locking the door as she went and wiping off the handle, smart of her to remember that, and went out through the backyard gate to the alley. After that, she came back to our place and put the gun in the drawer. She waited a while for us to come home so she could tell us what had happened, but that's when we were out in the country talking to Billy. She left that note on the counter and went back home."

"Yeah. The one that Mop and Broom played demolition derby with."

"Ended up chewed to pieces under the couch. Anyway, she didn't hear from us so she finally went to bed. By then, we'd gotten back and you'd been arrested. I didn't know until later, when I gave her the news about you being hauled into jail, what really happened."

"Bad timing," I said, relaxing a little. "Story of our lives."

Suzie looked up at me. "She wanted to confess all along. But you wouldn't hear of it."

"I was in jail." I said, thinking it over again for the millionth time. "I told her to wait it out. Once the trial started, if it looked bad, she could always stand up and tell the truth. Her knowing about the bullet hole in the ceiling was supposed to have cinched her testimony. Maybe they would have believed her, maybe not. But that option died with her. When I saw her lyin' there on the floor of the courtroom, she knew she was about to die. The life was goin' out in her eyes, her still knowin' her last chance to confess was gone."

"At least she got Mr. Garner here," Suzanne said. "That must have been some letter she wrote."

"I suppose. I never saw it."

"Whatever she said, it worked."

I give Suzanne a big squeeze. "I'd lie awake in jail, thinkin' about us, night after night, and the chances of me gettin' out of this. It scared me to death most of the time. I know you was worried, too."

"I couldn't imagine ever living the rest of my life without you," she said and gave me a kiss on the cheek.

I looked down at Summer's grave and thought again about losing her that day, how we got her little dress back weeks later. After B.J.'s buddy down state admitted to losing the evidence from her body, it was Suzanne that pulled the torn dress out of the plastic bag and went looking for a semen stain. After she found it and cut out the scrap of material, we had to get something of Reinhardt's to test it against. Her managing to accidental-like cut the man's hand in the restaurant and get the blood on a napkin was a stroke of genius. But it didn't give us the answer we wanted, not yet. Maybe one day we'll do the DNA test, but now, after what Cooter told me about Reinhardt, maybe the certainty of it don't matter anymore.

Suzanne stirred. "I've got to ask you something, sweetheart. Promise you'll think about it."

"What's that?"

"I know we said that there'd be no baby after Summer. But I've been thinking..."

"You want to have another one," I said.

She hesitated. "It wouldn't be like we won't remember Summer and how we loved her. Another baby wouldn't take her place in our hearts. It would make a new one..." Her voice trailed off.

"I want one, too," I said.

"You *do?*" Her face was up in mine, eager to hear the words again.

"Decided the same thing in jail and was tryin' to figure out a way to tell you."

"Oh, Edward, I *love* you!"

We kissed and hugged a while after that, two people making out in a graveyard, but somehow, in front of our family, it seemed like the right thing to do.

"You want to go home?" she said.

"Guess so."

We walked back to the truck and got in. I sat there and didn't start the engine.

"What's the matter?"

"I'm ready for something different," I said.

"You are?"

"I don't want to live here anymore. Way I figure it, most people liked things the way they was, even if it was corrupt. All they cared about was feelin' safe from their troubles. Now they're gonna have lots of changes a-comin', and we'll likely be blamed for any bad in that, too. By the time Barry and Mr. Garner get through soakin' all the money out of the taxpayers, there won't be much sympathy left for us."

Suzanne said, "By the way, the high school called. Said they must've messed up on the paperwork. You weren't fired, only on furlough. 'Cept they forgot to tell us until now. You can go back to work anytime."

I nodded. "Sounds like 'em. Maybe since I'm not a cold-blooded murderer, I can mop up the halls."

Suzanne looked out the windshield. "Sherry with the realty company called a few days after your momma died. She's got a client wants to buy the house and the lot next door and put in what she called a 'convenience store.' Said it was like a combination gas station and a little grocery store. You ever heard of that?"

"Nope. Not sure if that would work."

"Anyways, they want to try it. Sherry said it's a prime location, it being on the corner and all. I told them I was sure you'd want to move in instead, seeing as it's a better house than ours, and larger, but I'd ask."

"How much did they offer?" I said.

"Sixty-five thousand for the house, and another five for the vacant lot next door."

"Let's take it."

"But, Luther, that's the house you were raised in," Suzie said, surprised. "All they'll do is tear it down."

"People I cared about, ones that lived there and made it home, are all gone now, 'cept for me. I've got the memories of 'em stored in my head. It's time to start afresh."

"Really?"

"And when you call her back, tell her to list our house, too."

"But where will we live?" Her eyes went wide, not expecting any of this.

"Down the road a ways. Don't know where for sure. Maybe Galveston. You ever been there?"

"No."

"How about a vacation, baby? You could get yourself a bikini to wear out on the beach. We could get us some of those lounge chairs and sip us some margaritas, then spend the rest of the day up in the hotel room, naked."

"Luther!"

"It's *Edward*, dear."

"What are we going to do for money, *dear*?" she asked, but her eyes twinkled at the thought of it all.

"Got any on you?"

"A little. That's why I was late picking you up. The folks at the diner and the salon took up a collection for me. There's a hundred-fifty-nine bucks in my purse."

"Reach under the seat," I said. "Over on your side, up in the springs."

She bent over and fished out a worn envelope and counted out the bills. "Three-hundred-and-twenty-three dollars! Where the heck did you get this?"

"A wife don't need to know *everything* about her husband. It's my rainy-day fund, from workin' overtime waxing the floors last summer. You forgot to ask what happened to the money."

She giggled. "But I don't have any clothes packed. Neither do you. We'll have to go by the house, feed the cats..."

"Cats'll be fine. We'll call the neighbors, have them open some cans. The animals can find ways of amusin' themselves for a few days. And about those clothes, you won't be needin' any," I said. "First gear, woman."

My truck has a floor shifter, so we'd worked out this system where I'd drive with one hand on the steering wheel and the other snug around my wife's shoulder. I'd push in on the clutch and she'd shift. We got so good at it that it was as smooth as one mind doing it. But rounding the corner out onto the blacktop, she must've been thinking through what I'd said before 'bout what we was going to be doing in the hotel room, 'cause she missed the shift and the gears ground together.

"Sorry," she said, embarrassed-like.

"You know, what I figure I really need me is a new wife. Model that comes with the big titties and knows how to shift gears."

"You do that and I'll cut your pecker off," she said. "Besides, your big old leg was in the way. I couldn't get ahold of the knob right."

"Wasn't my leg, Miss Suzannie. My mind was on starting that baby tonight."

Her cute little face busted into a big grin and she threw back her head and laughed out loud.

It was the first time I heard her do that in a long, long while.

About The Author

Parman Reynolds' long and diverse career includes that of a utility engineer, consulting engineer, a university finance and economics instructor, and a writer. His outside activities include an interest in the arts, and he has served on various volunteer boards. He lives in Austin, Texas, with his wife, Mary.

NOTE FROM THE AUTHOR

Word-of-mouth is crucial for any author to succeed. If you enjoyed *All for Summer*, please leave a review online—anywhere you are able. Even if it's just a sentence or two. It would make all the difference and would be very much appreciated.

Thanks!
Parman Reynolds

We hope you enjoyed reading this title from:

BLACK ROSE
writing™

www.blackrosewriting.com

Subscribe to our mailing list – *The Rosevine* – and receive **FREE** books, daily deals, and stay current with news about upcoming releases and our hottest authors.
Scan the QR code below to sign up.

Already a subscriber? Please accept a sincere thank you for being a fan of Black Rose Writing authors.

View other Black Rose Writing titles at
www.blackrosewriting.com/books and use promo code
PRINT to receive a **20% discount** when purchasing.

www.ingramcontent.com/pod-product-compliance
Lightning Source LLC
Chambersburg PA
CBHW010728100726
47899CB00009B/2971